MASALA and MURDER

PATRICK LYONS

Published by
NIYOGI BOOKS
Block D, Building No. 77,
Okhla Industrial Area, Phase-I,
New Delhi-110 020, INDIA
Tel: 91-11-26816301, 26818960
Email: niyogibooks@gmail.com
Website: www.niyogibooksindia.com

Editor: Arkaprabha Biswas
Design: Shashi Bhushan Prasad
Cover design: Misha Oberoi

ISBN: 978-93-91125-15-8
Publication: 2021

To Malcolm and Ilka,
for the ball curry and coconut rice,
and to Olivia,
who really spiced things up.

PROLOGUE

The crew had assembled at the red sandy base of Uluru shortly after sunrise, fronting a growing queue of tourists eager to scale the famous rock before the ban on climbing was imposed. Animated chatter, a trilling of different languages grated against the silent still of the land. In the middle distance, a mob of kangaroos lazed in the long shadows cast from an outcrop of stubby bush, as if anticipating the heat to come.

She peered upwards through a squint, shading her eyes from the reflective brilliance of the rockface and grimaced at the steepness of the climb. A steel chain had been erected to help people with the first part of the ascent, though it didn't make climbing any more appealing. The last thing she wanted was to undergo any unnecessary physical exertion; she hadn't felt well again this morning.

It wasn't just the nausea this time, it was something more. Just a feeling, like an animal sensing a predatory ambush. Every now and then she would catch her breath, snap her head around and check behind her. There was never anything there, yet her spine would tingle and the hairs on the back of her neck would stand. The sensation lasted a few seconds, leaving her tense and uneasy. Her heart playing a wild rhythm.

Subhani Mehta, Bollywood's darling, tied her wavy black hair into a ponytail that reached down past her shoulder blades. She glanced back up at the steep embankment, took a deep breath and sighed. Several of the film crew surreptitiously watched as her T-shirt swelled when she inhaled. She was very watchable. Her 5/8' frame was perfectly proportioned, except for her perky breasts and large, teasing eyes. God had been generous to Subhani with these attributes. Some critics argued that she won the Filmfare Award for Best Actress, the Indian version of the Oscars, purely because of these assets. Subhani didn't give a damn what they thought, or most other people for that matter. Bracing herself with her right foot, she hoisted herself up and commenced the arduous climb.

An hour later she was sitting in a fold-out chair at the summit, holding a parasol against the sun and waiting impatiently while the film crew set up. Occasionally, she would stand up and glance around, squinting against the blinding horizon. Searching, scanning for what she didn't know. Instinctively, her hand would move towards the pendant around her neck.

When it was time, Subhani crawled into a small nylon tent that was set up as a make-do change room, but acted more like a hothouse. She emerged resplendent in a golden sequined sari with a matching midriff-length choli. A large costume diamond covered her navel. On each hand a collection of bangles jangled with her every single movement.

The film was much like all the other films she had been in—a romantic, action, musical, comedy drama. Elvis would've been proud. This time the film was set in Australia to capitalise on Australia's growing taste for Bollywood's 'Masala Movies'. This was the last scene, a dance sequence set on top of Uluru. She thought it a stupid idea to film up here, where they could only bring what they could carry, but the director called the shots. For now, anyway. She would make sure the imbecile wouldn't work again.

What was supposed to be a quick session had now stretched into mid-morning as the director made them repeat the scene over and over again, each time adjusting the location of the cameras or waiting for a break in the conga-line of climbers so that they would not appear in the background. Subhani wasn't used to being treated like this, being made to wait between takes in the heat like some common *chokri* from the slums. She strummed her fingers impatiently on the arm of her chair and rehearsed the ultimatum she would give to the film's producer. By now, the silk sari stuck to her back with sweat.

Finally, the director called them to attention again. This would be the eighth take and hopefully the last. The background dancers took their positions in a crescent around Subhani. The sequence was relatively simple, a fusion of traditional poses and modern funky dance moves that would end with Subhani crouching on the ground, and the background dancers folding in around her, like a flower closing up for the night. The speakers on the small stereo crackled as the high-pitched recorded music began to play. The full soundtrack would be dubbed in during post-production.

'Rolling', called the director, and pointed to the performers. They moved in unison.

The sequence was going well and Subhani's last move was to crouch down. It was then that she felt it. Her heart started to pound uncontrollably, painfully, wrenching itself against her ribcage, as if trying to escape. Wide eyed, she gasped for air, but her lungs refused to be filled. Her mind raced with adrenaline-fuelled panic. Instinct commanded her to flee, an instruction her body couldn't obey as her legs buckled beneath her. She gave a final, hollow scream, grasping for the pendant around her neck as she fell. Her sari folded in on itself as she crumbled to the ground, her bangles rattling as she hit the rock.

CHAPTER 1

It was my second death threat this year. Any more, and it could become a habit. I played the message again.

'You're gonna die, you bastard. You tried to take us down, now we gonna take you down. We know where you live.'

The voice was young, a strong Indian accent. He sounded agitated and nervous, racing to get the words out, making his pitch higher than what it might normally be.

'So, what do you think?' I asked Bec.

'Well, it sounds kinda serious. They know who you are and they've got your mobile number. I wouldn't be surprised if they really do know where you live.' Senior Sergeant Rebecca McAdam never beat around the bush, even when she was off-duty.

'If I were you, I'd stay away from that shack you call a home for a little while,' she said with a tone that meant she was only half joking. Bec leaned forward and placed her empty glass on the coffee table between us. She sat back and folded her legs up beside her on the couch, forcing her skirt to ride high on her thigh. I tried not to look but stole a glance anyway.

We'd graduated from the Victorian Police Academy at Glen Waverley together. Twenty-two and naive, proud to wear the blue uniform. Fifteen years on she was still enjoying the job, the uniform. I had lasted only six before going private, though not by my own choice.

'You think so?' I asked sceptically as I topped her glass with more wine.

Bec reached for her refilled glass, gasped in mock horror at the generosity of my pour. She held it up and peered through it, distorting her face from my perspective.

'I know what you're trying to do, Sam Ryder, and you're not going to get me drunk.' Her left index finger wagged at me slowly, playfully.

I put on my '*who, me?*' face, the same expression a child wears when caught red-handed doing something wrong. I was just as convincing.

'Yes, you can stay here tonight.' The finger stopped wagging and pointed to where I was sitting, 'On that couch!'

We shared a laugh. I had spent the occasional night here before, but never on the couch.

'Seriously though, do you want us to do anything about this?' She asked, after taking a long sip. There was a subtle change in her tone, a hint of concern.

I knew exactly who had left the message. 'No, it's just a gang of kids I pissed off during the last job. They'll cool off soon enough. But thanks, Bec, I will stay here tonight,' I said.

'You're welcome. After all, I wouldn't want them to hurt that pretty-boy face of yours.' Now she was taking the piss. On the force my nickname had been 'Brasco' because someone had remarked that I looked like a brown version of Johnny Depp in the film *Donnie Brasco*. I didn't mind the ribbing. It meant I was accepted as part of the group and, privately, I liked the comparison. We shared the same dark hair and eyes, high cheekbones and boyish smile, although I figured I was a little taller and bigger across the shoulders. I'd never been named as the 'Sexiest Man of the Year', however, so I guess Depp could rest easy.

Back then my partner was a guy called Brian McCann, a rottweiler red-head whose bite was definitely worse than his bark. Naturally, people called him 'Bluey'. Brasco and Bluey. Not quite Starsky and Hutch.

We worked well together, shared the same thinking. It helped us react quickly when trouble happened. In hindsight, perhaps we were too much alike? Both 'act now and suffer the consequences later' type of guys. Who knows, if we'd acted differently that day I may still be in the force? I'd wondered about that often over the years. Not that I regretted my actions, just the effect they had on my bank balance.

Since then I'd learned to be more circumspect, more cautious. You have to be in my kind of work. No partners, no backup. Although every now and then I regressed. A not-so-old dog with old habits. That's probably why I got the death threats.

The bottle had a few dregs, which I drained into my glass.

'Shall I open another?' I asked, holding up the empty one.

Bec downed her nearly full glass in one action, the trait of a long-serving police officer, and waved the empty glass in front of me.

'Splishy-splashy,' she said.

I woke up the following morning feeling a little woolly, looked across at Bec and remembered the first time I saw that little mole on her back, the sheet only covering her from the waist down. I traced my finger down the curve of her spine. She gave a small groan—hangover head—and turned towards me. Her long brown hair fanned out over the pillow and her green eyes took a little while to focus on me. In the morning light her face was soft, kind. Not the poker face she put on with her uniform. I liked her face, a lot. It was her eyes and her smile. They held a mischievous lustre. When she looked at me through the corners of her eyes, she was sexy. When she laughed, it was electric.

I missed mornings like this. That first moment waking next to someone that you care for, the bed warmed by two bodies. I moved closer and kissed her shoulder, then drew even closer and kissed her neck, then her cheek. Bec stroked my face, gently, like I was a puppy, then said the three magic words.

'Make me coffee.'

***

Bec's flat was just off Church Street, in the trendy part of Richmond. Once a hovel, where if the gangs didn't kill you the cholera would, Richmond was now the place to be seen pouting into your café latte. Occasionally, we would play 'spot the celebrity' and watch Melbourne's beautiful people prance between the apparel shops that lined the strip. I lived in the back streets of Collingwood, about 3 kilometres from Bec's flat. It wasn't quite as nouveau-riche as Richmond, but lately some parts of Collingwood had scrubbed up nicely. My part was still sleeping it off.

I arrived home about an hour later, freshly showered but in yesterday's clothes. My house looked the same as all the others down the street: a narrow, single-fronted weatherboard built before the First World War. Off-white paintwork with highlights of inner-city grime, a faded green tin roof pockmarked with rust. The house needed work when I bought it and needed much more now. It leaned a little to the left, much like me. In winter it would huddle up to itself so tightly, the front door would jam. In summer it would relax and sag, like a fat man undoing his belt.

There was no post in the letterbox, which was good. The only snail mail that arrived were bills and bank statements. One demanding amounts of money that the other informed I didn't have. I opened the front door and adjusted my eyes to the gloom of the windowless hallway that ran the length of the house. A blinking red light at the end of the passage grabbed my attention, like a lighthouse in the night. The landline was supposed to add a more professional and formal feel to my business than just a mobile. The flashing light meant it had been rung at least twice, with two messages waiting. Hopefully, there would be some work. My last case finished a couple of days ago and there was nothing else on the horizon. I walked down the hallway, pressed the button marked 'Messages'.

The first message was from a Vivienne Fredricks—a polite, efficient message. She left a phone number and asked me to call her back. The second message came from a familiar voice.

'We know who you are. You're a dead man.'

A chill crept down my spine. If they had my landline number then they definitely had my address. My first thought was to call Bec, in her official capacity. Then I thought again and figured I could handle it myself; give them a couple of days to settle down. Instead, I called Vivienne Fredricks.

CHAPTER 2

As usual for the morning rush, all six lanes of Punt Road connecting the north and south of Melbourne were choked and it took me an hour to travel the 7 kilometres from Collingwood to Saint Kilda, start–stop all the way. I hadn't been bayside for a while, there was no real reason to unless work brought me here. The beachside suburb's popularity had ebbed and flowed over the years, depending on which industry was in vogue; a constant churning between overpriced restaurants and oversexed nightclubs, on the one hand, and the underworld of drugs and prostitution on the other. I took a right onto Fitzroy Street, which led towards the bay. Ahead, I saw a man who staggered towards my direction along the footpath, his bare feet filthy. He wore a faded blue T-shirt and an expression that seemed both confused and angry. I kept my eye on him as I drove by, hoping he wouldn't stumble onto the street in front of me. I figured the tide must be out.

Vivienne Fredricks lived in a two-storey Tudor-style house with a view over the bay. I parked my Toyota behind the BMW convertible in the driveway. I was right to wear a suit, even if it was in need of urgent dry cleaning and shined my shoes against the backs of my trousers before walking to the front door.

A well-dressed lady answered the doorbell.

'Hello. Mr Ryder?' she enquired.

'Yes. Good morning,' I replied.

'I'm Vivienne Fredricks. Thank you for meeting with me.'

Vivienne Fredricks was similar to how I had pictured her on the phone—petite and refined. She styled her dark hair in a bun that accentuated her angular face. A minimal amount of makeup was all I could detect. Two thin strips of an earthy brown lipstick complemented her hazelnut eyes. She was wearing a casual chocolate brown skirt with matching jacket. Underneath the jacket was a glimpse of a cream cashmere. Occasionally, her delicate gold necklace and earrings would give off a glint, otherwise I would not have noticed them. Understated but classy. I pictured a younger Vivienne Fredricks wearing a head scarf and large dark sunglasses, a la Audrey Hepburn in *Charade*.

She led me through the entrance hallway into an ornate sitting room. The furniture was made from a heavily lacquered dark wood and a subtle hint of sandalwood spiced the air. Two brown, tufted chesterfield sofas formed a right angle. A scene of a Maharaja's hunting trip, comprised of different coloured ceramics, was inlaid into an ornamental central table. The prints on the walls were of the Taj Mahal and of the Lake Palace in Udaipur. Home away from home.

'Thank you for coming,' she said, and offered me the sofa adjacent to hers.

'Not at all, Mrs Fredricks. How may I be of assistance?' She'd refused to speak of any details on the phone.

Fredricks sat forward with her hands on her knees, legs pressed together. She was anxious, the way most people are when hiring a private investigator. Usually, I'd invite a potential client to call me by my first name. It helps with their nerves, making the situation feel a little more relaxed and normal. Not in this case, though. From experience I knew that Anglo-Indians of her vintage preferred formality, found a sense of comfort in it. She nodded once, as if giving herself permission to say something practiced beforehand. 'I'll be frank. I am considering using your services on a rather delicate and unusual matter. But first, can you please tell me about yourself and your experience?'

Fredricks was uncomfortable about asking such a direct question; a muted pink hue flushed across her cheeks. She needn't have been, most of my clients asked something similar. I had the spiel down pat.

'I'll keep it brief, Mrs Fredricks. I've got nine years' experience as a private investigator, the last six in my own business. I don't specialise, but mainly work on surveillance cases. I've been told, I've got a good sense of observation. Pick up things others don't see. That's not to say I don't do other types of jobs. Before that I worked for six years in the Victoria Police, the last two in the sexual crimes unit. If I could give you references, they'd tell you that I am reliable and discreet. Unfortunately, it's because I'm reliable and discreet that I can't give you any references.'

What I said must have pleased her. Her lips formed into a thin, aristocratic smile.

'That's excellent, Mr Ryder.' She paused. 'Now, do you remember the news about the Indian actress who died at Uluru a couple of weeks ago?' she asked.

I remembered scanning articles and seeing something about it in the papers, but not much detail. 'A little.'

'The name of the actress was Subhani Mehta. I am a friend of the family and I've known…knew… Subhani since she was a baby.' Her eyes became glassy. She blinked them dry. 'From what I understand, the authorities are saying that she died of natural causes.'

I nodded for her to continue. Her hands left her knees and came together on her lap, holding each other. 'Her family is distraught. They are struggling to come to terms with this and they cannot believe that she…died…naturally.' The last few words came out as forced whispers as she tried to keep control of her emotions. Her right hand darted into her left sleeve and pulled out a tissue. She dabbed her eyes.

Instinctively, I leant forward, about to place my hand on her arm, show empathy. Then experience kicked in and told me that such familiarity may not be welcomed from a person of Fredricks' background and age. I pulled back, thought about the implications of what she just said.

'I'm sorry for your loss, Mrs Fredricks. I know this must be difficult to talk about, but what exactly are you saying? Does her family think that she was murdered?'

She rolled her damp eyes and gave a defeated sigh. 'I don't know. Subhani was a fit, healthy young woman. She didn't drink much, didn't smoke, exercised regularly. It just doesn't seem normal for such a healthy young girl to die for no reason.'

I could see where this was going.

Fredricks faced me once again. 'The police investigation was wrapped up so quickly. They may have overlooked something,' she said.

'So you want me to double check?'

'Yes.'

I took out my notebook and wrote 'Vivienne Fredricks (client), Subhani Mehta (subject)' on the top of a new page.

'Tell me how Subhani died,' I said.

It only took about five minutes for her to give me an account of what happened at Uluru.

'I'm sorry, I don't know anything more.' She dabbed her eyes dry again.

On the face of it this job seemed like a straightforward reconnaissance, though for some reason there was something agitating in the back of my mind, like an alarm in the distance. With all the evidence pointing one way, why would the family think something else was at cause? Then again, it never surprised me how often people looked for a reason for death. Needing someone or something to blame.

Fredricks must have picked up on my thoughts. 'I know you will probably not find out anything new, Mr Ryder. But it would perhaps make the family feel better, knowing we did everything we could.' Her eyebrows knotted together in a plea, making her look desperate and pathetic at the same time. A look her face was not used to.

'I'm happy to take on your case, but I don't want you or the family to have any false expectations,' I told her. The truth was I had no other jobs in the pipeline and this looked like money for jam.

She looked relieved, sat back in her chair. 'I understand. Thank you.'

'I should tell you about my fee structure, Mrs Fredricks. My base rate is …'

Fredricks cut me off with a gently raised hand. 'Mr Ryder, I am acting on behalf of the Mehta family. Your fees will not be a problem,' she said. 'However, we are anxious for you to commence as soon as possible. I would appreciate it if you could meet me in one week's time with an update on the investigation.'

This was beginning to sound like the perfect job, a clear-cut case with rich clients. My daily rate had just doubled and I could think of a few expensive expenses. I was glad Fredricks came to me, wondered how she got my name.

'Just out of curiosity, Mrs Fredricks. How did you come by my details?' I asked.

She smiled. 'I belong to the same club as your mother. She told me to contact you.'

I had to stifle a laugh. The 'club' was the Anglo-Indian club of Victoria. My parents had been members for years. Whenever possible, the club preferred to keep things 'in-house'. Whether you needed a mechanic, a plumber, a doctor or anything else, there was always somebody's husband, son or daughter who could do the job. A community within a community, with mates' rates to boot. My expenses just became less expensive.

Every Sunday, after the morning mass, the club would meet at the hall of St Jude's Church in Dandenong, the centre of the city's south-eastern sprawl. The convention was that every family had to bring a meal for sharing over lunch. This usually turned into a competition over who made the best beef vindaloo, lamb korma or other spicy treats. For my money, nobody came close to my mum's tandoori chicken. Her secret was to add extra ginger, which gave her dish a rounded warmth that balanced the sharp heat of the chilli.

The competition also flowed on to children's occupations. The parents at the top of the pecking order had children who entered the church—Christian, from the British influence, not Hindu like most Indians. This was becoming a rarity, however, and so bragging rights were awarded to parents of doctors, lawyers and business people. The next tier of pride went to parents of teachers, nurses or children in IT. As far as I knew, my job wasn't even considered a real occupation and was a source of disappointment for my parents, in particular my dad, who thought I'd left a respectable and well-paying vocation and dived head-first into the sleaze business. I couldn't blame him for his view. He came from hard-working public service stock. And anyway, he was mostly right.

My father was a mathematics master in India, but his qualifications were not recognised in Australia. So, for as long as I can remember, he worked in the railways—shunting carriages, selling tickets. Gradually, he worked his way up the ladder high enough to sit in front of a computer. It wasn't glamorous work, but it was respectable and honest, and I suspect he liked the uniform. He saw those same qualities in the police force. The day I graduated, he was so proud he hugged me. I couldn't remember the last time he had done that. When I left the force, it was like a public humiliation for him. It was no day at the races for me, either.

The PI job didn't even come with a badge, let alone a uniform. Nonetheless, when someone needed the assistance of an investigator, or anything to do with security, my parents were quick to mention my name. Probably because they thought I was hard up for cash.

'So, Mr Ryder, have you worked for anyone else from the club?' Fredricks asked. Even though she asked this casually, I knew she was fishing. It was in her eyes.

'Yes, a few times. Advising on security equipment, marital and family issues. Things like that. You will understand that I cannot say more.'

'You *are* discreet. That's good. I am relying on your discretion also.'

'Absolutely,' I replied.

By the time I got back to Collingwood that distant alarm had returned, however its cause was annoyingly no clearer. From the look of things, the case seemed fairly cut and dry, though for some unknown reason I still felt uneasy, my head and gut not in alignment. I couldn't shake the feeling that the job could be more complicated than I first thought. Then again, complex cases took longer to solve, and I had rich clients.

CHAPTER 3

It was three days after the conversation with Vivienne Fredricks. I had only just managed to get a flight to Uluru, thanks to a last-minute cancellation. The plane was full, mostly older tourists who wanted to climb the rock before it was closed for good in two weeks' time. They spoke loudly to one another, even when they were close, like excited children on a school excursion.

The previous two days had been busy. The internet provided some useful background information on Subhani Mehta's death, mainly from archived newspaper articles. With Bec's help, I was also able to make an appointment with the local police in Yulara, the small town where most people stayed when visiting Uluru.

The flight gave me time to re-read the newspaper reports. Australian papers didn't say too much, just that an Indian actress died while on set at Uluru. It was far bigger news for Indian newspapers. I scanned the series of headlines: 'Subhani Mehta Dead', 'Tragedy Strikes Bollywood', 'Subhani Was Pregnant' and 'Subhani Mehta Cremated'. The article on the pregnancy interested me the most.

Subhani Was Pregnant

In yet another shock after the tragic death of Subhani Mehta in Australia, an autopsy has revealed that the actress was approximately three months pregnant when she died. Ms Mehta was not married and was not known to be in a relationship. The question of paternity of the ill-fated child still remains.

While not officially released yet, the autopsy has ruled out any suspicious circumstances surrounding the actress' untimely demise, but has also been unable to pinpoint the cause of death.

Ms Mehta's distraught father, Mr Aamir Mehta, owner of Mehta Paper Products, claimed his daughter's body two days ago and has brought her back to Mumbai. While the details of the funeral arrangements are yet to be advised, it is expected that Ms Mehta's body will be cremated within the week.

There were plenty of pictures of Subhani Mehta on the net. In the one I printed, she had her head cocked to the left, allowing her hair to fall over her right eye in a sultry pose. Her sharp nose looked small compared to her voluptuous, red lips that were parted in a seductive smile. I was surprised how fair-skinned she was.

It reminded me about my own childhood. How my cousins and I used to tease each other over who was the darkest. While other Australian kids were trying to get a tan during summer, we'd stay out of the sun, wearing long sleeved shirts and hats, afraid of getting darker. The lighter we were, the more we'd blend in. That was the theory, anyway.

The plane commenced a turbulent descent to Uluru and, after a stomach-turning landing, was soon taxiing to the terminal. Through the window everything looked clear and vivid. A mobile staircase was attached to the plane and when I stepped out, the hot dry wind knocked my head back with a searing uppercut. The pores around my face and neck prickled with the heat and a welcoming party of flies greeted me like long-lost family as I walked swiftly across the radiating tarmac.

My first view of Australia's red centre was through a squint. The sky was a crisp blue, marred only by the white smudge of faraway clouds. The land stretched in endless plains of powdery, rusty red dust, spotted khaki green by the outback scrub, the distant horizon vaporising in the heat.

My hotel room was basic, which was fine; I wasn't expecting any company. I was just grateful to find any accommodation during this tourist crush. The mattress wasn't too soft and the air conditioner worked. I dumped my bag and walked back to reception.

'Excuse me, can you tell me how to get to the police station?' I asked the woman at the front desk who had earlier checked me in.

She looked up, surprised and concerned. 'Is there anything wrong?' she enquired.

'No, no, everything's fine. I just have a meeting there later today,' I assured her.

She blushed, slightly embarrassed at her initial reaction and thumbed a stray lock of straight black hair behind her ear. 'It's about a kilometre up the road.' She pointed to the right. 'You can't miss it. The whole town is built in a big loop.'

It was 2 pm in the afternoon and my appointment with Senior Sergeant Davis was at 5 pm. 'Thanks. I think I'll take a walk around for a while and check out the town. Get something to eat.'

'It's way too hot to walk,' she said. 'It's only a five-minute drive to the town centre. There are plenty of eateries there.'

I looked out the window and saw the air above the carpark bitumen shimmering like a mirage.

'Thanks for the advice,' I said as I felt in my pocket for the hire car key.

According to the tourist map, it was a five-minute walk from the town centre to Yulara's five star resort, named Sails in the Desert, due to the overhead sheets of canvas providing shade. Fredricks told me Subhani Mehta had stayed there. I finished my burger and decided to brave the sun.

It was a bad decision. The maze of confusing little pathways and identical buildings conspired against me, leading me down false trails and making the walk take closer to fifteen minutes. The heat was omnipresent, pressing down from above and reflecting up from the concrete pavement.

By the time the resort came into view, my shirt was wet with sweat. I welcomed the cool air in the lobby by stretching my arms Christ-like, allowing the wet patches under my arms to chill. A group of elderly hotel guests watched me enter and shared an empathic smile with me.

'Hot out there,' said the receptionist as I walked towards her. She wore the same beige uniform as the lady in my hotel.

'Just a bit,' I said, flashing my best smile.

'How may I help you?' a Cheshire cat smile stretched across her face in response.

'I'd like to speak with anyone who remembered the Indian actress who stayed here not so long ago, the one that died,' I said.

Her smile dropped instantly. 'Why are you asking?' she queried in hushed tones now, so that none of the other guests could hear.

'I'm an investigator. I've been hired by the family to make some enquiries,' I responded.

'Ahhh,' she hesitated, raised a finger to me. 'Let me just page the manager for you.' She picked up the phone, pressed a button and spoke in a low, conspiratorial tone into the receiver.

'Mr Henderson will be with you shortly,' she said, hanging up the phone and moving to the far side of the desk. She found some paperwork to make herself busy with.

Shortly after, a tall, bald man approached from a passageway behind the receptionist's desk. From his pale complexion I guessed he hadn't been here very long or that he didn't go outside much. He wore the male version of the same uniform. From what I read, the whole town was owned by the one single company.

He walked around the desk to greet me. 'Hello, I'm Ian Henderson. I'm the manager here.' He offered his hand as he spoke, more out of habit than out of genuine intent. He was younger than I initially thought, the baldness adding years. Henderson's eyes darted over my shoulder, to the other guests.

'Natalie has told me what you're here about. I'm sorry but we can't help you. It's hotel policy not to talk about our guests.' Henderson spoke quietly, yet firmly. He hadn't let go of my hand yet. Instead, he placed his left hand on my arm and used his grip to gently guide me towards the front door. It was a lesson in Hotel Management 101—*How to deal with difficult people in front of hotel patrons.* It was time to become a little more difficult.

'That's very disappointing, Mr Henderson. It's not every day that a guest dies while staying at this hotel. I was really hoping you could help with the investigation.' I spoke loud enough for the guests to hear, though not so loud as to make it obvious.

Henderson cast a quick look around the lobby. The guests pretended to continue doing whatever it was they were doing, but by now their quiet conversations had thinned and they were all waiting to see what would happen next. Henderson's face flushed and a blue vein near his left eye pulsed. He let go of my hand.

'Okay. We can speak in my office,' he said with a broad smile that was meant for everyone in the room but me.

I sat on the other side of his bland desk in his inoffensive office. Blonde-wood veneer furniture, cream carpets, large postcard picture of Uluru hanging on the wall behind him. There were no personal touches, no family photos, no knick-knacks, nothing. Everything in Yulara seemed uniform, even the uniforms.

'That was a pretty cute stunt you pulled out there,' Henderson sounded annoyed.

'Thanks,' I said. 'I've found that sometimes I need to give people a reason to talk with me. Otherwise, I'd get lonely.' I gave him my card, which he glanced at before tossing it on his desk.

'Let's just get this over with, huh. What do you want?' he asked.

'Like I said to the lady at reception. I just want to know what Subhani Mehta was like. That's all.'

Henderson pursed his lips while he thought. 'Okay. But only on one condition. You leave the guests and my staff alone.'

'You tell me what you know, and I won't bother anyone here again.'

The negotiation over, we could get on with business. Without saying another word, Henderson turned to the computer that was placed on an angle on his desk and made some keystrokes. A printer behind his desk came to life and he grabbed the fresh printout.

'This is the register for that month,' he said as he ran his finger down a list of names.

'Only three members of the crew stayed here. Ms Mehta, Mr Singh and Mr Nadar. If I remember correctly, all the other crew members stayed at the Outback Pioneer.' He looked up at me. 'It's only three-star,' he explained, said it like it was a bad thing. It was the place I was staying.

'We don't get Indian movie stars staying here often, so we didn't know what to expect,' he recalled. 'We have had celebrities behaving badly before, so we are ready for that, but they were fine. Well, the two guys were anyway.'

'What about Subhani, did she do something wrong?'

'Oh, no, I didn't mean that. I just never got a chance to speak with her. Nobody did.'

'What do you mean?' I asked, intrigued.

'When she arrived, we were given strict instructions not to bother her at all. As far as I know, she never left her room, except for when they were filming. She even ate in her room. The only person allowed in was Mr Singh. Not even the cleaners.'

'That's weird,' I said.

'We just put it down to movie-star eccentricity.' He forced a smile that a mistimed blink would miss. 'Now, if there is nothing more, I would like you to leave.'

'Are you sure there is nothing else? I mean, you seemed very determined to get rid of me just before.'

From the movement underneath his cheeks I could tell Henderson was clenching and releasing his jaw over and over again.

'You may not have noticed, but this is a five-star hotel. Our guests pay good money to enjoy themselves, not to hear macabre stories about how someone died. Out in the lobby you insinuated that Ms Mehta died in this hotel itself. You saw how the guests reacted to that. You banked on it.' Henderson grew more animated as he spoke. 'The only reason why I'm talking to you now is to stop you poking around and disturbing our guests any further,' he said, jabbing a finger in my direction. He looked away from me, took some time to regain his composure. When he spoke again, he was back in control.

'Listen, important people from around the world have stayed here, politicians, celebrities, artists. They expect privacy and we give it to them. Imagine how they'd feel if one of our staff blabbed about what went on in their rooms, or someone's eating habits, or whatever. That's why we don't talk about our guests.'

I raised my hands as an offering of peace. 'Rest assured, Mr Henderson. Subhani Mehta won't be complaining.'

CHAPTER 4

It was close to 5 pm when I entered the Yulara police station. An electronic alert buzzed over the grinding hum of the air conditioner as I walked in through the front door. The officer slouched over the counter doing paperwork looked up.

'G'day,' he said, slowly straightening. His khaki uniform was much better suited to this environment than the navy blue I used to wear. I told him about my appointment with Senior Sergeant Davis.

'Just a sec, mate. I'll call him,' he said as he lifted the phone.

A short while later, a bulk of a man approached me, his belly drooping over his police issue belt.

'Mr Ryder, I'm Senior Sergeant Steve Davis,' he said in a high-pitched voice that didn't suit his build. From the strength of his handshake Davis had his fair share of muscle hidden amidst the mass. His short-cropped grey hair had traces of the brown it once was. He led me to an interview room out the back of the station.

'Thanks for meeting with me,' I said as I handed him a card. He looked at it casually before slipping it into his shirt pocket.

'Don't thank me. Thank that female officer friend of yours. If it weren't for her putting in a good word for you, I wouldn't have met you. I'm only doing this as a favour to a fellow officer. She said you used to be one of us?'

I nodded. 'That was a few years ago now.'

'So, what happened?'

'Basically, I got my arse kicked so hard you can still see the boot print. I'm not here to talk about me though.'

Davis weighed me up for a long ten seconds before smiling. 'I hope they were wearing steel caps,' he said, before offering me an instant coffee. I reflected on the hygiene levels of the kitchens in police stations I had worked at and politely refused.

We sat down at the table. Davis' shirt stretched across his ample belly and one button in particular looked to be under a great deal of stress. A small band of flies circled above us, occasionally bumping into the windowpane.

'First thing,' he said as he held up a chubby thumb. 'Everything I say is off the record. Okay?'

I shrugged. 'We're not even having this conversation.'

He smiled approvingly, dipped his head.

'So, you're looking into that actress' death, huh?' he said. Davis sipped some coffee, then smacked his lips. 'It seemed fairly straightforward to me. What exactly are you investigating about the death?' he enquired.

I told him what I was engaged to do. 'Judging by what I've read so far, I don't think there is anything more to this. But the family has the right to ask the question,' I said.

'Yeah, sure.' He took another sip. Davis placed the mug on the table, then held both hands together. 'So, what do you want to ask me?' he asked earnestly.

'You responded to the call. Can you tell me what happened?' I asked.

'Well, it was almost three weeks ago now. I checked the files before you came. We received a phone call from the Cultural Centre at about noon. A member of the film crew had run in telling them that someone was dying and that they needed help.'

He leaned back in his chair. 'Normally, when someone gets sick, they get stretchered off the rock. When we heard how serious the situation was, it seemed pretty clear that we would have to attempt an airlift.'

'I rang the National Parks Office and told them what was happening. Ten minutes later I was on a helicopter with two paramedics. We landed about 100 metres from where the film crew were. When we got there, she wasn't breathing. The paramedics tried to resuscitate her, but I could tell that they were wasting their time. She was gone.'

'What did you do?' I asked.

He drained his mug. 'Everyone up there was in shock. I secured the scene as best as I could. There was nothing much to secure though, just her body lying face up on the rock. From her positioning, I could tell that they had moved the body to try and resuscitate her. They crossed her arms over her chest when they knew it was too late.'

'Did you see or think there was anything unusual?'

Davis' hazel eyes fixed on the table. 'We see lots of dead bodies in this job. Mostly from car accidents, bloody idiots. We had a car roll over only yesterday. Speeding so that they could get to the rock five minutes earlier. Another fatality.' He paused, shaking his head. 'But we also have a few die trying to climb the rock.' He looked back at me. 'There was nothing unusual to me.' Davis shrugged, making his neck disappear into his shoulder blades.

'Nothing at all? No signs of a struggle?'

'No, nothing like that.'

'Are you sure? No bruises, no blood, no torn clothing, anything like that?'

'I'm sure because I saw the footage they were filming at the time. One minute she's dancing and the next the poor girl is dead.' Davis snapped his fingers. 'Just like that.'

'Can I take a look at the footage please?' I asked, thinking the film may answer all my client's questions.

Davis shook his head. 'Sorry mate, that wouldn't be appropriate. Besides, we don't have it anymore. Once the investigation was closed, we returned the footage. The film company made sure we didn't keep any copies. Something about it being their intellectual property.'

We both nodded sagely, as if we both understood intellectual property law. I knew at least one of us was bluffing. 'So, just to confirm, in your opinion was it natural causes?' I asked.

Davis winced. 'I guess so, but you can see the panic in the girl's eyes in the footage. It was as if she was fighting to stay alive.' Davis shook his head. 'It was not a nice way to die.'

'What do you mean by fighting to stay alive?' I asked.

'Well, fighting, struggling. Either way, it wasn't pretty.'

'So when you said that there was no signs of struggle, that's not completely accurate. She did struggle, but it was just with herself.' I clarified.

Davis looked away, then back at me. I could sense his patience wearing thin.

'Look, if we're getting into semantics then I'd probably call it a spasm. Either way, I'm telling you that there was no sign of...,' Davis' voice trailed away, for a moment his gaze drifted before focusing back on me. 'For what it's worth she did have a cut on the palm of her hand.'

'Her palm?' I questioned.

'Yeah, it seems when she died, she was clutching a necklace in her hand. From the footage it looked as if she tangled her hand while she was struggling,' Davis stopped, checked himself. 'I mean having a spasm and wrenched it off. Hard enough that she cut herself. She had a corresponding mark on the back of her neck. That's about all. Like I said, nothing much. Nothing suspicious, if that's what you're looking for.'

Davis had no more to add. The Is had been dotted, now it was time to cross the Ts.

'The newspapers mentioned an autopsy. Is there a Coroner's Office here?'

'Not here, we're too small for that. The body was taken to Darwin.'

'Darwin,' I repeated, 'Who conducted the autopsy?'

Davis chuckled. 'Her name is Julie Mahoney, but you're not going to get much out of her, if that's what you're thinking. Particularly after her report was leaked. She's really pissed off about that.'

'Leaked, huh. Did she find out who did it?'

'Not yet, but she will. She's determined about that.'

An idea came to mind. 'Can you give me her number?'

Davis shook his head. 'No. This is as far as my courtesy goes. We haven't even talked, remember?'

'Fair enough,' I replied, smiling. 'It was worth a try. Thanks for your time.'

I stood up, leaned over the table to shake his hand. 'For what it's worth,' he said, the coroner will be here tomorrow to look at the scene of that fatality that happened yesterday.'

By the time I got back to my hotel room and found the phone number for the coroner's office in Darwin, it was closed. I left a message for Julie Mahoney; said I wanted to talk about leaked reports, repeated my mobile number twice. After that I grabbed a pizza and a six-pack of beer from a take-away restaurant and walked up to one of the lookout hills scattered around the town. It wasn't a long hike, but even at this late hour beads of sweat trickled down my face and back from the heat. I sat on a wooden bench and twisted the cap off a beer. My ankles itched from walking through the needle-like spinifex plants. When I bent down to scratch them, I noticed that my boots and the lower parts of my jeans were covered in the fine rusty dust. It made them look old and worn, like everything else the dust touched. I wondered what it would do to me.

CHAPTER 5

By 9 am the next day I was at the Uluru carpark, nursing a mild hangover and brushing away flies from my face—the great Aussie salute. The base of Uluru was already full of tourists queueing to take their turn ascending the rock, including some of the elderly tourists from my flight. The line of people continued up the side of the rock, like a procession of ants following a scent trail. The rock dominated the landscape from afar. From up close it was intimidating, as if it had its own presence, own consciousness.

Up until then I hadn't really given much thought about climbing the rock. To be honest, I had deliberately avoided thinking about it. I knew the correct approach would be to check out the place where Subhani Mehta died. Not in the hope of finding any new evidence or clues, rather just to get a better feel of the place, to picture what happened. Instead, I spent the early-morning minutes staring at the majestic structure and prevaricating. A sign at the base asked people not to scale Uluru. It explained that for the Aboriginals this was a sacred place. A place where boys became men. A professional PI would climb it anyway, but it didn't sit well with me. It wasn't the cultural aspect that made me hesitate, rather it was about respect. This was their place, not mine. It was the second time my head and gut had disagreed during this case and this time I went with my gut. I looked for a reason not to climb.

The tourists didn't find themselves in the same moral quandary. I watched as they slowly and awkwardly defied gravity and age as they worked their way up. Their hoots and 'cooees' carried and echoed through the still air, making the place sound like a tacky theme park. It was all the reason I needed. I made my way to the Cultural Centre instead.

Built from thick earthen bricks, the Cultural Centre offered a welcome break from the burgeoning heat. It had just opened for the day, so I was the only tourist in the building. A young Aboriginal woman was pinning a poster onto a tall polished tree trunk that supported the high wooden ceilings. Light streamed in from a skylight above her, picking up the hues of the wooden beams along the way and flooding her in a honey-orange glow.

I waited until after she had straightened the poster and stepped down from the footstool. She was short and stocky, with long dark ringlets of hair. Her fringe was pinned back to keep it from falling over her round, chubby face. The name 'Anna' was printed on her badge.

'Hi, my name is Sam Ryder. I'm a private investigator,' I said as I gave her a card. 'Can I ask you a couple of questions? It won't take long.'

Anna looked down at my card. 'Suppose so, depends on what,' she replied, unconvinced.

'Were you working the day that the Indian actress died?'

'Um, yeah. But I don't know much about what happened.'

'Okay. I've only got a couple of questions. Anything you remember would be great.'

'Um, yeah…okay.' She smiled nervously. Her dark eyes scanned around the building, checking to see if we were alone.

'Thanks.' I smiled back, trying to put her at ease. 'I'm just doing some background checks. I understand that someone from the Cultural Centre called the police. Was that you?'

Anna nodded slowly, never taking her eyes of mine. 'First that guy ran in here. Then I made the call. Nothing else.'

'What did the guy say?' I asked delicately.

'I don't remember exactly. He was winded from the run, so we told him to breathe. When he could talk, he said the actress was dying, something like that.' She smiled nervously. 'We called the cops.'

'Do you remember anything else from that day?'

She shook her head. 'All I know is that it wasn't a good day. Never is when someone dies. We ask them not to climb. They don't listen. I don't know anything else.'

'Thanks for talking with me, Anna. Before, you said "we", was there someone else with you that day that I can also speak to?'

Anna glanced at the doorway marked 'Private' beside the information desk as she considered her response. A challenging look came into her eyes and she angled her face at me, cross-examiner style. 'Have you climbed Uluru?' she asked.

'No. I don't intend to.' I said, confused about the tangent she had taken.

Anna smiled and I felt as if I had passed some secret test. 'Uncle George was here that day. Follow me.'

Anna led me through the private doorway and out to a shack at the rear of the centre. A sign on the door said, 'Staff Only'. Anna opened it. Unlike the main building, the shack was made of weatherboard and the sun was slowly turning it into an oven, even at this early hour. Thick curtains covered all the windows in an attempt to keep some of the heat out. Instead, they just served to make the oven dark. It took a couple of seconds for my eyes to adjust to the gloom. She walked towards a figure in the shadows. 'Uncle George,' she spoke quietly, reverently. 'This guy wants to know about that actress who died.' After that brief introduction she left.

Uncle George sat on a chair at the far end of the shack. 'Come. Sit here,' he said, patting a nearby chair on his left. I sat down and took a closer look at him. It was hard to tell how old he was. His face, neck and arms were tough like weather-beaten leather, beef jerky. Tight silver curls of hair grew around the sides of his skull, leaving his dome barren. The same silver hairs covered everything on his face below his cheeks and his wide nose. He smiled at me, revealing a random gallery of yellowed teeth, as his face folded into a montage of wrinkles and crevasses. That was when I noticed his eyes. His left eye was a piercing brown, as striking as the day he was born. His right eye stole the attention though, the iris a ghostly white.

'What do you want to know?' he asked me in an ancient, grizzled voice.

I gave him the run down.

'Hmmm,' said the old man, his head slowly nodding. He paused for what felt like a lifetime. 'What do you know about Uluru?' he asked.

'I know that this is a sacred place for Aboriginal people.'

Uncle George reached with his left hand and clasped my right arm in a firm, but gentle way. With his right hand he made a broad sweeping movement.

'This place is a magical place for my mob. My ancestor spirits created it. They are still here today.'

Then, with a swiftness that caught me off guard, he turned towards me and gripped me across the shoulders with both hands. My face was inches away from his and I was drawn to his cataract eye.

'They're here now, watching us,' he whispered, his breath hot and damp on my face.

I fought the urge to free myself from his grasp, forced myself to relax as he continued to speak.

'The spirits talk to me. I hear them in the wind,' he said. 'I know why you're really here, even if you don't.' He let go with his right hand and thrust a finger into my chest. 'You gotta be careful.' With that, he slumped back in his chair, grew quiet.

It was clear he knew nothing that was of interest to me. I decided to stay for a little longer to be respectful. By now my eyes had adjusted to the dim and I watched a grey-green lizard about two inches long as it crawled along a wall. Every now and then it stopped to scan the room with sharp twists of its neck. Then it ducked behind one of the curtains and was gone. By now it was time for me to leave also. I made to get up off the chair when he gently rested his left hand on my right forearm again. 'Wait,' he said.

I let my weight fall back on the chair.

He set his one good eye on me. When he spoke, it was a more forceful voice than before—half angry, half fearful. 'That day, a bad spirit came here. Not our ancestors, it came with those people. The spirit took that girl.' He pointed outside, to where the rock would be. 'You be careful of that spirit, son. She'll take you too.'

We sat down for another timeless period of silence. This time Uncle George didn't stop me when I got up to leave. Anna was behind the counter of the Cultural Centre, keeping an eye on a couple of tourists admiring the Aboriginal art display in the far corner.

'Who is Uncle George?' I asked Anna as I approached.

She smiled, shrugged. 'George is George.'

On my way to the car, I noticed Uncle George had walked outside the shack. He slowly bent down and scooped up some of the red sand in his right hand. Saying some words that I could not hear, he let the sand sift through his fingers. He looked at me, nodded slowly and walked back inside.

***

I was already half-way back to my hotel but couldn't recall driving the distance, my mind still back in the old man's shack. It wasn't what he said that bothered me, I figured that to be just an old man's rantings; rather it was how he said it that I found disconcerting, his absolute certainty and the urgency of his warning. The scene replayed in my mind on loop until the sound of my mobile phone brought me back to the land of the living. I pulled over to the side of the road, the tyres kicking a plume of dust into the air.

'Sam Ryder,' I answered.

'Hello, this is Dr Julie Mahoney from the Northern Territory Coroner's Office. I'm returning your call from yesterday. You have some information about leaked reports?'

'Yes,' I lied, figuring this would be the only way she would talk with me. 'But I don't want to talk about it on the phone. Is it possible we can meet to discuss this?'

There was a weighty pause on the other end of the line. Eventually she spoke. 'Yes, okay. I am not in Darwin today but should be back tomorrow afternoon.'

'Actually, I am in Yulara. I understand that you are here also. Is there any chance we can meet later today?'

There was another pause, not so long this time. 'I'm not going to ask how you know about my whereabouts, Mr Ryder, but since we both seem to be at Yulara today how about we meet at Maxim's Café at 3 pm? It should be reasonably private. I hope you're not wasting my time.'

I drove back to my hotel, had the early afternoon to myself. Julie Mahoney's LinkedIn profile told me very little, apart from that she had been a forensic pathologist for fifteen years and had worked in Victoria and South Australia before her current stint at the Northern Territory. There was no picture.

The rest of the day was free and I spent most of it either in the hotel pool or lazing on one of the lounges that surrounded the pool. A family of four from the Gold Coast took up position on neighbouring lounges.

'Have you climbed Uluru yet?' asked the father, his attention shared between me and the children in the pool.

'No, don't think I will,' I replied. 'Have you?'

A victorious smile spread across his face. 'Yeah, climbed it today. I know they don't want us to, but I climbed it with my dad when I was a kid, and now I've climbed it with my boys. It's like a tradition.' I smiled at the irony.

'Tell me, how hard was the climb?' I asked, genuinely interested.

'The first part is brutal, almost vertical,' he nodded towards his sons in the pool. 'I wasn't sure they would make it past that bit. It gets less steep after that, but it is still hard, and it's also really hot. All in all, it almost killed us!' he said, his smile returning.

CHAPTER 6

Maxim's Café was in the middle of Yulara's cheap-eats strip, flanked by the burger joint I had eaten at before and a fish and chips shop that smelt of grease. The cafe was close to empty, being too late for lunch and too early for dinner. An Asian couple sat inside, looking over tourist brochures while two cups of milky coffee went untouched on their table. I arrived a quarter of an hour early. The air conditioning was almost non-existent, and I wanted some privacy; took an outside table, underneath the shade-cloth. A waiter sauntered over and handed me a menu. I asked for a beer.

'Mr Ryder?' questioned a confident voice behind me about ten minutes later.

I turned around and stood up. 'Dr Mahoney, thank you for coming,' I replied, shaking her hand.

Julie Mahoney was dressed in a stylish light grey pantsuit with a thin pale blue stripe that picked up the teal in her eyes. Her ash blonde hair was tied in a tight ponytail, revealing a pinched, narrow face. She was in her mid-forties at the most, but a smoker's harshness lined the edges of her eyes and mouth.

She sat down, noticed the half empty glass of beer in front of me.

'Would you like a drink?' I asked.

'I'm not here for a social event, Mr Ryder. I'm only here because of your phone call. What was it you wanted to tell me?' She spoke under her breath, but forcefully, the way married couples argue in public.

I just hoped what I was about to tell her wouldn't cause an argument now.

'Actually, I've been hired to investigate the death of Subhani Mehta. You conducted the autopsy on her that was leaked to the press. I think that maybe there is a link and perhaps we can help each other.'

Mahoney sank back in the chair. 'Shit!' She spat the word out. 'You lied to me. You don't know anything about the leak.'

'I know you're pretty pissed off about it.'

She moved to get up, the legs of her chair scraping on the pavement as she rose. I held my hands up in surrender. 'Listen, it's hot, and you're already here. Can I at least buy you a drink?' I asked.

She leaned forward, both hands propped on the table. I could tell she was angry, frustrated, but at least she was considering my offer. Then her head tilted back and her shoulders slumped as she sighed, she sat back down.

'Damn it, when we find out who it was, I'll have their arse,' she said, more to herself than me. She leant forward and jabbed at the table with a pointed finger. 'That report was supposed to be confidential. The media got it even before I had a chance to speak to her parents. Imagine how they must have felt!' Her face flashed an annoyed look, eyes wide.

'You know what else, what does it say about the professionalism of the Coroner's Office, of *me*?' She reached into her handbag and pulled out a packet of cigarettes and a lighter, used her left hand to shield against the warm breeze as she lit one.

It was clear, Mahoney's sense of professional pride had taken a battering because of the leak. I decided to play on that vulnerability. 'Look, I just want to know if what I read in the papers was accurate. If you can help me then maybe I can find out who leaked the report. After all, if you don't catch them, they could do it again. What have you got to lose?'

Mahoney took a deep drag and held it in, strummed the table with her left hand while she considered my latest offer.

She exhaled. 'I need that drink first,' she said and called over the waiter. 'A glass of the chardonnay, please.'

I smiled, at least she would stay until her drink was finished. She could do a lot of talking by then.

'Mr Ryder, you must understand that I am bound by privacy laws.'

I expected she'd say that. 'I know that, but you *can* tell me if what was reported is correct. That you could find no cause for death, and that she was pregnant?'

She sucked at the cigarette desperately, her face creasing along her smoker's lines. Mahoney kept the smoke in her lungs a long time before exhaling with a sigh. 'Look, I am very sorry for her family and friends, but that report was accurate. There was nothing that indicated a conclusive cause of death. Sometimes people just die. I could find nothing suspicious, if that's what you're looking for.'

The waiter returned with her glass of wine. She brought the glass to her mouth, exhaled smoke into it before taking a drink. The smoke twirled in the glass, trapped. Oak overtones with a nicotine finish.

'The baby, did you ever determine who the father was?' I asked.

'Mr Ryder, even if I did know the answer to that I wouldn't tell you.'

Mahoney took another deep, long drag, held it in, then exhaled. That done, she brutally stubbed the butt out in the ashtray.

'As it was, we had a real battle with the parents to conduct an autopsy at all.' She said before pausing to drink some wine. 'Something about the Hindu religion and desecration of the body. They had to be told it was the law in Australia that an autopsy had to be conducted on anyone who dies unexpectedly. You should have seen her dad when the report was leaked. He hit the roof. Especially about the baby.'

Her eyes widened. 'Mind you, I would have felt the same way if I were in his shoes,' she admitted.

I drank what was left of my beer. This interview was going largely how I expected. If the autopsy revealed nothing else this case was over.

'Is there nothing more you can tell me, Ms Mahoney? Was there anything in the report that wasn't mentioned in the media?'

'Why do you ask that?' she asked.

'Well, the leak obviously made a big splash in India. Someone would have been paid nicely for that. If there is any more information from the autopsy, I don't see why they wouldn't leak that also. Maybe they've held it back so that they can get another big payout. If there is anything else in Subhani's autopsy that hasn't been leaked yet, well, it may happen in the not-too distant future.'

'Another leak? Shit! That would completely ruin my reputation.' She closed her eyes and sighed.

I reached my hand across the table, stopping just short of hers. 'Was there anything else in the report, however small or insignificant?'

She looked away, as if recalling the report in her mind, then shook her head. 'No, that was all there was.'

I leant back on my seat, scratched my chin. 'So, she just died, huh?'

She leaned forward, placing both hands on the table. 'It's not as uncommon as you think. For example, some people are born with an abnormality in the heart called Long QT Syndrome. It's a defect in the genes that makes the heart beat irregularly.'

She patted her heart. 'It causes healthy, normal people to suddenly die. Unfortunately, the heart appears normal at autopsy, so we cannot identify it as the cause of death.'

'Are you saying Subhani Mehta may have died because of this syndrome?'

'Perhaps. We'll never know for sure. Do you know if she fainted often?'

'I don't know. Why?'

'That's usually a symptom of Long QT. Otherwise, there is very little to identify it with. Many people suffer from it without even knowing they have it. One minute they're doing something energetic, like playing soccer with their mates, the next they're dead. That's why it's also known as "Sudden Death".'

Mahoney finished what was left in her glass. 'So, what now?' she asked.

'Like I said, my focus is to look into the death of Subhani Mehta. If I find out anything that may help with the leak, you'll be the first to know. In the interim, I suggest you identify all of the people that may have had access to the report. People on lower salaries that may need some additional cash, also people with poor performance ratings. These are the people who are more likely to need an ego boost or have a grudge. If any of these people are also of Indian origin, I'd keep a close eye on them. It's all very general, but it's where I'd start looking.'

Mahoney nodded as I spoke, taking it all in, renewed determination in her eyes. I got the sense that she would follow my suggestions to the letter. I almost felt some pity for the leaker.

It was past 6 pm when I made it to the sunset-viewing area at Uluru. As the sun dipped lower into the horizon the colour of the rock transformed from rusty red, through various shades of scarlet and terracotta, before ending as a calm deep blue. The colour changes were like mood swings, passing through the five stages of grieving. Even though there were hundreds of people at the viewing carpark, I felt completely alone with my thoughts. The land was still, apart from a gentle wind that played with the plants. I began to feel how special this place was for Aboriginal people, for Uncle George, and wondered for whom the rock was mourning.

CHAPTER 7

I arrived back in Melbourne the following day, glad to be in familiar surrounds and a more moderate climate. The trip had gone as expected. The police and coroner both confirming that there were no suspicious circumstances to Subhani Mehta's death, although I wasn't quite sure what to make of the reclusive behaviour Subhani Mehta had shown. Uncle George was a distraction I tried to push out of my mind. My schedule was to provide my report to Vivienne Fredricks tomorrow. It would tell her nothing new, but I hoped it would provide some closure.

It wasn't until I got back to my house that I remembered to switch my phone off flight mode. It said there was one missed call and a new message. The call was from an unknown number, but the message was very familiar.

'When we're ready we're gonna fucking kill you. You're dead meat.'

It was the same Indian voice as the previous threat, though less high-pitched, more confident. A voice I first came across in my last case. It belonged to the leader of a gang of international students who were dealing drugs at a university campus. The university suspected something was wrong and wanted to keep it in-house with no police; so they contacted me, or more precisely my business—Australian Indian Investigations. I watched them over two weeks; four middle class kids playing gangster, a few pills here and there to make them feel badass. The pictures I took would probably get them a reprimand. I didn't think there was much more to it until I saw them beat up another student over what seemed like a transaction gone wrong. It wasn't so much the viciousness of the beating that stood out; I'd seen much worse. Rather, it was the way they attacked him without any fear of reprisal that made me think something more than a strict talking to was required. They jumped on the guy in front of his friends, just outside one of the cafes that surrounded the university. All four of them pummelled him with fists and kicks until he was a bloodied mass crumpled on the ground. Then the leader, a guy by the name of Sunil Devas, unzipped his fly and pissed on him as he tried to crawl away. They didn't care that people witnessed the assault, knowing nobody would dare come forward. I handed the university my evidence along with a strong recommendation to expel the students as part of their duty of care to other students. It seems they must have taken my advice.

For the first time in a long while I felt a little unnerved. Ideally, I figured I could take two of them out in a fair fight, then hope the other two would back down after that. Realistically, though, I knew the fight wouldn't be fair. They'd come armed, knives or bats. I checked the front door, double locked the deadbolt. Then poured myself a double scotch.

The next day I dressed in the same suit Fredricks had seen me in previously, only this time I had polished my shoes beforehand. The suit still needed a dry clean.

'Come in, Mr Ryder. It's very nice to see you again.' Vivienne Fredricks led me back to the sitting room. She wore a simple white dress. People paid extra for that kind of simplicity. Her hair was tied back in the familiar bun but this time I noticed more jewellery. Not much more, but enough to know she had taken some trouble.

An elderly man was already in the room, dressed in a dark blue suit, white shirt, matching blue tie.

'Mr Samson Ryder, please meet Mr Aamir Mehta, Subhani's father.' Mrs Fredricks paused before saying the last two words, said them with deference.

I was a little stunned at the introduction. 'Mr Mehta, please accept my condolences,' I said, offering my hand.

Mehta stood up slowly and shook my hand. 'Thank you, Mr Ryder,' he said in a frail voice that held the barest hint of an Indian accent.

Mehta looked to be in his sixties and in good shape. He was lean and when he stood up, he was slightly taller than me. His grey hair was cut short and parted to the side with military precision. The same grey hair was neatly clipped into a thin line above his top lip. His eyes were big, brown discs that drew you in and his lips would have made Angelina Jolie proud. It was not hard to guess where Subhani Mehta had got her looks. I was surprised by the fragility of Mehta's voice. A frame such as his would normally come with a commanding voice. But these were not normal times for Aamir Mehta.

'Please take a seat, Mr Ryder,' said Mrs Fredricks. 'Aamir knew you were giving me your report today and he wanted to be here. He caught the first flight he could.'

I recalled the newspaper articles; Mehta was a wealthy industrialist.

'Thank you, Vivienne,' he said. With that she left the room, dismissed. Mehta watched as she shut the door behind her, then he turned to me.

'Mr Ryder, I'm sure Mrs Fredricks has told you how much my wife and I have suffered during this time. I am grateful to you for investigating this sad business. I wanted to hear directly from you what you found out.'

He sounded so eager, so hopeful. I wasn't sure if he would like what I had to say.

'Mr Mehta, when I took on this case there were no promises about finding new evidence.'

He nodded quickly, keen for me to continue.

'Sir, I have spoken with the police officer who did the initial investigation and also with the forensic pathologist who conducted the autopsy.' Mehta winced when I said the word 'autopsy'.

I continued: 'From my investigation, I have to conclude that the findings of the autopsy report are accurate.'

Mehta opened his mouth to speak but I jumped in. 'What this means is that Subhani died from natural causes. There was nothing sinister in her death.' Instantly I realised that my comments were too callous, too matter of fact. This was his daughter I was talking about, not some stranger. My words hung heavy in the room and I could see the disappointment in Mehta's eyes. It was the same look my father had when I told him I had left the police force.

To his credit Mehta kept his composure. 'Thank you, Mr Ryder, that is some comfort,' he said, his hand knocking on the upholstered arm of the couch. 'However, I still can't help but feel there is more to this.'

I wasn't sure what he wanted, but felt I owed him more and wanted to ease his suffering.

'Sir, there was something else mentioned in the autopsy report. Something that I'm sure you are aware of.' Julie Mahoney told me she had given him a copy of the report.

Mehta rose slowly and walked stiffly around the room, hands behind his back.

'You are referring to the pregnancy.' He sighed heavily. 'Yes, I am aware of that. I have seen the medical report.' Mehta turned to face me. 'But that was not responsible for my daughter's death. There *has* to be more than just that.' He sounded like a man searching for the answers to a question he didn't know.

This whole conversation with Aamir Mehta had thrown me off script. I didn't expect to be speaking with him in the first place and now he wanted me to tell him something I didn't know. There was only one other thing I could think of.

'Tell me, did your daughter suffer from fainting attacks?'

'Fainting attacks? Of course not. She was a healthy young woman. Why are you asking this?'

As part of my preparation for this meeting I had researched Long QT Syndrome, or Sudden Death, online. It was just like Julie Mahoney had said. For a person with Long QT, their heart can suddenly begin to beat so quickly that it can't effectively pump blood around the body. Like a car backfiring. In mild cases it can lead to fainting attacks, but just as often it can lead to cardiac arrest. Usually it occurred when a person was undergoing some form of rigorous activity—like dancing on top of Uluru in the middle of a heatwave.

The article used a lot of medical jargon and diagrams to describe what actually causes it, most of which I skimmed over. The gist of it was that some people's hearts are wired a little differently from others. The tragedy was that the condition is hard to diagnose in the living, fainting spells being the most visible sign, and impossible to diagnose once a person is dead.

I explained what I knew about the syndrome to Aamir Mehta, which didn't take long.

'You're asking if my daughter was a genetic defect?' A rage flashed across his face before he regained control. He raised his right hand up in a conciliatory gesture, palm spread wide. 'No, no. You are right to ask such questions. It is why I am paying you.' He sat back down on the edge of the chair. 'But I know something is not right,' he said, shaking a clenched fist.

'Sir, the evidence suggests that your daughter died of natural causes. I know this must be difficult, but perhaps it is for the best if you accept this, carry on with your own life.'

'But is that the full evidence? Who else did you speak with?'

'Mr Mehta, there *is* no one else to speak with. The only other witnesses were the people involved in the movie and they are all back in India.' As soon as the words left my mouth I knew where he was going with this.

'I see,' he said. 'My wife and I will not be at peace until we know that every stone has been turned, every lead checked.' His voice grew in strength. 'Mr Ryder, please, come to India and finish the job.' He clasped his hands together in a plea.

I was losing control of the situation, not that I had much to begin with. 'Mr Mehta, believe me I would really like to help you, however I don't know if there is anything more I can find out. I also don't have a licence to operate in India,' I replied.

'I understand,' he said sadly. Then his face lit up like it was Christmas. 'What if you come as a tourist and work solely for me? Nobody would have to know.'

I hesitated. 'I don't know about that, Mr Mehta.'

'Please, Mr Ryder. I am begging you. If you come, you will be handsomely compensated. How about 10,000 USD per week, plus expenses?' he said.

For the briefest of moments I was stunned, my whole body flushed. Ten thousand bucks! He was a desperate man who either had no value for money, or, more likely, knew precisely the value of money. It made me cautious.

'That's certainly very attractive, but my problem is that I don't have any contacts or networks in the film industry there.'

Mehta had an answer for everything. 'Do not worry about that, Mr Ryder. I have some friends in the industry that will help.'

I still wasn't sure. 'Mr Mehta, why do you want me to do this? Why not hire someone in India to take on the case?' I asked.

He looked me in the eye. 'I know it would be cheaper to use someone from over there, but money is not my motivation. I feel I can trust you and you have come so far. This is important to me. If you find anything out, I know you will tell me, rather than the media. I could not be so confident about a local investigator.'

I didn't know what more Mehta thought I could uncover. Perhaps he was just after peace of mind? For 10,000 USD per week I'd try and get it for him. There was also something else about him, a sadness that I saw also in my parents, a sadness I would do anything to ease for them but couldn't. Maybe I could do it for him.

He smiled when I told him that it would take a few days to organise things. I gave him my business card and told him I'd be in contact. In return, Mehta gave me a cheque for my services provided to date and an advance on the first week. It felt hot in my hands.

CHAPTER 8

It took four days to get an Indian visa and book a flight. A couple of days before my flight I went to my parents' home for Sunday dinner, a ritual that my elder sister Anjali and I participated in ever since we moved out. My Father would lead prayers around the dinner table—taking literally the '*family that prays together, stays together*' motto—and then we'd eat. Significant partners were also welcome.

The only person I had ever brought to dinner was Caroline. We were pretty serious for a while but broke up about two years ago. At the time we agreed it was no one's fault, that we just grew apart, but deep down I knew that wasn't the case.

We had started off like all lovers start off, full of untamed sparks that could light a room as easily as torch a house. Everything was possible and our future full of optimism. We couldn't keep our hands off each other and pillow talk stretched deep into the early hours of the morning. Even when our relationship had matured and the spark became a steady flame, we were still engrossed in each other, lust growing to love. Then, around four years ago, a tragedy changed my life, changed my family's life, and I didn't know how to cope. Instead, I just closed myself down, overwrought with guilt.

It turned out that in punishing myself I was also punishing Caroline. She said that for our relationship to thrive we needed to be completely open with each other and that I wasn't doing that. She wanted to know how I felt about things, pleaded with me to let her inside my head, to share my grief and fear. I couldn't do that, couldn't let her know the anguish and the anger that was boiling inside me, couldn't let her see my weakness and shame, my impotence to act when I should have. I couldn't do any of that then and still couldn't do that now.

Anjali, on the other hand, had no compunctions about bringing different men to meet my parents, none of whom hung around very long. At times it felt like she brought a new guy for dinner every week and I worried what my parents must have thought about her lifestyle. Now, only I came to Sunday dinner and the house seemed smaller, darker, the atmosphere almost claustrophobic.

When I told my parents that I was going to Mumbai on a job they didn't believe me at first.

'Business must be booming!', called my mother from the kitchen. Despite living in Australia for half her life she still sounded Indian, with soft, rounded vowels.

'Do you know someone in your club called Vivienne Fredricks?' I asked.

She walked into the dining room, holding a large *handi* with oven mitts, steam billowing from the top. She placed the chicken curry on a tablemat, next to the saffron rice. The smell of turmeric and coriander filled the room.

'Oh yes, she comes to our church every now and then. I gave her your number. Did she call you?'

'Yes. A friend of hers wants me to do some work in Mumbai. I think I'll only be there for a week or so, but I've got an open-ended ticket.'

'Well, whatever it is, I'm sure you'll do a good job.' My parents preferred not to know the details of what I was doing, particularly if I was working for someone they knew.

My father listened on without saying anything, eyeing off the chicken curry. He waited until mum sat down next to him, reached out to her with his left hand and applied a gentle squeeze to her arm, a loving smile. His way of saying thanks. They had aged so much in the last four years. Since Anjali died.

Dad's hair was all but gone and his face had hollowed out. His cheeks had sunk, giving him a harried, haunted look. As for mum, her hair was still dark brown, but now it came from a bottle, and tell-tale signs of grey stood out near her scalp. She still had beautiful eyes, although the twinkle in them had faded. My mother had tried to deal with her grief through cooking. Every day she busied herself making elaborate meals for an almost empty house. Food that was mostly wasted. For his part, my father delved deeper into his faith, replacing the real world with online chatrooms about God. Both of them were diminished from the people they used to be, echoes, making me dread these home visits, where the repercussions of my failure were most palpable.

The ritual commenced. Dad began with the sign of the cross, we followed suit.

'Lord, thank you for this food we are about to eat. Provided to us through your bountiful glory. Please bless it and make it holy.' He started off every prayer session like this, followed it up with an 'Our Father' and a 'Hail Mary'. My mum and I recited the prayers with him, like backup singers. The last prayer was a recent addition. 'Lord, in your infinite wisdom you saw fit to take our darling Anjali. Please bless her and keep her safe in your glory.' He managed to say it this time without choking up. My mum shut her eyes tight. I turned away, my stomach in knots. Anjali's death had nothing to do with a so-called God's infinite wisdom, it was due to me and my inaction. I lived with that corrosive, damning knowledge every day, saw it every time I looked in the mirror.

I knew Anjali was taking drugs. We bumped into each other at a nightclub a few months before she died. Her eyes like dinner plates. She introduced me to her new boyfriend, said she really loved him. It was clear the love she felt that night came from a pill. It was no use talking to her then, so I called her the following day, late enough for the night's high to be over. She told me to relax, said it was only ecstasy, and that it was just a once-in-a-while thing and nothing serious. She made me promise not to tell our parents. As if I would. Four months later, she was found dead with a syringe still in her arm.

Since she died, I'd dreamt about Anjali often. It was always the same dream. She was twelve and I, ten. That was a difficult time for me with bullies and she helped me through it. Just by being there and saying the right words. The innocent, naive words only children can say. Words I couldn't recall when awake. I never wanted these dreams to end, wanted to grab hold of her tightly and drag her back to the land of wake. But the dream was never long enough and she was always out of reach. In that hazy, early-morning world between sleep and wake, I would try desperately to sleep once more, only to find my anxiousness driving me further awake and away from Anjali. In those mornings, I woke to wrenching feelings of sorrow and longing, desperate for the next dream, for another chance to bring her back.

I looked at my parents, grieving for a daughter whose death they didn't understand. It hurt to see what they'd become, knowing there was nothing I could do for them. They got some solace out of thinking she was with God. But that didn't help me one bit. If there was a Divine Being, it would have helped me stop Anjali's death. But I did nothing and now I couldn't talk about it, fearing that if I opened my mouth, others would blame me as much as I blamed myself.

Mum cleared her throat. 'You can each serve yourselves. Samson, the curry has extra chilli in it for you.' She managed a smile. I made light conversation as we ate. 'You want to hear something weird? I met this Aboriginal guy in Uluru the other day. He looked about a hundred years old. He told me that he spoke to spirits in the wind.' I forced an insincere chuckle. The fact was, the encounter with Old George still left me a little rattled.

My dad thought about what I said as he ate. 'Perhaps he does. After all, lots of people hear God's voice calling them,' he said.

'Yeah. But most of those people are in psychiatric wards,' I replied in between mouthfuls, attempting to use humour to steer the conversation away from religion.

'Not necessarily. The saints all spoke with God. And don't forget the vision of Our Lady at Fatima.'

My humour ebbed, replaced by frustration. 'Dad, you're a smart man. A mathematician. You *must* question all this stuff.'

He put his fork down and looked at me like he was about to punish a five-year-old. We'd had this conversation hundreds of times in the past. 'When you have faith, you don't need to question. All you need is discipline.' I couldn't tell if this was an inference to my lack of faith or lack of discipline. In any case, he was right on both counts. I let his barb go.

Despite being raised a Catholic, I was always agnostic, unable to believe without proof. For me, logic always came before the intangible. Asking questions was what separated us from the animals. That, and an opposable thumb. To me, religion was like a placebo, something that made you feel good without actually doing anything. The same way chocolate cake does when you're upset.

'When do you leave?' asked mum, in a bid to shift the conversation.

'In a couple of days,' I replied.

'That soon! You must let Mabel know.'

It was a good idea. Mabel could be helpful. 'Yes, I'll call her tomorrow,' I said.

On the way home I rang Bec, asked if she was up for a visit.

'Sure, but I'll be going to bed pretty soon.' She sounded tired.

'Thanks, I can do with some company tonight. I've just been to my parents.'

Bec knew how it was with my parents, understood how tough it could be for me. 'Oh, then you'd better come over straight away then. You've already eaten I gather?'

'Yes, chicken curry. I'll see you soon.'

She was in her pyjamas when she opened the door, kissed me when I entered.

'You smell of curry. How were your folks?' She asked, turning around and heading to the lounge.

I sighed, slumped on the couch, 'The same.'

'From the smell, I'd say the food was nice.'

'It was really spicy. I'll have to take you one day.'

'Are we getting *that* serious?' she joked while sitting herself next to me. At least, I thought it was a joke.

'I almost got into another argument with my dad again.'

'Really, what happened?'

Bec listened while I told her.

'Sometimes, I just want to grab him and tell him to wake up and smell the coffee,' I said.

Bec drifted into her own thoughts before speaking again. 'That Aboriginal bloke you met. He sounds like a Ngangkari to me. There were a couple of them around in Mildura when I was growing up. They're not the type of people you should take lightly.'

'What's a Ngangkari?' I asked.

Bec turned to face me. 'A Ngangkari is a traditional Aboriginal healer. Whenever someone from the tribe got sick, they would go to the Ngangkari before coming into town to see a doctor. They're supposed to have magical powers. Kind of like a witch doctor.'

'How do you know all this?'

'Oh, there was a big hoo-hah in the town when I was about thirteen. Something about two Aboriginal guys fighting over the same woman. Or maybe, one guy wanted the other guy's wife. I don't remember exactly. Either way, one of them pointed the bone at the other.'

'Pointed the bone?' I queried.

'You know, that's how they cast curses on each other. If an Aboriginal has a special bone pointed at them, they believe they are cursed and will die quickly.'

'Death curses?'

Bec continued: 'Anyway, the curse started to work, and this other guy was dying. An old Ngangkari man cured him by removing the curse. The local newspapers ran the story. I remember it because pretty soon all us kids started pointing sticks at each other. It wasn't a laughing matter for the guy who cast the curse though.'

'Why, what happened?'

'The other guy got retribution the traditional way.'

'What's that?'

'The guy who was cursed was allowed to spear the other guy in the leg. Eye for an eye style.'

'Sounds pretty harsh for just pointing a bone at someone,' I said.

'Not if you're the one the bone's been pointed at.'

CHAPTER 9

The in-flight PA woke me up, announcing that we would soon be landing in Mumbai.

I raised the shutter on the plane's window, my reflection ghostly against the dark night. Below, small dots of light punctuated the blackness. Slowly, the lights gathered in size and number until they formed a glowing stream of brilliance that outlined the coast.

The descent was so low over the city that I felt I could almost reach out and grab a poppadom from one of the outdoor stalls. Long lines of red became car lamps. Freckles of amber became house, shop and streetlights. Smaller pinpricks of lights clustered together like distant constellations, became slums. The long span of a dark nothing became the Arabian Sea. The blurring movement became people walking.

I'd been here a couple of times before. First, when I was eighteen, then again for a holiday at the age of twenty-four. My guidebook had described India as an assault on the senses. It was an understatement. The heat, the touts, the poverty and the never-ending noise and movement, all conspired to create a hurricane of emotions that left me physically and mentally exhausted, swearing I'd never return.

At the same time, India had somehow burrowed into my soul and I knew it would call me back. Mumbai was the land of my ancestors, the place my parents grew up and the place where I was born. Deep down, I felt a strong connection to the city. As much as it was foreign to me, Mumbai was also once my home and I wanted to learn more about who I was and where I came from. To find some place where I belonged.

The airport concourse was barren and long. The windows on one side overlooked the dark bitumen runway. On the other were row after row of waiting rooms, all empty and gloomy, lit by dull fluorescent lights. Welcomers were not allowed in the terminal, only the Airport Police. They milled about, looking self-important in their khaki uniforms, blue berets and white lanyards. Their machine guns aimed at the floor. The place echoed with the footsteps and murmurs of the excited passengers. Otherwise it was eerie, empty and silent.

Outside the terminal was a different story. First, the bitter, acrid smell hit me. A combination of diesel fumes, charcoal fires and urine. From experience it would take me a day or so to get used to it. Next, the chaotic crowds and the noise set in. Hundreds of people milled about, shouting instructions at each other, seemingly with little else to do. Up ahead, I could see the gathering of 'official' taxi operators, their eyes savouring the newly arrived tourists. I held back and scanned for Mabel.

Mabel was my mother's elder sister, my godmother. She lived by herself in an apartment overlooking Mahim Bay. I had stayed with her the two previous times I visited India. Her home was a peaceful oasis in the middle of Mumbai. Somewhere I could take stock, recharge and find my sense of humour again before heading back into the throng.

It wasn't long before I saw Mabel ambling towards me in a pink floral frock. Her arms open wide in preparation for one of her chest-crushing hugs. She hadn't changed much since I last saw her, except her hair was fully grey now, emphasising her sixty-five years. Her solid build reflected how much she enjoyed her food and the occasional tipple. She approached me with that crooked smile of hers. I smiled back and we embraced. She smelt of lavender. The top of Mabel's head came below my nose and I could see the taxi touts looking at us.

'What are you doing in town, you rascal?' she asked, emphasising each vowel lyrically. She had a throaty voice, the result of years of smoking, now over.

'Causing trouble.'

Mabel broke off our embrace and held me away. 'Let me take a look at you.'

I felt like a little boy being examined on his first day of school, almost expected Mabel to put some spittle on a handkerchief and wipe my face.

'Your hair is shorter and I can see some grey, but apart from that you look the same. You haven't put on any weight.'

'Thanks, I could say the same thing about your hair also,' I said.

'Cheeky bugger.'

Mabel used her ample bosom to part the sea of touts and led me into an adjacent carpark. We walked past a few Hondas and Fords, towards a rotund black car parked awkwardly across two bays. Owning a car in India was no easy feat and Mabel was justifiably proud. The car's body was rounded, no sharp angles or edges. An 'Ambassador' badge was attached to the boot. Overall, it gave the impression of being a 'polite' car, in that reserved, 1950s British, sort of way. It was perfect for Mabel.

There is only one rule on Indian roads—the bigger guy has the right of way. The only exception to this rule is if you are fast enough to zip through without being crushed. I braced my hand against the glove box as Mabel drove, using the lane markings as more of a guide than a rule. She swerved and zigzagged her way through the assortment of trucks, cars, bicycles, motorcycles, auto rickshaws and bullock carts, narrowly missing a family of four on a scooter.

She drove with one hand on the steering wheel and the other on the horn. The constant beeping and honking from the vehicles around us suggested that everyone else drove the same way. I spent the minutes taking in the images of Indian street life.

'You'll see better in the day. It's changed a lot since the last time you were here,' she said.

We slowed down as we crossed the bridge that spanned the mouth of Mahim Bay. Rickety shacks of tin and wood were built on stilts along the banks, lighting up the muddy plains with their low wattage lamps. Above them, near the billboard advertising *Kaun Banega Crorepati*? The Indian version of *Who Wants to Be a Millionaire?*, a tangle of illegal wires dangled dangerously from overhead power cables and draped into the slums.

On the other side of the bridge, large family groups sat along the kerbside in clusters, the women cooking on small kerosene stoves. Half-dressed children used the roads as their playground, running around, dodging cars and screaming with glee. I watched as a boy urinated against a tree, oblivious to anyone around him.

Mabel followed my gaze. 'Not everything's changed.'

Mabel parked near the darkened facade of a church across the main road from her apartment block. A rag-tag collection of beggars lined the church fence, palms open for some charity. They watched as I retrieved my bag from the boot and picked me for a tourist. Their appeal for alms intensified and focused on me but tonight I wasn't their 'Good Samaritan'.

The apartment had a simple layout. A central living space that led to three smaller rooms: bedroom, kitchen and toilet. By average Australian standards the place was tiny, though it wasn't much smaller than my place. It was also much cleaner and the walls were straight. The highlight of the apartment was a balcony that overlooked Mahim Bay. The lights from the high-rise apartments along the opposite shore reflected in the dark, murky water.

I looked down into the yard of what appeared to be a scaffolding company that neighboured the apartment block.

Workers dressed in nothing but worn cotton lungis that hung to their knees stacked long bamboo poles onto the back of an old lorry painted in vivid orange and green. It was almost 10 pm, yet they continued to work under the faint light barely radiating from globes suspended over the lot. This city never stopped, it just slowed down occasionally. Its pulse, the constant humming of traffic.

'Are you hungry?' Mabel asked. 'I made some crab curry. I knew you were coming so I put extra chilli.'

I smiled and came back inside. 'Sure.'

Mabel's cooking was second only to my mum's, and even then, it was a closely run race.

The furniture was the same as I remembered it. The same floral lounge suite, same scratched wooden dining table. The TV looked new, but it was in the same spot the old one occupied and was covered by a plastic dust protector. On the walls were fading pictures of my grandparents and other relatives. Pride of place in the centre of the room was a picture of Jesus, cherubic angels hovering above both his shoulders. A couple of brown, crispy crosses made from palm leaves were wedged in the frame—remnants of Palm Sunday ceremonies gone by.

To the right of Jesus was a picture of Mabel and Uncle Franky on their wedding day. The gold-embossed caption was starting to fade, '*Mr & Mrs Francis Bourne, 1977*'. I had faint memories of Franky as a child, before my parents emigrated. He was a big, smiling man. Even to a child they seemed the perfect match. Franky was an engineer on merchant ships, earning US dollars, which meant they were doing comparatively well in India. They were saving up to start a family.

Then one day Mabel got a message saying that he had been killed in a freak accident with a crane. They called it an 'Act of God'. His insurance was enough for Mabel to buy the apartment and keep her financially secure, but she never fully recovered from her loss. Mabel could have blamed God for Franky's death. Instead, she committed herself more deeply to the church. I never understood that.

'Come and get it.' She placed two heaped plates of curry on the table, each topped with a steaming red crab. I sat down beside her and she fixed me with an inquisitive look.

'Don't get me wrong, Sam. I am so happy to see you, but why have you come here so suddenly?' Mabel cracked a leg off her crab and sucked it like a straw.

It wasn't a surprising question, seeing that she only had one day's notice of my arrival. When I phoned, she insisted that I stay with her and it made sense. I couldn't speak Hindi or Marathi, so Mabel's language skills could come in handy. For that reason, I had already decided to bring her into my confidence.

By the time I had finished speaking, Mabel had devoured her crab and licked her fingers clean. My plate was still untouched.

'Do you know who the father of the baby is?' she asked.

'No, but that's really a side issue,' I replied.

Mabel soaked it all in. 'So what do you think happened to her?'

'To be honest, I think she just died. There is nothing to indicate otherwise. Perhaps her heart just stopped working. It's been known to happen.' A dissertation on Long QT Syndrome was beyond me at this hour.

While cleaning the dishes I asked Mabel to keep the reason for my visit secret, told her about the Mehtas' right to privacy and the fact that I was working while only on a tourist visa. She told me she would not say a word about my visit and mimed buttoning her lips.

'So, what do you expect to find out here?' asked Mabel.

'The father wants me to speak with some of the film crew that were with her when she died. I expect that they won't know more than what they told the police in Australia,' I replied.

'Will he be content with that?'

'I guess he will have to be.'

CHAPTER 10

The morning birdsong of car horns and jackhammers roused me from the camp bed Mabel had set up in the living room. I slipped on a shirt and walked to the balcony. Outside, a dirty, grainy haze settled in on the city, promising to keep the heat and humidity in.

Mabel joined me. 'How did you sleep?'

'Like a log,' I replied.

'So, what is your plan for today?'

'I have an appointment with Aamir Mehta at his home, somewhere on Malabar Hill.'

'Malabar Hill! Very nice,' Mabel said with an approving wiggle of her head.

'What have you got on today?' I asked in return.

'First, I'm going to mass. I will pray for your soul,' she joked.

'Good luck,' I replied.

It was the morning rush hour. The yellow and black taxi spent just as much time standing still as it did moving. All around me, stationary drivers honked their horns, either in frustration or out of habit, knowing it made no difference. From the back seat I watched as shopkeepers flicked water onto the pavement in front of their shops, wetting down the dust so that they could sweep it onto the road. No doubt they'd be sweeping the same muck from the front of their shops the next morning.

After what seemed like a circuitous route, my driver announced we were at Malabar Hill.

'Thanks,' I said, and gave him Mehta's address again.

'You would like to see Walkeshwar Temple? It is very popular with tourists,' he said, his eyes hopeful.

'Not today, thanks,' I said, reminding myself that even though I looked like a local, my voice gave me away as a tourist. So much for belonging.

From my research I knew that old money lived in Malabar Hill. I was wrong. Ancient money lives at Malabar Hill. The taxi pulled up outside a tall stone fence that hid any view of the house behind it. I paid the driver and got out. Directly across the road was a large, sprawling four-storey mansion with views over Chowpatty Beach. It was noticeable for its size as much as for its garish pink and white paint job. A brass sign near a guarded gate read 'State Guest House'. I hoped the State's guests were colour blind. The Mehtas kept good company.

The high wall that surrounded the Mehtas' property ended in a gated driveway, unlocked. I walked in, eyed the large three-storey house that intimidated rather than invited. Two imposing bay-windows flanked the entry doorway and stretched up through the various levels of the house. The peaked roof was covered in brown, aged shingles, splotched with green-grey lichen. At one time, a creeping vine must have covered the entire stone facade, perhaps in an attempt to soften its inherent harshness. It had since been removed but the traces remained, like scars or wrinkles on an ageing face.

I pressed the button near the door and a slim, young lady with cynical eyes answered the bell. She had typical Indian features: long dark hair woven into a tight plait, dark brown skin and a heart-shaped face. Her sari was worn in a way that exposed a midriff as taut as a snare-drum. On her forehead was a bindi. She raised her hand up in a gesture for me to wait, then closed the door behind her.

'Good afternoon, Mr Ryder. I trust you had a pleasant flight?'

Aamir Mehta was wearing a traditional churidar kurta, white cotton pants with an oversized white cotton top. For some reason I had expected to see him in a suit, like the first time we met but what he wore made more sense in this weather. He had brown leather chappals on his feet, his toes protruding from the end.

'Yes, the flight was fine, thank you.'

The hallway was long and had several doors coming off either side. I waited until he showed me the way.

'Just here, to the left,' he said.

I walked into what must have been a formal welcoming room. The shutters on the bay-window were closed, making the room much darker than the entrance hallway. The room was sparsely furnished for its size. A lacquered wooden coffee table separated two dark brown leather sofas. The heaviness of the furniture reminded me of Vivienne Fredricks' home, but the dim lighting gave this room a glum, constricting feel, like it was in mourning. It reminded me of my parents' home.

On the walls were pictures of a Hindu god, splashed with colours of red and gold. In the far corner, hidden amongst the shadows, was a shrine to a deity too dark to make out. Two pistols were mounted on the wall immediately to my right, their silver barrels crossed over. At the corner of one of the couches, a diminutive, elderly woman sat with her hands between her knees.

'Mr Ryder, this is my wife, Rekha Mehta.'

Even though she stood up to greet me she was still tiny. Rekha Mehta looked much older than her husband. Her hair was beyond grey, almost white, and matched the simple white sari that she wore. The redness around her eyes spoke of her grief. She clutched a handkerchief the way an alcoholic grips a bottle.

'Hello, Mrs Mehta. I am sorry for your loss,' I said, trying hard to not see glimpses of my mother's grief in the lady before me.

She tried to smile but was unable to through her pursed lips. Instead, she nodded and dried her eyes with the handkerchief. Aamir Mehta motioned for me to sit across from him and his wife. I noticed that they sat apart, formal rather than familiar. Without a word, Rekha Mehta poured me a cup of tea from the tray on the centre table. He watched her like a master watches a servant. I gathered he was the dominant one in the relationship.

'Mr Mehta, before we go much further, I would like to take stock of where we are at with the investigation.' I said this for me as much for him, needing to confirm what his expectations were of me.

'You have a report on my findings from Australia. Based on my investigation so far, it seems clear that your daughter died of natural causes. There is nothing to suggest otherwise.'

Rekha Mehta let out a muffled moan. She bit her lips to stop from making any further noise.

'Yes. That is what your report concluded. But as I told you in Australia, not all the witnesses have been interviewed. There are those who were there when my daughter died.' He sat rigidly, with fists clenched so tightly his hands resembled cauliflowers. She silently dabbed at the stream of tears tracking down her face.

Looking at the couple before me I couldn't help feeling sympathetic. Their only child was gone. Perhaps they blamed themselves and were now looking for someone else to point the finger at? I didn't think there was anything more to learn in India, but if it helped this couple come to terms with their grief it would be worthwhile. Something I couldn't do for my parents, or for myself.

'You're referring to the film crew in Australia. You were going to provide me with some contacts that I could follow up. Are you able to do that, sir?' I asked.

'Better than that. I have arranged for you to meet with Mr Davindar Singh. He was the producer of the film in which my daughter was acting. He is also a family friend.'

Aamir Mehta gave me a piece of paper with Singh's address and phone number. 'He is expecting you tomorrow at 2 pm.'

That was fast work. Singh was one of the other two people who stayed at the five-star resort in Yulara, the only person whom Subhani let enter her room.

'Thank you. Before I go, I need to ask you some further questions which may assist with the investigation.'

'By all means. What do you want to ask me?'

'I just want to double check with you about Subhani's health. You told me before that Subhani was in fine health, that she never suffered fainting attacks. Now that you have had some more time to think about it, are you still sure that she hadn't fainted before? Maybe even when she was a child?'

Aamir Mehta shook his head. 'No, Mr Ryder, Subhani was a healthy child who grew into a healthy woman.'

This question needed to be handled delicately.

'Mr Mehta, you know that your daughter was pregnant at the time that she passed away.'

He nodded sharply.

I continued: 'Do you know who the father was?'

Rekha Mehta squeezed her eyes tightly shut while Aamir Mehta answered. 'Mr Ryder, neither my wife nor I was aware of the pregnancy. We were not even aware that Subhani was in a relationship. She did not tell us.' He glanced at his wife, turned back to me. 'That *damned* leaked report has caused us great shame and embarrassment,' his voice flashed with anger. I let a couple of seconds pass before I spoke again.

'One final question. Did Subhani have any close friends that I may speak with? Someone she may have confided in?'

'The film industry is full of people who want to be your friend when you are popular, then forget you when you need them the most. Subhani didn't keep such company. She was too professional for that.' He cut the air with his palm, emphasising his point. 'Subhani confided in her mother and me. We were all the friends she needed.'

'Thank you, sir, I will try and…'

'Anveeta Khan,' Rekha Mehta said in a soft, trembling voice. I turned my attention to her. 'Subhani was good friends with Anveeta Khan some time ago. They acted together.'

CHAPTER 11

Mabel was washing the grit from a large bunch of spinach in the sink when I got back.

'What are you making?' I asked.

'Palak paneer, except I forgot to get the paneer from the cheese-wallah. I'll get it later. How did you get on with the Mehtas?'

'Okay. They've already arranged for me to meet with the producer tomorrow afternoon.'

'Poor people. It must be so difficult for them. She was such a beautiful girl.' Mabel paused. 'Like your sister. Tell me, how are your parents? I speak to your mother every week, but I can't tell how she's coping.'

'Mum's good at putting on a brave face every now and then, and dad spends much of his time online, but it has shattered them. I think they take it one day at a time.'

'And what about you?'

I faced away from Mabel so she couldn't see the damp building in my eyes and walked into the lounge while answering, 'Same, I guess. Sometimes, I can't get it out of my head and all I want to do it just scream. I get so angry at her for what she did and then I get angrier at myself. Sometimes I picture whoever it was that gave her the drugs and what I would do to them.' I dropped onto the sofa, suddenly weary. 'Then, sometimes, if I am busy, I can go for days without thinking about her. Then I do, and I get angry at myself for letting myself forget.'

Mabel dried her hands on a dishcloth, tossed it on the kitchen table. She came over to me and rested her arm on my shoulder.

'You will never forget, Sam. Believe me. Even now, so many years after Franky has gone, I will suddenly get upset and cry. Just like that.' She sighed. 'But I know he is at peace and with God's help, I have been able to carry on.'

'Hmm,' I nodded approval for Mabel, knowing relying on God's help would get me nowhere.

Mabel sat down beside me. 'There's also something else I have to tell you, Sam,' she said, sheepishly, changing the subject. 'I was talking about you to the ladies after church this morning…'

'Mabel, I thought you agreed to keep things quiet?' I interjected.

'I know, Sam, I'm sorry, but I am just so happy you're here and on such an exciting case. It just blurted out of my mouth,' she continued. 'The problem is, I forgot that Lucy Patel's son works in the police. His name is Vincent. Anyway, when she returned to her home, she told him what you were doing. Apparently, he was not very happy and Lucy called me just before you arrived to tell me that Vincent wants to take you to meet his boss tomorrow. He will phone here to make arrangements later tonight.'

I couldn't believe it. 'Mabel, I don't need these distractions right now.'

'I understand, Sam. Actually, I am surprised I forgot about her son. She is always talking about him. Vincent this and Vincent that. She goes on and on.'

I couldn't help but think that Lucy Patel wasn't the only one who was good at talking.

'It's okay, Mabel. Just, please, don't tell anyone else.'

'Absolutely, Sam. From now on, mum's the word!'

***

By 9 am the following morning, I was standing on the steps of a double-decker bus alongside Officer Vincent Patel, the vibrations from the engine travelling up through my feet. Patel was a metal rod in build and demeanour: tall and thin, and with about as much personality. Like most police officers, Patel was clean-shaven, except for his brushy moustache. From this intimacy I could smell the almond essence from his aftershave. He looked like most other Indian men except his skin was a velvety brown, like caramel, and his face bore deep acne scars that spoke of an awkward adolescence.

Patel wore his uniform with pride. You could shave with the creases on his khaki pants and shirt. People gave him a wide berth, a luxury in cramped buses like this. Even the conductor, who squeezed his way through the crowd while clicking holes in paper tickets, let Patel ride for free.

We continued the journey in silence until he tapped me on the shoulder.

'Move towards the exit. We get off after two stops,' he said.

Despite people making an effort to get out of the officer's way, it took a long time to shuffle our way through the throng of morning commuters.

'Ready? On the count of three we hop off.'

As we approached the stop the bus merely slowed down, rather than stopping. We jumped off and ran to a stop, trying not to bump into those running to hop on at the same time.

We walked beside a high brick wall topped with coils of barbed wire until we came to a gated entry. A sign said 'Colaba Police Station—Lion Gate'. Patel led me around the lowered boom. The officers on guard measured us up quickly before continuing their conversation. Patel's uniform was all the ID they needed.

Police Headquarters was an old colonial building that had seen better days. The once cream sandstone facade was black with age and pollution. The turrets that rose on either end of the building now only served to house flocks of pigeons. A type of moat circled the building, revealing that in addition to the three stories above ground, there was one story below ground level. Noticeably, the basement had barred windows.

As we walked towards the entrance, two military-style personnel-carriers raced past us and screeched to a halt outside the entry. Patel held an arm out, signalling me to keep back. A driver from one of the vehicles jumped out of the car and called for assistance from inside the building. Within seconds a troop of officers surrounded the two jeeps, each carrying a rifle. A short, fat officer wearing a peaked cap and carrying a pistol opened the large door at the back of the jeep and called out something to the passengers.

One by one, three bent men stepped out of the jeep, their clothes torn and dishevelled. Each man shackled by the hands and legs. From the way they were blinking and looking around disorientated, it seemed that they had been in the jeep for quite a while. One of them raised his hands to shield his eyes from the sun. This was all the incentive the peaked cap officer needed and he pistol-whipped the defenceless man. A muddled, cracking noise echoed through the grounds. The man screamed with whatever part of his jaw still worked and fell to his knees. His two companions joined him on their knees, cowering. Two men in a similar state were removed from the second jeep and all five were dragged inside. Patel and I watched this dishing out of justice in silence.

Once inside, Patel led me up an imposing flight of white stone stairs that ended in a curved flourish, the type of stairs beautiful girls in fancy dresses normally walk down in Hollywood movies. The second floor was one large open room with about one hundred officers sitting behind desks, smoking. Dozens of fans hung from the high ceiling, blowing the stale cigarette smoke back down. Compared to the action I just saw outside, this floor had all the excitement of a bingo hall. Patel told me to take a seat on the wooden bench near the doorway while he spoke with his Super.

The hard bench seat was uncomfortable. I got up to stretch. Dirty green linoleum tiles peeled off the wall behind me, adding to the decaying atmosphere of the building. Above the tiles was a wooden noticeboard with sliding glass panels. A range of posters and official looking documents were pinned to the board, some in English.

One poster caught my attention. It called for people to come forward with any information on dowry deaths. According to the poster, the practice of marrying a woman for her dowry, then killing her shortly after, usually by burning her, was on the increase. The grieving husband usually blaming the death on a faulty petrol stove. It sounded heinous.

Reappearing about twenty minutes later, a rather flushed looking Patel came for me. I gathered he had been at the receiving end of a tirade from his boss.

'Superintendent Rao will see you now,' he said.

Patel led me through the room of desks and knocked on the door etched with the title 'Santosh Rao, Superintendent of Police, Colaba Division'.

'Enter.'

Superintendent Rao sat behind his mahogany desk. It was oversized and made him look small by comparison. The only item that appeared to be used on the desk was the ashtray, which held several filter stubs from past cigarettes. The computer was switched off. A map of Mumbai was pinned to the wall behind him, demarcating the city into several zones. To his left was a large window with an air conditioner attached to it, not currently in use.

I was not important enough to warrant him to stand. Sitting down, Rao's body seemed to melt into a fat, rotund ball. His face was dark brown, with even darker circles around eyes the whites of which were tinged yellow. Long strands of artificially black hair were pasted in place over his balding crown. His peaked cap hung on the hatstand near the door. The pistol he had used on the prisoner wouldn't be too far away. I took an instant dislike to him and wanted to get this over quickly, decided to take control of the meeting.

'Good morning, Superintendent Rao, my name is Samson Ryder.' He took the card I offered, looked at it fleetingly before flicking it onto his desk.

Rao rubbed his face with both hands, irritably. 'Officer Patel tells me you are working on a case here in Mumbai. This is very unusual and requires special permissions. Show me your passport.'

Patel had made sure I brought my passport with me. I handed it over to Rao. He looked at my identification. 'So, an Australian citizen, but you were born here in Mumbai.' He looked up at me 'When did you leave India?'

'My parents decided to leave when I was three. I had no choice in the matter,' I responded, feeling like Rao wasn't really listening. He thumbed through my passport, stopped at the page with my visa. 'A tourist visa,' he looked back at me, 'You're not supposed to be working on a tourism visa.'

'I'm sorry, I must have made a mistake. I can get it fixed. Is there a fine I can pay?' By fine, I meant bribe, but there were no takers.

Rao placed the passport near to my business card, then placed his elbows on the table and massaged his temples. 'Tell me about your client and the matters you are investigating,' he said, eyes remaining closed. His body language smacked of self-importance. A man who liked authority. I'd come across people like this in the Victorian Police Force.

At the first mention of the Mehtas, he looked up at me and started to pay attention. Occasionally, his jaundiced eyes would look over my shoulder to Patel, who was still standing behind me.

'I must say, I am surprised that Aamir Mehta did not see fit to inform me of this investigation', he said, clearly annoyed. 'The Mehtas are a very important family and we were all sad to hear of their daughter's death. If they have asked you to investigate, then of course we will tolerate your presence.' He gave me a smile that turned ugly, pointed a stumpy finger at me. 'I'm warning you, though. Do not cause me any trouble.'

Rao's eyes looked behind my shoulder again. 'Officer Patel, see Mr Ryder out.'

'Well, that went well,' I said once we were outside the building.

'What did you expect?' challenged Patel. 'How would you feel if you were the superintendent and you learnt that a prominent Mumbai family has gone to a private detective rather than the police force for help? And what makes it worse is that they choose an NRI, rather than a local.'

He checked himself, changed his tone. 'Look, I don't care about Rao, but something like this is an insult to the whole police force.'

He was right, the truth was Mehta didn't trust the police.

'NRI, you mean Non-resident Indian, yeah?'

'Some say it means not really Indian,' he said, smiling. It was the first time he seemed to relax.

Patel pointed me in the direction of the bus stop, gave me his number and told me to keep him informed of the case.

'One more thing,' he called out to me as I was walking away, 'if you ever try to bribe another officer again, don't do it in my presence.'

CHAPTER 12

From the look of his house, Davindar Singh lived the high life in Bandra, the mecca for Mumbai's nouveau riche. While not as impressive as the Mehtas' abode, the new concrete two-storey bungalow had a clean, fresh look about it. Big glass windows gave it an open, welcoming feel. A driveway led to a shiny black Mercedes saloon being worked on by two mechanics. I wondered how wealthy you needed to be to have mechanics do house calls, figured I would never be that rich.

It was just after 2 pm when I rang the doorbell and listened as a voice on the other side of the door grew louder. The door opened and a tall, broad man opened the door while speaking on a phone. 'Haan, chalo' *yes, goodbye*, he said and flicked the mobile shut.

'Mr Singh?'

'Hello Mr Ryder, Aamir Mehta told me you would be in touch.' At a guess he was six foot five, six-six. I shook hands with the giant in front of me, his hand swallowing mine and hungry for more. He wore jeans and a light blue collared shirt, the top two buttons undone revealing a heavy gold chain caught amongst tufts of black curly chest hair. A sports jacket and brown loafers finished the ensemble. Half business, half pleasure.

Singh looked past me, to where the mechanics worked and said something in Hindi, said it firmly. The response must have pleased him, he waggled his head as the men started to pack their tools. 'They are fixing the brakes but you need to show them who's the boss or they will take forever', he said with a smile.

Singh guided me to a large room towards the rear of the house. Three rectangular windows filled it with light, and colourful Picasso-*esque* pictures adorned the walls. Steps in the corner led to another floor. I sat on the cream leather couch, reflected on the contrast between the casual, modern style of Singh and the formal, traditional approach of the Mehtas.

'Scotch?' He was already pouring himself a glass from the decanter on a side table.

'Yes, thanks.'

He gave me a tumbler with a generous pour of malt, then sat at an angle so he could see me, or more likely so I could see him. He rested his left arm on the back of the sofa. Two heavy, gold rings gleamed on his fingers. His right leg crossed over the left—a laid back, confident posture. King of his domain.

He was probably in his late forties but looked more youthful than that. Singh had a manly face that was held together by a strong nose and a firm, square jaw. His sleepy eyes caught my attention, adding a touch of vulnerability to his appearance. Overall, he was on the right side of handsome.

Singh combed his left hand through his thick, black, brushed-back hair and aimed an infectious smile at me, flashing perfect teeth. I smiled back. He took a drink from his glass, then spoke.

'Aamir Mehta is a good friend of mine. I will do whatever I can do to help him and Rekha during this sad time. What do you want to ask me?' His voice was friendly, disarming. The kind of voice a used-car salesman would kill for.

I put my glass on the table and pulled out my notebook. 'You were there when Subhani died. Can you tell me what happened?'

'It's like I told the police. One minute she was dancing, the next she was dead. Just like that.' He snapped his fingers.

'What do you think caused her death?'

'I don't know.' He took another mouthful of scotch and looked up at the ceiling, recalling the past.

'It was a really hot day, and we had to climb up that rock. Do you know how tiring it is to climb that thing?' He looked back at me.

I shook my head.

'We had to carry everything up. Cameras, lighting, costumes, the lot. We took only what was necessary, so we didn't take a lot of extra water. It was supposed to be a quick shoot. None of us expected to be up there that long.'

'How long were you up there?'

'A few hours.'

'And there was no drinking water?'

'Not much, no. We also didn't know Subhani was pregnant. She kept that to herself.'

'What happened when you found out she was dead?'

'Well, when she didn't get up from the ground, we realised there was a problem. We all ran to her. Someone even gave her mouth-to-mouth.' He sighed. 'It was no use. We wanted to call for help but there was no mobile reception. So we sent someone down.'

The rest I knew.

'The manager of the hotel that you stayed in said that Subhani was very reclusive and would only let you into her room. Was that normal for her?'

Singh took in a deep breath and let out a long sigh.

'No, that was not normal. In fact, it only started when we arrived in Australia. Usually, Subhani was the life of the party.' He looked away, eyebrows furrowed. 'Actually, thinking about it, she was a little jumpy. As soon as I would enter her room, she would lock the door behind me. The curtains were always drawn. Like she was scared or hiding.'

'Scared? Of what?' I asked.

Singh shrugged. 'I really don't know.'

'Is there anything else you remember? Did Subhani ever feel faint or pass out before she died?'

'No. She was always very healthy.' Singh looked away into the middle distance, twirling the ice in his glass. He came back to me. 'I'm sorry there is nothing more I know. I really feel for Aamir and Rekha. Subhani was a beautiful girl and a talented actress. In fact, I am dedicating the movie to Subhani in her honour. We are editing it now.'

'I know you are a busy man and I appreciate your time. There's just a couple more questions. Is there anyone else who was at Uluru that I could talk to?'

Singh combed his hair with his bling-ringed hand again. 'By now most of the crew will be scattered around India on other shoots. Jogesh is here, though.'

'Jogesh?' I queried.

'Jogesh Nadar. The director of the film. He is overseeing the editing. I am going to see how he is progressing after this. If you like, you can come.'

'That would be useful, thanks.'

'Anything for Aamir and Rekha.' Singh closed his eyes and shook his head.

I waited until he looked back at me. 'Do you know an actress called Anveeta Khan?'

'Anveeta, yes I know her. Why?'

'Her mother said she was a friend of Subhani's. If possible, I would like to speak with her. Subhani may have told Anveeta Khan something she couldn't tell her parents.'

Singh drummed his fingers against the back of the couch.

'I don't think they were really very close. You'd be wasting your time talking with her.'

He said it without looking at me, giving the distinct feeling he would prefer it if I didn't speak with Anveeta Khan. It made me more keen to speak with her.

'Perhaps so, but Mrs Mehta requested that I speak with her specifically. She said you would give me her contact details.' I figured he wouldn't check with Rekha Mehta, he didn't strike me as a details type of guy.

'I see.' He drained his glass. 'I can give you her secretary's number and you can make an appointment to see Anveeta. It just so happens that Anveeta has replaced Subhani in a new film of mine. Right now, she is in Goa.'

Singh placed his empty glass next to my full one. The contrast looked impolite so I drank mine in a couple of gulps and endured the burning sensation immediately after. He seemed impressed, asked me to join him in another. It would be rude not to accept. He took the glasses and walked back to the side table.

'Australia is a nice place. Sydney Harbour, Opera House, *and the girls on Bondi Beach.*' He smiled from the corner of his mouth. Singh liked the ladies and with his job and his charisma, I didn't think he'd have a problem meeting them. I was right about half business, half pleasure.

He returned to the couch with the refilled glasses. 'You're a handsome-looking man, if you want, I can find a part for you in my movies.'

I laughed. 'That's very kind of you, but I can't speak Hindi and I sing and dance like a midnight drunk.'

He chuckled. 'We can teach you how to dance. The singing and Hindi we can dub in later. You would be good as a love interest. I'm sure you have had plenty of practice at that.'

'Davindar, leave the poor man alone. He's not here to talk about his personal life.' The stern voice came from behind me. I turned around, focused on the woman on the staircase.

'Hello, Mr Ryder, I'm Leela Singh. Please excuse my husband's prying,' she said from where she stood. She spoke like she could've given elocution lessons to the Queen of England.

Leela Singh had side-parted dark hair that fell just to the top of her neck, almost a bob. Her face was elongated, and her facial features looked ill matched, as if they were taken from other people. Her eyes were a little too close and struggled to look past her large beak-like nose, giving her a cross-eyed affect. Unlike her husband, Leela Singh was no looker.

'Hello, Mrs Singh. Your husband has been very helpful.'

'I am glad Davindar has been of use to someone.' She took a quick puff from her cigarette, not enough to get any effect. Despite her looks she oozed a regal confidence. Not the superficial, wide-smile type that her husband had. Hers seemed inherited, entitled.

Davindar Singh's face grew taut, his neck rippled around tensed sinews. He knocked back his scotch. 'Well, I'm going to the studio now. Would you still like to come?'

'You should go, Mr Ryder. After all, it is not every day you get to see a cinematic genius at work,' she scoffed in an icy tone that could reverse global warming.

CHAPTER 13

The Merc was impressive. It felt like we had floated over the potholed roads leading to the studio. The car also came with a driver, swanky uniform and all. Singh flashed a pass and the obligatory smile to the beret-wearing guard at the entry of the studios. The man touched his forehead with the back of his palm in salute and swung open the large iron-spiked gate.

Namaste Studios wasn't what I expected from a Bollywood studio. There were no exotic sets, no colourfully dressed performers. Just rows of warehouse-like buildings stitched together by a black bitumen drive. Romance was reserved for in front of the screen. Singh parked outside the bunker marked with a large '6' in black paint.

Inside was cavernous, just a few wooden frames that could be clamped together to look like a room, the odd piece of furniture and lots of dust balls. A staircase to the left led to a mezzanine level of what looked like offices. Singh sensed my disappointment.

'This is where we do all our internal shoots. We hire most of our equipment and props as we need them. The editing office is up there.' He walked towards the stairs with me in tow.

Singh led me into the first office, although to call it an office was an exaggeration, more like a cell. The room was so small you'd have to take turns to breathe. A narrow table was placed along the left side of the room, carrying two computers. The only light came from the flicker of the monitors. An oscillating fan at the far corner rattled and struggled against the hot, stale air.

'Jogesh.' Singh walked up to the seated man in front of the monitor and clasped his shoulders from behind. 'This is Mr Sam Ryder. He is working for Aamir Mehta. You know, Subhani's father. He wants to ask you some questions about her death.'

Jogesh Nadar was slightly built, which was convenient considering the proportions of the room. Sitting in the swivel chair he looked more like a schoolboy than a man in his mid-thirties, his legs barely touching the ground. His hair was parted at the side and held in place with some type of oily lotion, tainting the hot air with the smell of coconuts. He dressed similarly to Singh—jeans, a white collared shirt and a jacket that was slung over his chair—but Nadar couldn't pull off the same debonair look. He seemed to fade into the gloom of the editing booth. In an industry full of beautiful, fair people, Jogesh Nadar was definitely a 'behind the camera' guy.

'How may I help you?' he said in a voice that sounded more like a husky female than a male. Nadar's account of Subhani's death was similar to Singh's.

I looked at my notes. 'Mr Singh said that it was a hot

day and the shoot took longer than expected. Why was that?' I asked.

Nadar shot Singh a look of betrayal, then turned back at me.

'What exactly are you investigating?' He said defensively.

'Just the circumstances in which she died. That's all.' I tried to make it sound like nothing unusual.

'That figures.' He snorted. 'Everyone makes a fuss over Subhani.' Nadar looked at me. 'You didn't have to work with her.'

'What was she like to work with?' I asked.

'Honestly, she was a bitch. It was either her way or no way. She thought she knew everything, but she had no idea about the *art* of making a film.'

The room felt like it got warmer with his outburst. It was about time something heated up.

Nadar looked over his shoulder at Singh. 'I knew she was plotting to get rid of me.'

'Come on, Jogesh.' Singh squeezed Nadar's shoulders reassuringly.

'I know it and you know it, Davindar.' Nadar smiled. 'Thank god you didn't have to make a choice.'

Nadar took a breath, looked back at me and spoke like a repentant child. 'Yes, it was hot, and we were there for longer than I planned. It was so bright I had trouble with the lighting and then we also had to wait for all the other climbers to be out of shot. It took a lot of effort to get up there in the first place, so I didn't want to go down until we had the shot right.

Of course, if I knew Subhani was pregnant, I would never have made her do it.'

'You didn't know Subhani was pregnant either?' I asked.

'No.'

'Is there anyone else that may have known about the pregnancy?'

The two men looked at each other. 'Judging by the stir that it caused, probably not. Maybe that's why she kept it a secret. Because of the scandal,' said Nadar.

'Yes, but the secret would have been out soon. She was already three months pregnant. Tell me, do either of you have any idea who the father may be?'

Nadar shook his head.

'I can't think of anyone,' said Singh.

Nadar made a point of looking at his watch, anxious to get back to work. I wasn't quite finished though.

'Is there anything else from that day that sticks in your mind? Anything unusual?' I asked.

'No. Not really. To be honest, I've had so much trouble with the footage from the Australian shoot that I haven't really thought much about that particular day.'

'What type of trouble?'

'It's a continuity thing. Making editing difficult. Look, it's easier if I show you.'

Nadar turned to the computer in front of him and typed something into the keyboard. A digital clock appeared on the screen. He used the mouse to manipulate the time.

'It starts from about the eighty-third minute of the film,' he said.

'Must just be the opening credits, then?' I joked, as I joined Singh to watch the screen over Nadar's shoulder.

Nadar ignored my quip, clicked on the green 'Play' arrow on the screen. The movie began to play, soundless.

'See here,' he said, pointing to an image of Subhani Mehta. 'Look at her neck, nothing. This is where we stopped filming in India. Now keep watching.'

The screen faded to black, signifying the end of a scene. Almost immediately the screen lit up again with a close-up of Subhani, this time from another angle.

'Now, this is supposed to happen straight after the last scene but look at her neck.' Nadar touched the screen. There, resting against her larynx, was a dark, heavy pendant of a menacing face with grotesque oversized eyes and a sharp beak for a mouth. Judging from its prominence on Subhani's neck, it was about an inch in size. It was attached to what looked like a black chain, made of tiny links.

'She only started to wear this ugly thing when we came to Australia. We had already shot most of the movie here in the studio. So now I have to go through every scene and digitally remove it. It's a bloody nuisance.'

'Why did she start wearing it?'

Nadar shrugged his shoulders again. 'Search me.'

'I asked her to remove it. The character she was playing would never wear something like that,' added Singh. 'She wouldn't listen to me. She said she'd leave the film if I forced her to take it off.'

I stared at the screen, conscious that both Singh and Nadar were looking at me. Senior Sergeant Davis said she clasped a pendant in her hand when she died, had wrenched it off in a spasm. This must have been it. It didn't look expensive, or attractive, so why was she so precious about it?

I looked down at Nadar. 'I know this sounds terrible, but do you have the footage of Subhani just before she died?'

Nadar's eyes lingered on me, then he looked at Singh for guidance.

I turned to Singh. 'Mr Singh, if you have it, please let me see it. It may be important.'

'You understand that this footage will never be released,' Singh said.

'I understand. I wouldn't ask to see it normally. It's just something the police mentioned in Australia that Subhani did just before she died. Something I want to check.'

Singh nodded to Nadar. 'Let him see it, Jogesh.'

Without a word Nadar changed the on-screen clock once again.

'Here, watch,' he said distastefully. His attitude was understandable, it was as close to a snuff film as I would ever want to get.

I watched as Subhani Mehta's life ended in front of me. A dance sequence that seemed so innocent and full of joy. It was hard to keep the context out of my mind and focus on Subhani's movements.

'Stop.' I pointed to the screen. 'Can you play that bit again in slow motion?'

'Okay, yes,' said Nadar, reluctantly. He replayed the last part of the film, this time frame by frame. There it was again. It was hard to make out, but in the middle of her fall I could just see her right hand reaching towards her neck. Senior Sergeant Davis was wrong. It wasn't a spasm; it was the final conscious act of a dying woman. I wasn't sure what it meant, or how it could help my case, but that pendant was surely very important to Subhani Mehta.

CHAPTER 14

I spent the trip back to Mabel's house lost in my thoughts. Nadar had given me a close-up printout of Subhani wearing the pendant. It looked horrid and I wondered why she would wear it, refuse to take it off, purposely reach for it in her last moments. Singh also confirmed the unusual behaviour of Subhani that Henderson told me about at the hotel. Apart from that, the information they provided had filled some holes in the sequence of things, but nothing they said threw any new light on how Subhani died. I wondered whether Mehta would be satisfied with the autopsy findings now.

The taxi braked sharply as it veered towards the kerb, the jolt rousing me back from my reflections. I looked blankly at the dashboard until a small statue of an elephant-headed deity came into focus. It was adorned with a garland of orange and yellow marigolds.

'Ganesh,' said the driver, following my gaze. 'God for good prosperity.'

Ganesh would've been pleased with my tip.

I really needed to talk to someone, share my thoughts and be distracted, but Mabel wasn't home. I hadn't shown it in front of Singh and Nadar, but watching the video of Subhani really drained me, another young woman dying needlessly. I wanted to compartmentalise the images so that they wouldn't invade my thoughts at random times, the way thoughts about Anjali ambushed me. It was just past 5 pm, almost noon in Melbourne. I washed the clammy Mumbai grime off my face, then rang Bec's mobile. She answered almost immediately.

'Hey, I was just thinking about you. How's India?' From the background noise I figured she was at the station.

'Noisy and humid. How are you?'

'All good here, busy though. I can't talk long. How's the case going?'

'Pretty much as expected, Bec. I got to speak to the producer and director today. Neither had anything much to add to what I already knew. It looks pretty straight forward, so I guess, I'll have to speak to the parents again pretty soon.'

'Nothing new at all? That's strange, given they were the only ones who were actually there when Subhani died.'

'Yeah, I was hoping for more too. The producer did confirm she was acting strangely, like she was scared, and the director complained about a necklace she suddenly took to wearing, but apart from that there was nothing new.

'That's a pity. It's interesting that he thinks she was scared. Did he know what she was scared of?'

'No. She never spoke about it to him.'

'What's the deal with the necklace?'

'Oh, you should see it, Bec. It's this really ugly pendant on a black chain. She only started wearing it when she came to Australia and wouldn't take it off. In fact, it was the last thing she grasped for before dying.'

'Do you know that for sure?'

I sighed, rubbed my face with my free hand. 'Bec, I saw the video of her dying. Over and over again. She was dancing one minute and the next she's dead.'

Bec could sense my discomfort. 'Are you alright, Sam?'

'I'm fine,' I said, trying to regain composure.

'Are you sure? You know you can always talk to me.' The concern in her voice genuine.

I closed my eyes, pictured Bec, her face, her eyes, that smile.

'To be honest, I just felt so helpless watching that video, Bec. Knowing someone's about to die and not being able to do anything about it. I couldn't help thinking of Anjali.'

There was a pause before Bec spoke. 'Sam. What happened to Anjali wasn't your fault. Deep down you must know that.'

'Thanks, Bec. It's just good to hear your voice.'

'I care for you, Sam.' It came out of nowhere.

'I care for you too.' For a while we both remained silent. I wasn't sure if we'd entered into a new phase of our relationship, wondered if Bec felt the same way also.

'The video, Sam. Was there anything suspicious?' Bec asked, professional again.

'No, nothing suspicious. If I showed the video to her parents they would have to agree. I couldn't do that, though. I don't think they know the footage exists. The director seemed very protective of it.'

'So that's it, then. Case closed. I hope the parents can accept the news and move on. By the way, it didn't take you long to speak to the key witnesses.'

'Actually, there's one more person I could speak with. Her name is Anveeta Khan, she was a friend of Subhani's.' I made a mental note to follow this up.

'Was she at Uluru when she died?'

'No, but she may have background info on Subhani's health, and that may be useful.'

'That sounds plausible. It also doesn't hurt to stretch this job out for as long as possible, does it? How much is he paying you again?' Now she was teasing.

'Now, now, Bec. You're getting cynical in your old age.'

Bec's laughter filled my ears and I urgently wanted to hold her, to smell her, to see those green eyes and the mole on her back. Speaking with Bec made me feel better, but I still needed to clear my head. I decided to take a walk; needing a change of scene.

CHAPTER 15

By now I'd grown accustomed to the constant cacophony of noise and the pungent smell, it was the heat that was tough. It wasn't a dry burn like at Uluru, where enough shade and water would see you through. Here, the heat was wet and would cling to you. Making everything heavier, even breathing. It was the type of heat that drove sane people mad. 'Going troppo' they called it in Darwin.

The footpaths had long since stopped performing their designated duty and were now busy shopping malls in their own right. In some parts, brightly coloured clothing hung from makeshift bamboo frames extending across the paved path. In others, vendors stood next to wooden carts, some filled with fruit, others with linen, others still with plastic toys and storage containers. They shouted out their wares like it was a closing down sale—everything had to go. Like all the other pedestrians, I was forced to walk along the edge of the road, maintaining an unnerving balance between the bustling traffic and the filthy gutters on either side of me.

Makeshift food stalls occupied most street corners, dishing out savoury smelling *pani puri* and *sev puri* on little paper plates and in plastic bags that would one day end up in the Arabian Sea. An old man with one leg and no teeth sat against the corner of a road. He said something in a squeaking, hissing voice and shook his bowl at me as I passed. I dropped in some coins, didn't know how much, except that it would never be enough.

I kept walking. Past the guy who was holding up a tiny mirror while getting his hair cut on the street. Past the cripple who wanted to shine my shoes. Past the three filthy-looking women clearing rubble from a ditch. Past the guy who juiced sugar cane stems and sold the grassy coloured liquid to waiting customers. Past the man paying homage at a road-side shrine to a monkey-faced god. Past the *paan-wallah*, who wrapped a betel nut and spices in a leaf and passed it to an eager-looking toothless man.

Through all this I felt removed, distant. As with my other trips to India, it was like I was granted limited access to watch but not participate, to see but not understand. The minute I opened my mouth, people would brand me a stranger and raise their guard as well as their prices. I wanted to feel at home, like I belonged, but instead I felt mute and alone in this noisy, crowded city. So far, the walk hadn't cleared my head or lifted my spirits. I decided to catch a rickshaw back to Mabel's apartment when my mobile rang.

'Hello, Mr Ryder. My name is Naina Krishnan. I am the crime reporter for the *Voice of India* newspaper.' Her rapid-fire voice sounded well educated.

'Mr Ryder, a contact has told me that you are here on an interesting case. I was hoping to interview you about it.'

This was all I needed. 'I don't think so, Ms Krishnan. My...'

Krishnan anticipated my reticence, cut me off.

'That's okay, Mr Ryder. I was hoping to interview you, but I can write an article on what I know without your help. Of course, without your cooperation I will have to embellish some things...' She left it hanging, playing hardball. Time for damage control.

'Okay, Okay. When and where?'

'How about tomorrow?10 am at Aladdin's Bar in Colaba? Do you know where that is?'

'Aladdin's Bar at 10. I'll find it.'

'Shit!' I swore under my breath as I ended the call.

Her contact could only have been either Singh, Nadar, Patel or Rao. Singh was a family friend and wouldn't want to cause any trouble for the Mehtas, so I ruled him out. From our last exchange I figured Patel was an honest cop, so I scratched him from my list also. That left Nadar and Rao. Nadar didn't have much time for Subhani Mehta and it had felt like Rao had even less time for me. Then I remembered that Rao had my card, which was probably how Krishnan got my number.

Mabel's chat with the church ladies had resulted in me coming to the attention of the police and my investigation about to make the news. Aamir Mehta's worst nightmare was coming true and he'd have to be told. I started to dial his number. Then stopped. Better to find out what Krishnan knew before upsetting the old guy. Instead, I rang the number Davindar Singh gave me for Anveeta Khan and left a message.

***

'Busy day?' Mabel was home when I returned, a cup of tea on the table in front of her. The man sitting next to Mabel wore a dog collar.

'I think interesting would be a better way to describe it,' I replied.

'Interesting? Hmm.' She tilted her head, inquisitively. 'Sam, come meet Father Joseph.'

'Hello Father,' I said, walking towards him.

The priest stood up to shake my hand. 'Please son, call me Joseph.' He spoke in a voice made for laughing and shook my hand with both of his. I decided to stick with calling him 'Father'.

Late fifties, squat and rotund, Father Joseph resembled the image carved in the tiny statues of a Laughing Buddha. Fine black hair covered the sides of his head and his smiling eyes were magnified by the thick lenses in his black glasses. Deep laugh lines around the corners of his mouth gave him an endearing disposition.

I sat down opposite them, declined the offer of tea.

'So, Mabel tells me you are a private detective. That sounds very exciting,' he said, smiling.

'Sometimes, yes. It has its moments.'

'Is it like on TV? Do you use lots of high-tech gadgets?'

'Father, nothing is like what it is on TV.' I laughed. 'And no. I'm a very low-tech type of guy. As they say on TV, just the facts.'

Father Joseph grew more interested. 'How did you become a PI?'

'It's a long story, Father. I used to be in the Police. That's how I got started.'

'Ah, a policeman. That is a worthy calling. Why did you leave?'

'Father, you would make a good PI.' I was dodging the question but he got the message and let it be.

'You think?' He chuckled. 'And now you are looking into the death of Subhani Mehta?'

I looked at the priest, then fixed a stare at Mabel. She gave me another sheepish look in return. So much for 'mum's the word'!

'Yes, but I can't really speak about that. Client confidentiality.' I hoped that would be the end of the story.

'Don't worry about Father. He listens to confessions. That's real client confidentiality,' said Mabel. I counted to ten in my head, got to twenty before calming down.

'What is that photo of on the table?' asked Father Joseph, breaking the tension.

I looked across and noticed the photo of Subhani Mehta. I had left it on the table while I went for my walk.

'It is a picture of Subhani Mehta.'

Father Joseph lent across, picked up the photo and studied it for a couple of minutes.

'She was a very pretty girl. Such a waste. I do not care for the talisman she is wearing though.'

'Talisman?'

'Yes. Here on her neck.' He pointed to the pendant.

'You mean the pendant?' I asked.

'I don't know about pendants. But most religions have important symbols.' He put his hand in his shirt and fished out the crucifix around his neck. 'See?' he smiled.

Mabel lent towards the priest, looked across at the picture in his hands. 'Such a horrible thing! What do you think it is a symbol of?'

Father Joseph took off his glasses and drew the picture close to his face. Subconsciously, he started to make disapproving 'tut, tut' noises.

'What's the matter, Father?' I asked, my interest aroused.

He put his glasses back on. Raised his head to face me slowly.

'I've seen something like it before, not exactly the same, but close.' His voice was different now, distant, more serious.

'Really? Where?' I asked.

Father Joseph placed the picture on the table, lent back in the chair. He breathed in deeply.

'Many years ago, when I was a young parish priest at Bhusaval, one of the village leaders suddenly took ill. He was a big, powerful man, but in a matter of days he went from being as strong as an ox to wasting away on his bed. His skin became covered in a terrible rash and he developed a high fever. What was even worse was that during the night he would start to have nightmares and scream at the top of his lungs. The sound he made, dear Lord. It was not human, more like an animal being tortured. From what I heard he would writhe about in his bed, sometimes so violently that his sons had to hold him down. His screams could be heard right down the street. And then, when the sun came up, he would be like a vegetable again.

The family was wealthy and spared no expense, but the doctors could not find out what was wrong with him, or how to cure him. For weeks he just lay on his bed, howling and withering away. When finally it looked like he was going to die, the family invited a pujari to come and pray for him.

When the pujari arrived at the family home he immediately felt that there was a curse on the man. He ordered the family to check every part of the house, inside and out, for the source. Finally, one of the sons found two tiny chicken bones tied together and wedged into a crack in the bottom of one of the walls. The pujari took those bones outside the grounds of the house and said a few prayers over them. He then burned the items.' Father Joseph's eyes grew wide. 'You wouldn't believe it, but within days the man started to improve in health. The nightmares ended and after a week he was almost back to normal.'

Father Joseph looked across to Mabel then back to me. 'The problem was nobody knew who sent the curse, so the culprit could not be caught and was free to strike again. Being a village leader, many people had visited the man's home and could have hidden the items. To protect the man, the pujari gave him a talisman similar to this one.' He pointed to the photo lying on the table. 'I spoke to the man shortly after he recovered. He said he had felt as if a demon had taken over his body. He showed me the talisman the pujari had given him. He wore it for the rest of his life.'

The story got the appropriate effect from Mabel, who instinctively made the sign of the cross. She picked the photo up and looked at it carefully.

'Are you sure what that man was wearing was the same as the one around Subhani's neck?' she asked.

'Not one hundred per cent, no. But it looks similar to me,' he replied.

Father Joseph looked at me quizzically. 'Tell me, why was this girl wearing the talisman?'

'I don't know. All I know is that people around her said she was scared and that she wouldn't take it off. I didn't even know it was a talisman.'

'Perhaps I can help you. Do you have something to write on?'

I gave him my notebook and pen. He scribbled something down.

'This is the name and address of a Hindu pujari I know. Take the picture to him and ask him what he thinks. He will know much more about the talisman. He is a good man and will be able help you.'

I took the notebook back. 'Thanks, Father. Can I ask how come you know so much about Hinduism?'

Father Joseph smiled. 'Christianity in India is not like in Australia. Here, we are a minority religion. For us to do God's work we cannot afford to be naive about how the majority of people think and act. Besides,' he said with a grin, 'it pays to know your competition.'

CHAPTER 16

I stood at the balcony, looking over the scaffolding company. Just like the night I arrived, the yard was bustling with activity. Two lorries were being filled with long lengths of bamboo, carried by an assortment of barefoot men wearing filthy lungis. A portly man, dressed in slacks and an untucked collared shirt, shouted out instructions in between dragging on a cigarette. I wondered if he owned the company, or whether there was an even better dressed man shouting directions at him. For a moment I was glad to be my own boss, walk my own path. Then I thought about Aamir Mehta and his cheques, leading me back to India. My new boss, for a week or so anyway.

Mabel joined me at the balcony, followed my gaze to the yard next door. 'What did you think about Father's story?'

I shrugged, said nothing, kept looking straight ahead. He seemed like a nice guy, but his story was ridiculous and I didn't want to upset Mabel by saying so.

Mabel turned towards me, put her hand on my shoulder so that I would look at her. 'I know what you're thinking. I can see it written on your face. All I can say is that Father Joseph is a very good and smart man. He was the one who kept me sane after Franky's death.'

'I'm not saying he's not a good man. It's just all that stuff about curses....'

'You think it's rubbish, but why else would anyone wear something like that?'

'Don't tell me you believe in that mumbo-jumbo?'

She let me go, turned back towards the yard and lent on the balcony wall. 'I've never been to Australia, but my India is a spiritual place. Things are not so clear-cut as in your world. I think it is possible that Subhani may have been cursed.'

'You really believe that?'

'The Bible tells me that evil is real. Remember, Jesus cast out the demons into a herd of pigs.'

Mabel looked back at me, maternal concern in her eyes. 'I want you to be careful. You may not be taking this seriously, but I do. Curses are real. There are people in the community who cast spells over people. People pay them to put a curse on their enemies. Sometimes they can even kill people with a curse. These black magicians are very dangerous people.'

'Black magic?'

Mabel nodded. 'It's a growing problem. It's become so bad that the government has passed a law to ban people practicing black magic.'

'Are you serious?' I scorned.

'Yes. Everybody is scared of being cursed, particularly those who live in the villages. There are many stories like the one Father Joseph told you tonight. In retaliation, many people have been killed because they are suspected of being witches or evil magicians. Every week there are reports of people being beheaded or burned alive because they are supposed to be practicing black magic.'

'Okay, okay. I'll be careful,' I was only half mocking, but Mabel didn't appreciate my tone. She turned and walked inside to her dining table, opened her laptop and called me over. I watched as Mabel typed in 'black magic legislation in India' and ran a search.

'Here, sit down and look through these', she said, walking away.

She was right about the government trying to outlaw black magic. I skimmed over a copy of the *Maharashtra Prevention and Eradication of Human Sacrifice and other Inhuman, Evil and Aghori Practices and Black Magic Act, 2013*. It was fascinating. From what I could gather, the intent of the Act was to protect people from falling victim to con artists claiming to have supernatural powers. It also tried to protect people from being persecuted as witches or black magicians. It wasn't the pros and cons of the legislation that interested me. I was more engrossed by the vitriol that the Bill stirred up amongst supporters and detractors. Some claimed it was anti-Hindu, while others responded arguing it was pro-progress. The same battle was being waged on a number of fronts, from the influence of western culture and standards, to the influx of American fast-food chains. The lines were being scratched deep into the sand.

The fact that the government passed such contentious legislation into law made me realise just how seriously black magic was being treated. I thought once again about what

Father Joseph had said, about Subhani being scared and about her not taking the talisman off, if that was what it was. Then the warnings of a cataract old man came back to me and, despite myself, a shiver skipped down my spine.

I leant back on my chair, unsure what to think. It all sounded so ridiculous, but Mabel's question was valid. Why else would Subhani wear the talisman? If it was a talisman. Father Joseph and Mabel seemed convinced. Maybe another opinion would help.

I found Mabel in the kitchen, grating a bucket load of carrots. 'What are you making?' I asked.

'Halwa,' she replied without looking at me. 'For the church fete.'

I remembered halwa from my youth, a surprisingly sweet dish. 'Oh, that'll be good,' I said, then continued. 'Listen, maybe I will talk with Father Joseph's Hindu friend.'

'I think that's a good idea.'

'Would you mind coming with me? Just in case I need a translator.'

Mabel stopped grating and looked at me with her crooked smile, making me feel like the prodigal son returned. 'That's fine with me. If you like I can make us an appointment?'

'Thanks Mabel, you're one in a million.'

'Actually, in India, I am one in a billion!' she replied and started to chuckle.

'Thanks, that would be great. I've got something on at 10 am, so any time after midday would be good for me. If he's free tomorrow.'

'Oh? What are you doing at 10 am?' she asked.

Mabel pursed her lips as I told her about my phone conversation with Naina Krishnan and my suspicions about Rao. 'Bloody Police, they're as corrupt as everyone else. That's the curse on all of India.'

I was about to give Mabel a hand grating the carrots when my phone rang and vibrated in my pocket. It was the number I had rung for Anveeta Khan. I answered as I walked into the lounge room for privacy.

'Hello Mr Ryder, My name is Silvia Dias. I am Miss Khan's personal assistant.' She spoke melodically, taking her time with every word.

'Thank you for returning my call, Ms Dias.'

'Not a problem, Mr Ryder. I hope you don't mind but I had to ring Aamir Mehta to verify who you were and what you were doing before I passed on your message to Ms Khan.'

'No, that's completely understandable.'

'I am ringing to tell you that Ms Khan is happy to meet you.'

'That's great, thank you. Can you tell me when and where?'

'Unfortunately, Ms Khan is not able to leave Goa until the end of next week. You can either wait until then or, if you want, you can meet her in Goa itself.'

I'd been to Goa the first time I'd travelled in India, with Mandy, a gaunt, fair-haired British girl I had met in a Delhi backpackers' lodge. We were headed in the same direction, so we decided to travel together. We ended up spending a week swimming, drinking coconut water, smoking pot and having sex before we went our separate ways. No strings attached. Goa was that type of place. I hadn't planned to be in India until next week. I told Dias I'd meet Anveeta Khan in Goa and took down her details.

I found Mabel back in the kitchen, speaking on her mobile. She held one finger up to indicate she was nearly finished.

'Mabel, how quickly can I get a plane to Goa?' I said after she ended the call.

'Goa! Why do you want to go there?'

'Subhani Mehta had a friend called Anveeta Khan.'

'I've heard of her. The actress, yes?'

'Yeah. I need to speak with her, but she's in Goa.'

'What do you hope to find out?'

'Not sure. I just hope she can shed some light on who Subhani Mehta was. What her health was like. Her parents haven't been helpful in that regard. In fact, Subhani's father didn't think she had any friends outside the family. I know that can't be right because Davindar Singh told me she was usually the life of the party.'

'You can book airline tickets on the laptop.'

'What? You mean I don't have to queue up for three days and fill out a million forms?' I joked.

She smiled and waved her phone. 'By the way, that was the Pujari I was just talking to.'

'You called him already?'

Her smile grew wider. 'I knew you would change your mind. He said we can meet him tomorrow afternoon.'

CHAPTER 17

It was a little after 10 am the next day when I walked into Aladdin's Bar. The Arabian-style café was popularised by an almost equal mix of well-to-do locals and European tourists. Dark furniture, large soft cushions, heavy velvet drapes and dim lighting gave the place a warm, cosy feel. The odd patron smoking from a bubbling hookah added to the theme. The sickly sweet aroma of apple tobacco stopped just short of being nauseating.

I didn't know what Naina Krishnan looked like, but the lone woman sitting in the corner booth seemed like a good bet. She was looking in my direction.

'Ms Krishnan?'

'Mr Ryder. I was wondering if that was you. Please take a seat.' As with our previous conversation, she spoke quickly and sharply. A bony arm extended and pointed to the cushioned chair. Naina Krishnan was late-twenties and kitten-esque in appearance. Her large, round eyes overwhelmed the rest of her impish face. Cute, rather than pretty. She wore a camisole underneath her short-sleeved white-collared top, probably out of modesty, and a frilled pink skirt. The combo worked well against her mahogany skin.

A waiter came over and I ordered a short black. It matched my mood. She asked for another cappuccino, this time with lots of froth.

Krishnan started off slowly, skirting the reason she brought me here. 'So, have you been in Mumbai long?'

'No, I've only been here a couple of days. How did you know I was in town?'

'You know I can't reveal my sources,' she said, smiling.

I didn't want to play her games.

'Ms Krishnan, I have a busy day ahead and I don't want to waste time. Why did you want to speak with me?'

My frankness didn't faze her. She was used to uncooperative sources.

'Okay,' she said, shrugging nonchalantly. 'I understand that you are here to investigate the death of Subhani Mehta. Is that correct?'

'Where did you hear that, Ms Krishnan?'

'As I said, that's confidential.'

I decided to take a punt. 'That's okay. I know who your source is. As you are aware, Aamir Mehta is a powerful man. When I told him what you planned to do, he was outraged. He intends to speak with Superintendent Rao himself. I also understand that he wants to contact your editor.'

Her ears tinted pink and she leaned back ever so slightly. So it was Rao! I guessed that her editor didn't know what she was doing either. Krishnan would change that the minute she got back to the office.

'You see, Ms Krishnan, the Mehtas are still grieving over the death of their daughter and just want to be left in peace. They were very upset with the newspaper reports of their daughter's autopsy. Mr Mehta will do anything to stop that type of harassment happening again.'

'That wasn't harassment. I just reported the facts,' she said, riled.

I didn't realise that she had written the article. Maybe meeting Naina Krishnan wasn't a complete waste of time. It was my turn to ask some questions.

'So you saw the autopsy report?' I queried.

'Yup. I got a copy of it.' She smiled proudly.

'How?' I asked. A certain coroner in Australia would also like to know.

'Once again, that's confidential.' Krishnan smiled, flashing a set of snow-white teeth.

'Fair enough.' It was worth a try.

'So you know about Rao, huh?' She said. 'He told me about what you were doing. Sounds like a good story. Tell me, what do you expect to find?' It was a different question but seeking the same answers. Krishnan was a professional.

'I'm sorry. I don't know what Rao told you, but I'm not going to discuss why I'm here with you.'

We both fell silent as the coffee arrived. I raised the glass to my mouth, drank it in one gulp. She just watched me, stirring sugar into her cup.

'That's fine. I know what I'm going to write. I only had two questions.'

She counted with her fingers. 'One. What is it about Subhani's death that you are investigating? And two. Why you? Why would Mr Mehta hire a PI all the way from Australia?'

Krishnan was good. I still wasn't fully clear on those questions myself.

'Perhaps you should ask Superintendent Rao for the answers.'

Krishnan pushed her cup towards the middle of the table, then picked up her bag and sidled her way to the edge of the booth.

'I can see that I'm not going to get very far with you, Mr Ryder. Nevertheless, this has been a useful conversation. Thank you.'

She forced a smile as she stood up, then walked away. I sat in the booth for a while longer and watched her cappuccino lose its froth, wondering what she would write.

***

Mabel's apartment smelt of bitter-sweet vinegar when I arrived back. Mabel was sitting at the dining table, leaning over the crossword in the daily papers. 'What have you been cooking?' I asked.

'Beef Vindaloo. Do you want some?' Mabel replied, putting her pen down.

'Not just yet, thanks.' My appetite had started to wane in the heat. I walked behind Mabel, looked at the crossword from over her shoulder.

'Fourteen down. Cosmic Body. Seven letters ending in "r". Try "stellar"' I said.

Mabel was no longer interested in the crossword. 'So, how did it go with the journalist?' She asked.

I walked around the table and sat opposite her. 'Not sure. She knows why I'm in town and admitted that it was Rao that tipped her off. I gave her nothing new.'

'That's good.'

'Yes, but now I have to tell Aamir Mehta that the media is aware of the investigation. He's going to be pissed off.'

'That's not your fault.'

'It doesn't matter. Mehta will blame me. All he wanted was discretion and I couldn't deliver that.'

'Well, we have to go to see the pujari soon. Maybe he will have some good news about that pendant that you can give to Mehta?'

'Mabel, whatever that pendant may or may not be, I'm pretty certain the news won't be good.'

CHAPTER 18

The taxi dropped us off near an ancient entrance archway made from large blocks of stone the colour of dried blood. The grounds of the temple lay on the other side. A group of hawkers had set up shop selling petal garlands, colourful candles and tacky plastic images of fantastical gods. Other vendors tended to the more earthly pleasures of ice-cream, soft drinks and candy bars.

A group of urchins, each dressed in their Sunday worst, stopped chasing each other and made a beeline for us, putting on sad puppy-dog faces along the way. They crowded around us like seagulls around a chip, their hands outstretched.

'Please sir, ten rupees. Please sir, ten rupees,' the oldest girl repeated. Another boy crept along beside me and shyly tugged at my shirt, holding out his other hand.

'Hold on to your wallet. These little buggers will steal it without you even knowing,' said Mabel. She began to shoo the children away, unsuccessfully.

I felt sorry for the kids but didn't want to encourage them to beg for money. Instead, I walked over to one of the hawkers who sold bags of chips and frozen icicles. The urchin group split in two, some coming with me, others staying with Mabel. In the front of the shop was a tray of deep-fried discs of dough. They looked more filling than anything else on offer.

'Onion *bhaja*,' said the vendor. 'Five rupees, one.'

I counted the number of kids and paid the guy for eight *bhajas*. The vendor wiggled his head and placed the snacks into a plastic bag.

I turned to the eldest girl. 'Here. One each.'

She looked disappointed. 'No food. Only rupees.'

I shook my head, gave the bag to the little boy instead and walked away. He took the bag and ran to a group of older women watching events from underneath a large tree. I wondered if there'd be any food left for him after the adults had their share. The other urchins drifted away, realising they'd done their dash with us.

Three flights of marble stairs, worn smooth and grey with age, led to the temple itself. On each landing a handful of wretched-looking beggars pleaded for alms: some old, some maimed, some with leprosy. My moral high ground regarding begging failed at the sight of these broken people, their lives mostly behind them and my change was exhausted by the second flight.

The temple was part of a larger complex. At the front stood the mandir, its gleaming marble tower reaching 20 feet above the inner sanctum. Fierce statues of Hindu gods with blazing eyes stood on guard, as they had done for hundreds of years. Bamboo scaffolding still attached to the tower hinted at a recent cleaning and explained the brilliant reflection of the sun, making it painful to stare at.

Surrounding the tower was a large marble hall where an idol of Nandi, the bull, faced the darkened inner sanctum of Lord Shiva. Someone had respectfully laid a rich red shawl across the back of the black bull. Worshippers, pilgrims and holy men hung around in the cool of the hall, talking in quiet groups, meditating in silence or reflecting on what life's all about. In a corner at the back of the hall a middle-aged man slept soundly, his right arm used as a pillow and his left shielding his eyes from the light. His gentle snore sounded like a resonant mantra.

Completing the complex at the rear was a plain, two-storey building built more recently than the temple itself. On each floor was a series of rooms with numbered green doors. Living and administration quarters for the temple pujaris. Some of the rooms were open but it was too dark to see inside. A line of drying clothes hung from the second-floor balcony railing, mostly of a saffron orange colour. Holy men needed to do laundry too.

We left our shoes at the front, hoping they would be there when we returned, and walked into the hall. We stepped carefully, avoiding the slippery residue of rotting flowers on the marble floor—yesterday's garlands. Instantly it felt quieter and cooler, as if the outside world was not allowed to enter this hallowed place. Large, chimney-like incense burners gave off a spicy smoke. In the inner sanctum a handful of people were devoutly performing their puja, bowing deeply with their palms pressed together near their forehead. I felt like an intruder and headed for the green door numbered 4.

Sri Sarmaravi Chandrapathy was in his forties, though it was hard to tell from his baby face and short crop of thick, black hair. He looked too skinny for his height, like he'd been stretched in a taffy machine. He had regular features except for his crooked nose, which implied a break that was never tended to. He dressed simply, just an orange lungi, and wore a cotton string across his honey-coloured chest—a symbol of his Brahmin heritage. In the middle of his forehead, above his clear brown eyes, was a smudge of orange flanked by two vertical white lines.

His room was small and simple: a low bed with folded linen at the foot, a chair and desk directly opposite, a chest of drawers near the door. On the desk was a picture of an elderly man, perhaps his father or his guru. It was hard to make out any resemblance. A collection of books lined the back of the desk, against the wall—some in Hindi, some in French, some English—all speaking of good education. The wall above his bed had a poster of a benign-looking Lord Shiva sitting cross-legged, one of his four arms holding a trident. On the opposite wall was a picture of the Indian cricket team.

Mabel and I sat on his hard bed in silence, our knees up near our chests. The hushed murmur of devotees faded away like white noise, leaving a stillness that was only punctuated by the resonant sounding of the temple bell, its random toll never failing to give me a start.

The pujari wedged the door open with his large foot and studied the photo in the light. After a while he took a long step in and handed me the picture.

'You say Father Joseph thinks it is a talisman?' he asked in a reedy voice.

'He wasn't sure. That's why he gave me your details,' I replied.

He took the photo back from me and crumpled his face in a squint. 'It is very difficult to say. The picture is not very clear.'

He studied it for some more time, moving the photo up and down and looking at it from different angles, as if it were three-dimensional.

'To me it looks like it could be a talisman, but I can't say anything more about it from this picture. You see, anything can be a talisman. It's not the physical shape that is important. It's the blessing that it contains. Without actually touching it I cannot be one hundred per cent sure. Do you have it with you?'

'No, the photo is all.' That got me thinking, where was the pendant?

He shut the door gently, making sure it didn't make much noise, then sat down on the chair opposite us. His legs extended between Mabel's and mine.

'Getting a talisman is not as simple as you think. Sometimes, it can take weeks to decide what the right spells and prayers should be. It all depends on what it is used for,' he said.

'What do you mean?' I asked.

'Well, some people use talismans to promote good luck or to find love. Others use them to help with health problems,' he paused. 'And some use them to protect against curses. If this *was* a talisman, why do you think she was wearing it?'

'Like you, I don't even know if this is a talisman. She died shortly after getting it, so if it is one then I'm thinking perhaps for health reasons,' I said.

'Or maybe she thought she was cursed,' added Mabel, eagerly.

'If it was for health then we will never know now,' he said, shaking his head. 'But if she was cursed there is one other way to find out.'

'Really, how?' asked Mabel, her voice lowered conspiratorially.

'Take me to where she lived. If she was cursed, I will know.' He said it without any pomp, like this was nothing new to him. I looked up at him, wondered at the world he lived in where curses and black magic were as normal and humdrum as cheese on toast.

'There's no need for that. I saw how she died. She wasn't cursed, her heart must have given out. That's all.'

'Well, if you are certain, then why are you here?' enquired the pujari.

'Because her parents believe there is more to it than that, don't they Sam?' Mabel directed her response to me, making a point, rather than answering the pujari. 'That's why they engaged you. I know you only want to see light and dark, Sam, but this is India and there are lots of shadows. You owe it to her parents to find the truth.'

Mabel's interruption wasn't welcomed by me, even though there was some truth to what she was saying. Subhani's parents did believe there was more to it than the coroner's findings and nothing I had already told them would change that, would help them heal. Then I thought about my own parents, how their grief was corroding their lives and how I was powerless to act. I recalled the room at the Mehta's house, the picture of a Hindu god on the wall. They seemed like religious people and may feel the same way about curses as the pujari. I figured if I could dispel any concerns about black magic then they may be better able to accept the facts. I couldn't do it for my own parents but this was my chance to give someone else's parents some peace.

'Let me talk with Aamir Mehta.'

CHAPTER 19

'We have to get him inside Subhani Mehta's home,' Mabel whispered excitedly, cautious of what the taxi driver could hear. I wound down the window and let the dirty air whip against my face, thought about how best to approach Aamir Mehta. I knew he was going to hit the roof when I told him about the newspaper article and now I was also going to ask him to let a pujari visit Subhani's home. I wasn't sure how he'd take the suggestion and didn't want to lose my best paying client, my only client. He knew the official findings, but was paying me to find more evidence, explore other leads. I needed to remind him of that and hope that his desire for answers would outweigh any ridicule or contempt for the idea. It would also be a good opportunity to check out Subhani Mehta's house, look for any medications that may suggest a heart problem.

I reached for my mobile and dialled Aamir Mehta. He told me to meet him at his club and gave me the address. I tapped the taxi driver on the shoulder, got his attention.

'Marine Drive,' I said. He wiggled his head, spat a streak of red *paan* juice out of his window and made a U turn.

The entrance to the Marine Club was not well signed. Instead of an ostentatious building built for Mumbai's elite, which was what I had expected, all we could see was a tall, white, brick wall topped with broken shards of glass. A wide entrance gate across the driveway was left open. Our taxi driver missed it on the first pass and had to make a circuit around the block for a second attempt. The driveway curved around to the front of the building. Hidden behind the wall, the squat, white-washed hacienda building failed to take advantage of its commanding view over Chowpatty Beach. Dwarfing it on both sides were large concrete apartment blocks—monstrosities of architecture. Tables and chairs were placed underneath tall palm trees throughout the manicured garden, a respectable distance kept between them.

'I never knew this building was here,' said Mabel, staring through the window.

'I think they like it that way,' I said, opening the rear door. 'I'll see you back at your place.'

'If you like, I can book your flight to Goa,' she said.

'Thanks. For as soon as possible, please.'

Mabel's gaze drifted over shoulder and she pointed behind me with her chin. I turned around to see a middle-aged man in a black suit, so worn that it shone, approaching me. He had a snooty 'I don't think you belong here' look on his face. I asked for Aamir Mehta before he could finish clearing his throat. Told him to take me to him *jaldi,* quickly.

He led me onto a large veranda that took advantage of whatever sea breeze made it past the front fence. Aamir Mehta was the only person in this part of the club. He was sitting in a high-backed wicker chair, reading a broadsheet.

He was dressed in a suit and tie again, this time in matching grey. He finished what he was reading before acknowledging my presence. A half full glass of whisky sat on the side table, near the cigar that was leaking delicious smoke.

Mehta looked up at me from his seated position. 'Mr Ryder. I was not expecting to see you today. Do you have some news?'

'Thank you for meeting me at such short notice. I just needed to ask you a few more things,' I replied.

'Oh, well, in that case please take a seat.' He folded the paper and placed it on the table, then picked up his cigar.

I sat in the matching chair, not sure of what I was going to say to him. My throat became dry.

'So, what more did you want to ask me?' he said.

'First of all, thank you for arranging for me to meet Mr Singh. He and his director, Mr Nadar, were very helpful. I also hope to interview Anveeta Khan in the next couple of days.'

'That is very good. Have you discovered anything?'

'When I spoke to Mr Singh, he told me that Subhani seemed to be scared of something when she was in Australia. He said she acted as if she was hiding. Did she say anything to you about being afraid?"

Mehta took a puff from his cigar, held in the smoke while he thought about it. 'No, the last time I saw her she was happy, looking forward to going to Australia,' he said through wisps of smoke.

'Did she say or do anything at all that worried you?' I asked.

He shook his head.

'Has anyone been to her house since she died?'

'Just some workers.' He paused. 'To clear things up.' His head tilted down and his eyes closed for a second. Holding back the tears he was too proud to shed.

'With your permission, I would like to visit Subhani's house. There may be something there that can help with the investigation. Perhaps something that may shed light on Subhani's state of mind.'

'Of course, but as I said she was in good spirits.'

'Thank you.'

He took another puff from the cigar, let the smoke escape before speaking this time.

'I must say I don't see why you had to come all this way, Mr Ryder. You could have asked me this on the phone.'

'There is one thing. I would like to bring someone with me,' I said.

Mehta sat slightly straighter in the chair. 'Who? I hired you to work alone.'

'A pujari. His name is Sri Chandrapathy.'

'A pujari! Whatever for?'

I pulled out the photo of Subhani wearing the talisman, handed it over to him. He put the cigar down.

'Have you ever seen the pendant your daughter is wearing in this picture before?'

He looked at the picture with tender eyes, gently running his fingers across the image of his daughter's face, then focused on the pendant around her neck.

'I'm sorry, I've never seen this thing before.' That was unexpected, I figured Mehta would have received it along with all of Subhani's other possessions when he collected the body.

'You didn't receive it as part of Subhani's belongings?'

'No, not that I am aware of. It may have been packed along with everything else, but I can't remember it specifically.'

'Your daughter started wearing this pendant when she went to Australia. For some reason it was very important to her. She wouldn't remove it.'

I leaned in towards him. 'Are you sure it doesn't ring any bells?'

'No. I have never seen Subhani wear this. I am sure my wife hasn't either.'

'That's a pity,' I said, wondering what happened to the talisman.

'What is so important about it?' He kept the photo on his lap.

'Mr Mehta, all I know about this pendant was that Subhani placed a great deal of value on it.'

I shifted in my seat, uncomfortable with what I was about to say.

'Before coming here, I showed the picture to the pujari and asked him what it was. He said it could be a Hindu talisman.'

'A what? Our family is Hindu, but we have never heard or seen anything like this before.' He picked up the picture again.

'I'm not an expert, but I've been told that people who wear things like this often do so to protect themselves from poor health or, sometimes…a curse,' I said.

My words seemed to hang in the air for an eternity. Aamir Mehta put the picture down slowly and stared at me.

'Curse! What do you mean *curse*?' He looked confused.

'Mr Mehta. I know this sounds ridiculous. But the pujari thinks there is a chance that Subhani may have been cursed. If you allow him to check Subhani's house, he will be able to tell for sure.'

'Are you saying my daughter was killed by a curse?' His brows knotted with the question.

'No. All I'm saying is that this is something we should investigate along with any other leads.'

Mehta's face grew flush and he shot up from the chair, paced about the room.

'You come here to tell me this!' he said, aiming an accusatory finger at me. 'After all your questions, this is what you have come up with? Is this what am I paying you good money for?' I couldn't blame him for his reaction, I'd have reacted the same way if the tables were turned.

'I'm sorry. I know what you must think. I'm not convinced myself. But right now, everything that I'm finding out, the forensics, the eye-witnesses, leads me to believe that Subhani died of natural causes. If Anveeta Khan doesn't shed any new light then that's the dead-end. If you truly believe that there is something more to Subhani's death then what do you have to lose?'

That seemed to infuriate Mehta more.

'I've already lost a daughter and you ask what more do I have to lose? How about whatever is left of my family's dignity?'

He stood behind the wicker chair, leaned heavily on its back and took time to regain his composure. 'I am not stupid, Mr Ryder. You are telling me that this investigation will not proceed much longer unless either you discover something from Ms Khan or this...pujari...finds something, aren't you?'

I nodded. 'I'm just trying to cover all the angles.'

'Then it seems I have little choice. You have my permission, but I will be there when the pujari arrives. 12 noon tomorrow.' He gave me Subhani's address.

'Thank you, Mr Mehta.'

Mehta sat down again. He lent forward, his elbows on his lap and his chin in his hands. 'Who would curse my beautiful daughter?'

From his faraway look I knew the question wasn't meant for me.

'I'm sorry Mr Mehta, but I also have some bad news.'

He focused back on me. 'Bad news. After what you just told me? What more bad news can you have?'

'A journalist from the *Voice of India* newspaper found out about the investigation. I think we can expect an article in the next couple of days.'

'A journalist!' Mehta thumped the arm of the chair. 'How did this journalist find out?'

'I'm not sure,' I lied, deciding not to let him know about my visit to the police station. 'It could have been anyone I spoke with, or maybe someone that they told afterwards. It is hard to say.'

'I told you before, you cannot trust anyone in India.' He wagged his finger at me briskly, like he was admonishing a naughty child.

'Like I said, I'm sorry. I tried to scare the journalist off by reminding her you are a powerful and influential man.' Strategic sucking-up never did any harm. In this case it didn't help.

'From now on you report only to me. No one else. Understand?' Spittle flew from his mouth as he spoke.

CHAPTER 20

It could have been worse. Mehta would still be angry, though. I read the article again.

> *It has come to this newspaper's attention that Mr Aamir Mehta, father of recently deceased actress Subhani Mehta, has secretly recruited the services of a foreign-based private investigator to scrutinise the incidents leading to the Bollywood star's tragic death.*
>
> *The autopsy on Ms Mehta found no suspicious circumstances contributed to her death. The precise nature of the investigation, therefore, is unknown. Neither is the reason why a foreign investigative firm has been engaged to undertake this work.*
>
> *While this paper acknowledges the Mehtas' desire for privacy, Subhani Mehta was dear to the hearts of millions of Indians. Any questions surrounding her death are of interest to the public. Any further developments on this matter will be reported by the Voice of India.*

The private investigator in question, Mr Samson Ryder of Australian-Indian Investigations, refused to be formally interviewed for this article.

I folded the paper angrily and threw it on the dashboard of the taxi. The traffic was moving so slowly that a young boy selling bootleg copies of novels kept pace with us, knocking on the window. He was a shoeless scamp with a businessman's brain. At Rs 50 per copy, Kiran Desai's *The Inheritance of Loss* was a real bargain. I wasn't in the mood to read and instead reached into my pocket and offered him a handful of coins. He grabbed them as if he were doing me a favour, then asked for a coin from my country. On current exchange, one of mine equalling thirty of his. I took a liking to this roadside entrepreneur, a future Richard Branson. For a while he let me forget what we were about to do.

The pujari chuckled from the back seat, his knees up near his ears. 'You know, it's supposed to be a good book. You should have bought it.'

I turned around and cocked an eyebrow at him, then looked at the large canvas bag on the seat next to him, sagging like a half-deflated balloon.

'What's in the bag?' I asked

'Things that may be of use,' was all he said, shifting his gaze out the window.

The traffic moved lazily, like a sloth after a feed.

Both Aamir and Rekha Mehta were waiting in their car outside the gates of Subhani's home, their driver poised at the wheel. We pulled up alongside. Aamir Mehta looked across at us, his lips pursed. We both got out of our vehicles at the same time.

'Have you read the newspapers?' Mehta shouted as he stomped towards me. 'My phone has been ringing non-stop.'

I raised my arms to placate him. 'I'm sorry, Mr Mehta. I'll make sure it won't happen again,' I said, though not sure how I could guarantee this.

Mehta stopped about a metre away from me and exhaled deeply. His shoulders slumped as his anger dissipated and he looked lost, spent. He looked at the pujari in the back seat.

'I'm not sure about this, Mr Ryder,' he said, quietly.

'Neither am I, Mr Mehta. But we're all here now.'

The pujari stepped out of the car, adjusted his orange lungi and walked around to us. Aamir Mehta eyed him suspiciously. I did the introductions and the two men shook hands. A car door closed and we all turned around to see the shell of Rekha Mehta walk towards us. Her feet dragged across the dirt, creating swirls of dry grey dust that settled on her once-white sari. Unkempt mats of brittle hair framed a red, raw face that had dark echoes for eyes. She had aged ten years since I last saw her, years she could not afford to lose.

'Please excuse the sight of my wife, gentlemen. She is suffering greatly,' said Aamir Mehta apologetically. 'I would have preferred her not to come.'

Two tall iron gates formed a barred archway leading to the home that Subhani Mehta once lived in. A watchman's box that was built into the large brick fence was no longer manned. Aamir Mehta was about to unlock the gates when the pujari held out his hand and asked him to stop.

Moving close to the gate, the pujari closed his eyes and began to chant something inaudible over and over, his lips barely moving. Slowly, gently, he swayed his head from left to right, repeating his mantra. I watched this ritual quietly, not knowing exactly what to think. Then, abruptly, the pujari stopped and turned to Aamir Mehta.

'I believe beauty has turned ugly here', he said, solemnly.

Aamir Mehta had tears streaming down his face. 'Are you saying my daughter was cursed?' he asked.

Sri Chandrapathy held his hands together and bowed his head. 'With your permission, I will cleanse this house. Only then can your daughter continue her *samsara*, the cycle of life'.

CHAPTER 21

The gravel driveway crunched under our shoes as we walked up to the house. We approached reverently, the way people walk in a church, or a cemetery. The front yard was mainly grass, with thick, green hedges along each side fence. Four large trees had been planted in the part of the garden that caught the afternoon sun. Their branches had been trained together to form a natural arbour of bright green foliage. Underneath, a white wrought iron bench collected dead leaves.

The two-storey building was made of a creamy-brown brick, the colour of damp beach sand. It was largely conventional in shape except for the middle third of the façade, which jutted out from the rest of the building like buck teeth. Eight white-trimmed windows lined up on the ground floor. Two on the protruding façade surrounding the front door and three each on the recessed wings. The second storey had nine windows; a door not being required. The house had a solid, aristocratic feel to it.

Aamir Mehta opened the door and entered the house, the rest of us following. The layout took me by surprise. The rabbit warren of little rooms that the façade promised wasn't there. Instead the ground floor comprised a large entertainment area. A bathroom, kitchen and laundry came off this main room. The house was empty of Subhani's personal effects and had been freshly painted in vivid white, making the place feel cold, soulless.

Upstairs were three double bedrooms, each with an ensuite. The staircase continued up to a rooftop garden with views of the Arabian Sea. Downstairs, large glass doors at the rear of the entertainment area opened out into a rambling garden, the front part of which was paved and led to an empty swimming pool.

The pujari placed his bag near the front door and called us all to gather.

'This house needs to be searched. We need to find what was used for the curse,' he said.

I was out of my depth, and felt exhilarated and scared at the same time, like watching a horror movie through his fingers. This was not like the death threats, which I could understand and deal with. This was something irrational, alien, completely out of my control. I took a few breaths to calm my nerves, reminded myself that we were only acting on the pujari's hunch, nothing more. He was insistent, though.

'What should we be looking for?' I asked.

The pujari shrugged. 'It can be anything that looks out of the ordinary—animal bones, different things tied up together. Anything that you feel doesn't belong.'

'All the furniture is gone. Perhaps what we're looking for is no longer here?' I said.

The pujari shook his head. 'What we seek is still here.'

'Mr Mehta, if you look outside, I'll check inside,' I said.

Aamir Mehta gave me a single nod, more like a shallow bow, and went out the back door. The pujari sat down on the floor next to Rekha Mehta, holding her hand and spoke softly.

The rooftop garden was a barren, concrete slab with a concrete railing coming up to my hip. In the corner a large pot held the withered remains of a plant. There was nothing unusual. In the distance I could make out the white frothy lines that etched the waves of the Arabian Sea. Two small fishing boats swayed with the waves, their masts moving in time, like metronomes.

The three bedrooms on the next level down were empty. Marks on the carpet the only clues to what furniture they'd held. The ensuites smelled of bleach. If this house held any of Subhani's secrets they were long gone by now. Aamir Mehta told me they'd cleaned up. They'd done a good job.

The downstairs rooms were just as bleak. Nothing seemed out of place because nothing was in place. Rekha Mehta and the pujari were still sitting on the floor.

'There's nothing inside, I'll help outside,' I said to them.

The garden was large and I figured Aamir Mehta would appreciate a hand. He wasn't in the back when I checked and had probably moved to the hedges in the front yard. I strolled through the back half of the garden, past the paving and the pool. This section was populated with large banyan trees, their roots springing out from overhead branches and spilling over smaller, woody shrubs and purple bougainvillea. In parts, the canopy was so dense that the house was barely visible. It even felt a couple of degrees cooler. The earth was kept damp by a succulent, dark green ground cover.

I stood in the shadow of the banyans, wondering where to look next, when something seemed odd. Hidden behind the tangled trunk of a large tree a small section of earth lay bare while the lush groundcover grew all around it. Being behind the tree it couldn't be seen from the house. I walked over and squatted down for a closer examination. From above it looked like a dirt crop-circle surrounded by a field of green. The ground had recently been disturbed.

A sense of exhilaration surged through my body. I jumped up and ran back into the house like a kid who'd overdosed on sweets.

'I think I've found something. Is there a shovel?'

Rekha Mehta turned her weary eyes to me. 'Everything is gone,' she said in a dry, husky voice.

I ran back to the spot at the rear of the garden, fell on my knees and began to dig with my hands. Others joined me and watched on over my shoulders. The soil was loose and came away easily. Not far from the surface was a piece of brown material. I reached down and tried to pull it out but it was still partially buried. It took some effort before a sodden hessian bag came away from the earth.

I placed it on the ground and looked up at the pujari. 'Is this what we're looking for?' I asked.

'Perhaps, let's see,' he replied and squatted next to me.

I stood up and took a couple of steps back, flicked the soil from my hands as the pujari closed his eyes and whispered some words.

He carefully untied the string that sealed the bag and tipped it upside down. A plastic bag covered in mud slid out. The dirt camouflaged its contents. The pujari looked up at all of us, then back down at the plastic bag. He untied the end on the bag and we were instantly forced back by the pungent, putrid stench of rotting meat. It reminded me of the smell of dead kangaroos strewn along country highways. Roadkill.

The pujari turned away momentarily to clear his throat and take a fresh breath, then he upturned the plastic bag. First, a slimy, viscous liquid dribbled out. Then, once the bag was almost completely upside down, a lump of solid matter flopped out and the rotten smell intensified. Acid rose in my throat. I swallowed to keep it down. Rekha Mehta gargled a scream and her legs buckled from beneath her. I managed to grab her and keep her from falling, smudging her sari with my dirty hands. We both looked down at the lump on the ground. It was hard to make out at first, but then the shapes started to fit together.

The foetus would have been about three months old. The main features of the human body were clearly developed. I could see its head, big indentations where the eyes would form, arms, fingers. Three iron nails punctured the foetus and pinned it to a shrivelled lemon. The image and the smell burned themselves onto the hard-drive in my mind.

I assisted Rekha Mehta back inside. She dropped to the floor and sobbed. I didn't know what to say to her; so left her on the floor and walked back outside. Aamir Mehta was trembling with rage. The pujari was telling him that he would dispose of the items but Aamir Mehta didn't seem to be listening, he turned his back on him and literally ran towards me.

'You see now, Mr Ryder.' He had furious wide eyes and flaring nostrils. 'I was right. This proves it. Someone *did* kill my daughter.'

I didn't know what to think. Images raced through my mind, trying to make sense of what I had just seen, though no sense would come. My head told me that this proved nothing, my gut told me differently, again no agreement.

'I don't know what this proves but leave it with me. I'll check it out.' I said.

That wasn't good enough for Aamir Mehta. 'I know I'm right. And I know who it was.' He flailed his arms wildly, spittle spraying as he spoke.

'You do? Who?'

'Whoever was the father of Subhani's baby.'

'The father? How do you know this?'

'You saw that thing…that dead baby.' Aamir Mehta pointed to where we dug. 'It is symbolic. The father wanted to kill Subhani's baby. That is why he used a dead baby.'

He moved in on me, his crimson face inches away from mine.

'Find me the father. He deserves to burn in hell's fire,' he whispered coldly.

CHAPTER 22

The pujari retrieved a clear plastic bottle and a packet of matches from his canvas sack. Inside the bottle was a transparent blue liquid. I watched from a distance as he doused the foetus with the liquid while Rekha Mehta's sobs faded to whimpers in the background. The chemical smell of petrol wafted in the air.

The pujari lit a match and took a step backwards. He then tossed the match onto the foetus and a violent ball of flames instantly erupted. A bitter, black smoke seemed to swirl around the pujari and drift away in the wind. He stood still until the pile of rotting fuel was well alight. Then he turned and walked back towards me.

'What should we do now?' I asked him as he joined me.

'We wait until the fire dies down,' he said.

'Is that part of some sort of ritual?' I queried.

'No,' he replied with a smirk, 'it is to make sure the house doesn't burn down.'

We stood silently, side by side, for another ten minutes while the fire slowly exhausted itself. We then made our way through the house and out the front door.

Aamir Mehta was pacing by their car. 'Finished? Good,' he said impatiently to the pujari before turning his ire towards me. 'You. I want the name of the father immediately.' His eyes were wet and wild, sad and angry.

I nodded. 'I'll do my best.'

'It had better be good enough,' he said as he stepped into the car. I peered in the back seat to see Rekha Mehta lying, curled up in a corner.

We drove back, silent in our thoughts. The taxi pulled over near the archway that led to the pujari's temple.

He patted me on the shoulder. 'You're having difficulties with this, aren't you?'

'Is it that obvious?' I said, managing a smile. 'Everyone expects me to believe that people can die from curses, that spirits or demons can be summoned to kill people, and the stuff we just saw back there, well I'll be honest that scared the shit out of me. But I just don't buy it. It makes no sense.'

'You are not a spiritual person, which is a great pity.' He stepped out of the car. 'But you will need to open your mind if you are to understand. Come with me,' he said, closing the door.

We sat facing each other in his tiny room, him cross-legged on the bed, me on the chair, the door shut. The only light came from the bulb dangling from the exposed wires that snaked along the central joist in the ceiling.

'Okay,' I said. 'Even if I assume Subhani was cursed. How can black magic kill a person?'

I wasn't sure what type of answer I was looking for.

'I cannot explain to you the philosophy of Hinduism in one afternoon. What you need to know is that there are some mantras that, if used by the wrong people, can cause great harm, like the *Baan Mara* and the *Baan Jala*. These mantras are known as *dhanurvedam*, or bow and arrows. Someone well trained in these mantras can use them to strike down an opponent wherever they are.'

'You mean like sticking a pin in a voodoo doll?' I asked.

'Not exactly. People who do that believe they are directly causing the pain the victim suffers. What happens in a curse is that a magician summons up a spirit to do their wishes.'

Once again, the warnings of Uncle George haunted my thoughts.

'What was the baby and the lemon all about?' I asked.

'Different magicians use different items. The lemon is sour, bitter. Its acid eats away at the flesh of the baby. Destroying creation. It was buried there so that the spirit could be centred on the actress.'

'Where would a person get things like that, the foetus?' I asked.

The pujari sighed. 'These items are available to anyone who knows where to find them. Some villagers make their living this way. Digging up the recently dead, perhaps even resorting to murder. Sometimes, when a woman dies while pregnant or during childbirth, it is considered such bad luck that the body is butchered and buried in different places far away from the village. The belief is that the evil spirit won't be able to find its way back to the village.'

'You're kidding,' I said.

He shook his head. 'It would not be hard to get a foetus that way.'

He spoke in a matter of fact fashion and once again I reflected on his world view, where the concept of curses and spells was part of culture, a part of life. I was beginning to see why the government had banned black magic.

'The magic in that house was strong. So strong I believe only a powerful magician could create it.'

'Do you know who?' I asked over-eagerly. As soon as I spoke, I felt a wave of embarrassment wash over me, ridiculed myself for taking it too seriously.

He screwed up his face, shook his head. 'If the girl were alive, I could channel the spirit and find out who sent it. But not now.'

'So, we're back at square one,' I said.

His eyes glazed and drifted over my shoulder. There was a long pause before he spoke again.

'Tell me, what do you know of Tantra?' he asked, using a schoolteacher's tone.

'Nothing.'

'Tantra is about union with the cosmic consciousness. The Shiva and the Shakti.' He shaped a globe with his hands. 'For tantrics, the ultimate aim of years of practice, meditation, and prayer is Nirvana.'

'Most tantrics follow *dakshinacharya*, the right-handed path. These people abide by a strict code of conduct, called the *yamas*, and are very good people.' He wiggled his head approvingly. 'There are also a few people who follow *vamacharya*, the left-handed path. These people partake of things that are forbidden in *dakshinacharya*, such as meat and alcohol and sexual rituals. Usually, they also have a female partner, a *shakti*, with which they perform these rituals. Such things are forbidden in *dakshinacharya*.'

I was starting to wonder where this was all going, why I should be interested.

The pujari continued: 'Both paths are equally valid if followed correctly. But *vamacharya* is very strong, with the potential to give its practitioners immense powers very quickly.'

He shook his head. 'Some *vamacharya* tantrics become so obsessed with the power that they give up on ever attaining Nirvana. Instead, they focus on the flesh. Some have been known to do terrible things with corpses, sleeping with them and eating their flesh. These people can end up using their powers for more base purposes.'

My interest picked up again. 'Like black magic?'

He nodded. 'Black magic and sex go hand in hand. Because of this, many fallen *vamacharya* tantrics end up practicing the dark art. Sometimes for baksheesh.'

I caught on to his line of reasoning. 'Are you saying one of these *vamacharya* tantrics killed Subhani?'

He looked at me with his clear, brown eyes. 'If so, then they're a very dangerous one.'

He wasn't able to give me any more information on the tantric's identity, except that whoever it was probably worshipped the goddess Kali. He trawled through his books to find a picture of the dark, fearsome idol. She had a hideous face with three glaring eyes and a large red tongue that poked fun at the world. Around her neck was a chain of human heads and her belt comprised of dismembered arms. A savage-looking sword was held aloft by one of her four hands, another holding a severed head. She looked powerful, vicious, unstoppable.

'Despite how she may look, Kali is not an evil god,' he said, looking at the bewilderment on my face.

'Unlike Christianity, our gods are neither good nor bad. The important thing is how worshippers use the gifts the gods give them. If someone asks Kali to do terrible things on their behalf, eventually terrible things will happen to them also. That is the nature of karma.'

CHAPTER 23

Mabel sat on her couch nursing a whisky as I narrated the day's events. She shuddered when I described the sopping mess in the hessian sack.

'So, he believes Subhani was cursed by a powerful magician?'

'Yes, well, it's hard to disagree when you find an unborn child pinned to a lemon buried in someone's backyard. It's not a normal circumstance,' the cynicism in my voice was meant for myself. I finished my drink, instantly wanted another.

'Mabel, this is the first hard piece of evidence I have that suggests there may have been more to Subhani's death than the official account. This is what the Mehtas are paying me to uncover,' I shook my head, turned away from her. 'But if I take this at face value and follow the lead, then I'm basically acknowledging that Subhani was cursed and that is how she died. I just can't believe that.'

'You know, it's not what you believe that's important. It's what they believe,' said Mabel, thumbing towards the door, meaning the world outside. She took a sip of the malty, golden-brown liquid. 'For us Indians, belief comes before everything else.'

I got the strong feeling she meant *Indians* exclusive of me.

'Most Indians believe in curses and will go to great lengths to protect themselves and their families.' She stood up and walked to the balcony.

I poured myself another drink and followed.

We stood side by side, leaning on the balcony wall.

'You're like Saint Thomas. Always looking for proof.' She took another swig and stared out over the bay. The lights from the apartment buildings along the far shore were slowly coming on and the Muslim call to prayer wafted gently in the heavy air.

'I can't prove that curses exist, but I can show you proof of belief.'

'What do you mean?' I asked.

'Tomorrow, when you go to the airport, take a look at what people tie to their cars. You'll see a lime and some chillies tied together with a piece of string. It's usually on the grille or tied near the exhaust. People believe that charm wards off the evil eye.'

Mabel had come good with the flight to Goa and Anveeta Khan could fit me in tomorrow afternoon.

'A lime and some chillies?'

'Yes. It's a simple thing, but it means so much to these people.' She turned towards me, her face half in shadows. 'You know, in the villages, where the people are less educated, the belief in magic is even stronger. If a cow suddenly dies or a crop fails it is because they are cursed. These people will do anything their local witch doctor tells them to do to remove it—even if it means sacrificing someone. They have nothing else to turn to.'

'Is this why the government banned black magic? To stop things like that happening?' I asked.

'I don't know what their intent was. How can they decide what is right and what is wrong? After all, what is superstition to you may be faith to someone else. For instance, I believe that Jesus rose from the dead but for many people that is nonsense. Who am I to judge? That is God's role. In the end the government is trying to protect people from themselves. But do the people want protection?'

She shrugged her shoulders. 'I don't know much about curses, but I do know that if you believe enough in something, it just might come true.'

'Say that again,' I said.

'It's belief. If you believe enough in something then it will come true.'

'Mabel, you may be on to something there.'

'I am?'

'Listen to this. After what we found in Subhani's garden, there is no doubt that someone cursed Subhani. We also know that Subhani started to wear the talisman, so she probably knew she was cursed. That also matches up with what Singh said, that she was scared. What if she was so scared about the curse that it set off something else?'

Mabel looked thoughtful. 'You mean someone scared her to death?'

I nodded impatiently. 'I don't know if they wanted to kill her or scare her. But knowing you're cursed would make you incredibly stressed, particularly if you believed in curses. And we know she believed in curses because she got the talisman as protection. She was also pregnant and could not hide that much longer, so that would also make you stressed. And then there she was, dancing on the top of Uluru in the blazing sun with not much water. More stress. What if all those factors contributed to something more real, more tangible, like a heart attack?' Or Long QT Syndrome, I thought.

It made sense, reconciled the stuff that I had witnessed at Subhani's house with the findings from the autopsy, the witness statements and what I knew about Long QT Syndrome.

The look on Mabel's face told me not to pop the champagne cork too quickly.

'I'm not sure. If someone wanted to scare Subhani, why would they take the trouble to bury the curse where she wouldn't find it? How could she be scared of something she didn't know about?'

Mabel was right. The hessian sack was well hidden. Even Aamir Mehta had overlooked it. It was just luck that I had stumbled upon it. Even then, it took a lot of effort to retrieve it.

'If you ask me, whoever buried the bag really believes in the power of black magic. They were not interested in just scaring her and hoping that she would die,' she said.

I had to agree with her thought process. 'What you're saying makes sense. However, Subhani got the talisman as a guard. Which means that even though she never found what was buried in her garden she knew she was cursed. So she could still have been under enormous stress.'

'Yes, that's true,' said Mabel. 'It also means someone told her she was cursed.'

CHAPTER 24

Mabel was right about the chilli and lime charm. I looked at the grilles and undersides of the traffic on the way to the airport. At times, it felt like every second vehicle—car, truck, motorbike or ox driven cart—had the charm attached somewhere. The Indian equivalent of fluffy dice.

'Goa is not good now,' said my taxi driver on the way to the airport, looking at me through the rear view mirror more than he did at the road. He had a friendly round face with chubby cheeks, hooded eyes and a thick moustache underneath a flared nose. The red mark on his forehead told me he had already done his morning puja.

'I know. It's going to be very humid,' I said.

'Humid yes. Also, the tourists are now gone. The shops will be closed.'

I hummed in agreement, looked at his dashboard. A gold compact disc hung from his rear-view mirror, spinning slowly with the movement of the car. Around the edge of the windscreen was a border of red-coloured globes. This car would look like a brothel at night.

There were stickers of several different deities stuck over his glove-box. I recognised Ganesh and Hanuman, couldn't see the vicious-looking Kali.

'Who is this?' I said, pointing to a picture of a blue-coloured God with four arms, one holding a golden mace.

'This is Vishnu. Most divine,' he said, reverently.

'These Gods protect you?'

'Always,' He said with a beaming smile.

'What about that?' I pointed to the car in front, idling while the traffic stagnated. Three saggy green chillies were strung to a grimy lime and tied to a hook near the spluttering exhaust. 'Does that also protect people?'

The smile dropped and he pretended not to hear. Instead, he dredged his throat, lent over so his head stuck out of the side window and let the phlegm drip from his mouth onto the street.

'Which country?' he said when he sat back in his seat, changing the conversation.

I got the picture. 'Australia,' I replied.

'Ah. Great cricket team,' he said. 'Terrible thing about the sandpaper, though.'

I agreed, and we drove on without another word being spoken. What I saw drove home Mabel's point, though. It's not whether curses are real or not, it's what people believed.

It took longer to get from Goa's small airport to my hotel room than it did to fly from Mumbai to Goa. The roads seemed to meander to their destination, take their time getting there. It was the same relaxed attitude that the people of Goa seemed to share. Slowly, slowly.

I didn't mind too much either; sat back in the airport shuttle and took in the view. The van was air conditioned, which was a blessing, as it was muggy enough to poach an egg. The driver took me down some back roads, said that they would get me to the hotel quicker. I almost believed him.

The traffic lanes were single file and bordered by steep ditches on either side, meaning you either gave way to oncoming traffic, or danced a hazardous tango, inching past each other, two wheels on the road, two wheels off. The ditch just an untimely sneeze away. Either way it was slowly, slowly.

We drove past huge acres of sunken rice paddies, their thick carpets of grass grazed on by skinny bullocks and goats. Egrets stepped tenderly through the fields with their long, slender legs, occasionally darting their spiky beaks into the thick green morass. Dense forests of palm trees reached for the sky, replacing the concrete skyscrapers of Mumbai. Old, crumbling churches and tiny chapels occupied strategic intersections, reminders of the Portuguese Catholic influence.

The road skirted along one of the many beaches that made Goa famous. I asked the driver to stop and took a look. White sand, palm trees and thatched huts faced froth-topped waves thundering in from an aggravated ocean. In peak season these beaches were crammed full of pasty Europeans slowly turning pink on beachside sun lounges. Now, only a few lounges dotted the beach.

Three chocolate-skinned girls in bright, colourful saris walked from sunlounge to sunlounge, holding out tie-died sarongs. An end of season sale. They zig-zagged their way along the beach, spruiking to the few remaining tourists, like sand-crabs scurrying for a morsel of food.

The van driver said this was Zeebop beach, a 'very nice beach'. I asked him if he knew the place Anveeta Khan was staying in and whether it was very far from my hotel. He said that we were close, walking distance, that her hotel was the best hotel in Goa, a 'very nice hotel'. According to him everything was 'very nice' in Goa.

It was close to 2 pm by the time I checked in at the Colva Seaspray Hotel. Anveeta Khan told me to meet her at her trailer at 5 pm. The town had changed a lot since I was here last. Far more developed, far more Western, far more soulless. Doof music instead of Bob Marley. My hotel was one of the recent, bland developments built to cater for Europeans desperate for a week of sun. Not much more than a bunch of cheaply made apartments circling a pool.

I killed some time by visiting Old Goa, the white-washed heart of the once Portuguese colony. In reality it was little more than a collection of empty churches and cathedrals, connected by wide, colonial streets. A town square would have once occupied the middle, where markets would have traded, edicts been read out and people were hanged. Now it was just a large expanse of grass, sand and weeds.

The humidity was almost overwhelming. I undid another button on my white cotton shirt, blew cold air down my chest. My linen trousers were also white, making me look like Don Johnson a la Miami Vice. All I needed were the loafers. It wasn't just me who was uncomfortable in the heat. Hawkers took up position wherever there was shade, selling luke-warm water and cheap cloth hats. I bought the coldest bottle of warm water and headed to the biggest building.

The immense Basilica of Bom Jesus, with its baroque red and white stone facade, was also the main attraction for a tired-looking group of middle-aged tourists, resting in the building's shade. They sat in the pews, some waving hastily fashioned paper fans, others tugging at their damp tops, listening to their tour guide's description of the cavernous interior. His voice bounced around the hollow, vaulted room.

The chief feature was the gilded shrine that contained the remains of Saint Francis Xavier. I eavesdropped as the tour guide spoke of the dead saint's miraculous healing powers, amazed that it still brought thousands of ill pilgrims to the church every year hoping to be cured, clinging to the power of belief. Eventually, the group continued their tour, moving on to the cloisters. The echoes of their footsteps faded away in the building's void, leaving me alone in the comparative cool of the church.

I walked up to the front, passing sandalwood saints along the way and sat on the first pew, alone. The hush of the Basilica seemed surreal. In front, the three-storey altar was brilliantly gilded, marking a stark contrast against the faded dullness of the rest of the building. Twisting pillars drew my eye up to a large baroque sun, flanked by two angels. Above the sun stood the ever-watchful trinity; Father, Son and Holy Ghost. In the middle of the altar a large figure of a saint stood astride an infant Jesus. The rest of the detail was lost in the gilding. The grandeur of the Basilica was impressive, yet the symbolism of its altar gave me no great insights. I just looked at it, like I would at any other piece of art, and pretended to understand.

I couldn't remember the last time I'd willingly been to church, weddings and funerals excepted. For me, mass was a chore. The rapture others seemed to get passed me by, as if it knew I was a fraud, my own passover. That's why I stopped going. The basic premise of Christianity was sound enough—treat each other well—and I tried to do that. But in the end, for me, it wasn't enough to base a whole religion around, particularly when the men of the cloth failed that lesson far too often themselves.

I knew why I came this time. To test myself. The last couple of days had shown me the power of belief and I wanted to know if anything had changed for me, to see if I could open myself up, to accept and understand. I had dreamt about Anjali again last night. The same dream, me being bullied, crying and she comforting me. When I awoke I had that same feeling of being cheated; that what was real in my dreams could not be real in my wake. That's why I wanted to believe that an afterlife existed. To know that there was something more. For me, sure, but mostly for my sister. I wanted there to be more than just death for her. I wanted the chance to say sorry. Sorry for all those stupid sibling rivalries growing up, sorry for not doing something sooner when I found out about the drugs, sorry for not saving her, sorry for causing our parents such pain.

The stuff about black magic and curses had unnerved me. I knew it was nonsense, but I still had that niggling feeling, a hesitancy. Like that uneasy feeling you get after watching a ghost story, despite yourself. That little voice that puts reason aside. Now, I challenged myself to hear that same little voice about God. I looked up at the Trinity and tried to believe. But there were no miracles for me. In the end I didn't, couldn't, believe without proof. Mabel was right about me and Saint Thomas.

Why was it that those ill pilgrims could have faith, yet I had none? What was it that kept Mabel and my parents so firmly committed to their God? Salvation? Fear? Even the taxi drivers, with their candy-coloured idols, spent this life preparing for the next. I didn't know if I was jealous of them or felt pity for them. At least they found some comfort in the unknown. The unknown was just that to me.

CHAPTER 25

The film shoot was taking place on the beach at the end of Colva's main drag. I crossed over the concrete bridge that spanned the moat protecting the town from monsoonal storm surges and joined the small group of onlookers behind the roped-off fence. There was still a half hour before my appointment with Anveeta Khan.

Up high on the beach, where the sand was dry, a group of about twenty people sat on sheets underneath a large green tarpaulin. The women were dressed in a rainbow assortment of saris, the men in white baggy trousers and blood red shirts with frilly sleeves and necklines. I guessed they were background dancers. They all looked hot, taking big gulps of water from plastic bottles.

Lower down on the beach, where the sand firmed up, four men with their trousers rolled up to their knees moved a rig that held a large camera into position. A fifth guy stood in front, irritably calling out directions. On the right of them, two men followed a wire that led from a control panel to a set of large speakers. One checked the connections while the other ran back to the panel. He pressed a button and a thumping beat filled the air. The guy near the speakers gave the thumbs up and the music cut out.

Right down the bottom of the beach, where the waves lapped the sand, two shirtless young boys in soggy shorts raked the ground smooth with large scrapers.

The onlooker I was standing near tapped his friend on the shoulder and pointed to where the dancers were sitting. I looked over. A fat man in shorts, t-shirt and a New York Yankees cap, was speaking with the dancers, using his hands to emphasise what he was saying. From the way they paid attention to him I figured he must have been the director. Satisfied with his pep talk, he clapped his hands and ushered them back to their positions. The male dancers put their white turbans on and joined the ladies on the smoothed section of the beach. They formed two lines, women in front of men.

About five minutes later two more women appeared. One dressed in a magnificent plum sari with gold trims, the other in bottle green with purple frills. They carried themselves like royalty, walking barefoot on the sand as if every step was distasteful and knowing that everyone was watching them. They took their positions without acknowledging the dancers behind them. After them came a young man with big hair, the hero of the film. He was dressed the same as the background male dancers, except his shirt was blue and he wore no turban. He casually tossed his sunglasses in the director's direction, laughed when they missed the mark by a considerable distance and took his place between the two starlets.

'Which one is Anveeta Khan?' I asked the guy next to me.

'The older one in the red. The one wearing green is Priya Salwar,' he said with a lecherous smile. There was no doubt which star he'd come to see.

The director pointed to the audio guys and the tabla began to play again, this time accompanied by a floating melody and a piercing voice that sounded like Kate Bush on helium. He then said something inaudible and pointed to the dancers. The girls jerked their hips in time with the beat, their arms held high above their heads and their hands twisting like vines reaching for the sun. The two lead females began to lip-sync to the song.

The men danced behind the girls, holding on to their hips. The lead actor spent most of the routine dancing behind Anveeta Khan. Then the other lead female star dropped her hands and made wavy motions with her arms, like a Hawaiian dancer. This caught the attention of the lead male, who sidestepped to the beat and took up position behind her.

The director clapped his hands and the music stopped. He walked over to the dancers, said something and then walked back. The scene was repeated. This happened another five times before the day's shoot ended.

It took some convincing before the guard allowed me to enter the sealed-off section of the carpark where all the trailers were. He led me to the one with 'Anveeta Khan' written in large black type on the door. An older lady answered his knock.

'Mr Ryder, I'm Silvia Dias, Ms Khan's secretary. Please come in.' Dias had a homely face topped by a mop of curly dark brown hair just starting to turn grey. She wore her pink blouse loose over a dark blue skirt that covered the top half of her dimply knees. Her black shoes were built for comfort, open topped and low heeled. I stepped up into the air-conditioned trailer.

Anveeta Khan sat on the padded bench that curved along the back wall of the trailer. A small veneer table was fixed in place in front of her, holding a well-used ashtray and a half-filled packet of cigarettes. She had dark, luxurious hair with highlights of henna. Her round, deep brown eyes were heavy with mascara and her cherry-glossed lips had a sensuous pout. The sari was tight around her lower torso, emphasising her generous bust. From her straight-backed posture I could tell Khan was a confident and powerful person. It was hard not to be attracted to her.

'Ah, Samson Ryder, private investigator,' she said. 'Please sit down,' She moved along the bench to make room. I sat down to her left. From up close she looked older, closer to my age than Subhani's.

'Tea, coffee?' asked Dias.

Khan looked disinterested. 'Do you like gin, Mr Ryder?'

'Yes.'

'Two G and T's, Silvia,' she ordered. Dias nodded and walked to the front of the trailer.

'Thank you for meeting with me, Ms Khan. I saw some of what you were doing out there.'

'You did? What did you think?'

'It looked good, really colourful.'

She laughed. 'Yes, but what did you think it signified?'

'Well, it looked like one guy and two girls. A love triangle?'

'Spot on. Such a simple plot.' She shook her head. 'You know, this one dance sequence has three more locations. Even one in Spain! We spend more time and money on the dances than we do on plots. But you're not here to listen to my gripes.' She smiled.

Dias returned with two glasses and an ice bucket. 'The ice is made with sterilised water,' she told me reassuringly, then walked back to her desk opposite the front door. I took a glass, didn't risk the ice.

Khan leaned on her right arm, framing her strong face with her index finger and thumb. 'Now, you're here to discuss poor Subhani's death. What can I do for you?'

'Subhani's mother told me you two were close friends. I was hoping you could tell me what you knew of Subhani.'

'Yes, we were close. When she first entered the film industry, I took her under my wing. She was completely overwhelmed, poor thing. But we have not really spoken for some time now. I was devastated when I heard she had died.'

Khan reached for the remaining glass, filled it with ice and took a drink.

'What was Subhani like?' I asked.

Her eyes seemed to be looking into the past, a smile formed on her lips. 'Subhani was always smiling, laughing. She knew how to have a good time.'

'So, she had a lot of friends?'

'Plenty, *yaar*. We all loved her.'

'Was there anyone special in particular? A boyfriend perhaps?'

Khan turned her head away from me, squinting in an attempt to recall a memory.

'She was friendly with a guy some time ago. It was nothing she ever took seriously.' She smiled slyly. 'Apart from his body. He was quite cute really. They met on a film set. I forgot which film it was. He was a background dancer.'

'Can you remember his name?' I asked.

'Let me think about it. I remember telling her that she was being stupid. You know, if the media found out. Ah yes, his name was Pradeep...something. I can't remember. Silvia...,' she called out to her assistant. 'Do you remember the name of that dancer that Subhani was seeing? The one she tried to keep secret.'

'Sorry, Ms Khan. No,' said Dias, her face tinged pink, embarrassed at knowing things she shouldn't know.

'Find out, will you? And give it to Mr Ryder here.'

'Certainly, Ms Khan.' Dias wrote a note to herself.

'Thanks, that will be really helpful.'

'Now, any more questions? I have a function to attend tonight and I have to prepare,' she said.

'Just a few. Did you ever see Subhani faint, or feel weak?'

She shook her head so that her hair swung rhythmically. 'No, not that I recall.'

'Is there anyone else who may know? Perhaps Subhani had a secretary, like Ms Dias?'

'No. Subhani didn't need to have a secretary. Her father took care of all her affairs. He was her manager.'

Aamir Mehta had already told me he knew of no health problems.

Khan said she hadn't spoken to Subhani in a while, so it was no use bringing up the pendant. I went with a more general question.

'Was Subhani superstitious about anything?'

Khan jerked a little back from me and gave me a puzzled look. Dias also looked up from her desk.

'What a strange question!' Khan said rhetorically. 'The truth is, everyone in this industry is superstitious about something or the other.'

'Even you?'

She laughed. 'Yes, especially me!'

'Do you mind if I ask what about?' I inquired.

Khan's eyes narrowed as she considered her response. She hunched slightly over the table. 'You see, in this business there are lots of people who are jealous of you. Some of them are even mad enough to try and curse you. Just to spite you.'

'Curse you?'

'Yes. Absolutely!' She placed her hand on the table as if it were a Bible.

'So what do you do?'

She smiled, sat back. 'I know you will think this is silly. Every month, my mother performs a ritual to cleanse me from any curses. First, she takes some dried chilli, ground mustard seeds, salt and a strand of my hair and wraps them in a piece of paper. Then she circles it around my body three times, first clockwise, then anti-clockwise, then clockwise again.' Khan mimicked the motion with her right hand. 'Then she burns it. Usually, it smells bitter when it burns, which is good. If it doesn't smell, then there was a curse on you that has been removed.'

'That's fascinating. Do you really believe in it?' I said.

'Better to be safe than sorry. You know Priya, in the other trailer? She wears a black spot of charcoal behind her ear to ward off the evil eye. She thinks nobody knows.'

She reached for her glass. I did the same.

'Thank you, Ms Khan, you've been really helpful.'

Khan laughed nervously. 'You know, I've never told anybody else that.'

I smiled back. 'Don't worry, your secret is safe with me. Tell me, do you think Subhani believed in curses?'

A broad grin spread across her face. 'You have to believe in curses if you want to survive in this industry.'

Subhani didn't survive.

I was almost out the door when a thought struck me.

'Ms Khan, you said everybody in your industry believes in curses. Does that include producers and directors?'

'*Yaar, everybody*,' she said.

'Even Davindar Singh and Jogesh Nadar?'

Now she looked at me suspiciously. 'Why do you ask?'

'No particular reason. I just want to understand the industry and the people Subhani worked with.'

'I don't know what you're looking for, Mr Ryder. I can tell you, Davindar Singh is a wonderful man. The way he treats his stars.' She moved her head in a figure of eight, smiled. Singh obviously treated her the way she liked to be treated.

'I don't know too much about Jogesh. Although his last couple of movies haven't been successes. Perhaps he's been cursed? Who knows?' She spoke about Nadar as almost an after thought.

CHAPTER 26

The sun had set by the time I left Anveeta Khan. The main street back into the heart of the town was dark except for the amber glow from the far-too-rare streetlights. The road ahead looked like a checkerboard, alternating between large sections of darkness and light. I walked to where the lights huddled together, where the few restaurants that remained open were.

The place was half full, mainly Brits by the sound of the chatter. A local entertainer had set up a karaoke machine against the back wall. Thankfully, it was still too early for the guests to bang out a tune, more courage from a bottle being required. Until then, he regaled us with his versions of songs by *Air Supply* and *The Beatles*. The waiter had a chiselled, angular face, more Portuguese than Indian. He said the house specialty was called Goan Chilli Fry. It came with a small basket of naan bread. I ordered a beer to go with it and thought about the meeting with Anveeta Khan.

Khan confirmed lots of what I already knew. She also intimated that Subhani would have been superstitious. Hell, according to Khan everybody in Bollywood believes in curses. Which means that anyone in Bollywood could have cast the curse on Subhani. I hoped Dias would come through with the name of the boyfriend. He was the next step, maybe even the father of Subhani's child. The specialty turned out to be a spicy chorizo-like sausage cooked in a thick gravy made of onions and tomatoes. On my chilli scale it was a tongue tingling seven out of ten. Anything above eight induced sweat and saliva. I mopped up the last of the thick gravy with the naan bread and shovelled it in my mouth, finished the last of the beer. The handful of flimsy notes I left on the table would be enough to cover the meal and a reasonable tip.

My hotel was down a dark road that came off the main street. Along one side, between the road and the beach, entire families sat in front of ramshackle wooden huts, illuminated around open fires. The women hunched over large aluminium pots, stirring, while the men sat in groups and talked, perhaps planning the next day's fishing. A gang of children played a game trying to keep a plastic bag in the air with their feet. Dogs, goats and chickens free ranged.

On the other side of the road large nets had been erected over makeshift timber frames. Thousands of small fish lay drying on the ground inside the net cages, oozing a heady, salty reek into the still, muggy air. A silhouette of a bird of prey, a hawk or an eagle, stood perched on top of one of the bamboo poles that comprised the frame, looking for a way in.

It was then that the contrast between rich and poor struck me. On a small, dark street in Goa, where the minutiae mattered. Not in Mumbai, where it was so easy to get overwhelmed by the magnitude of the inequality that it never really sunk in. The tip I'd left in the restaurant may have been more than what these people would earn in a week.

A teenage girl saw me and approached from the gloom. She wore a patchwork outfit of heavy cotton, far too warm for this time of the year. Little pieces of mirror were inlaid into her garment, giving her a glittering effect. The plaits in her hair fell forward, over her forehead, and a golden chain linked the ring in her nose with a large hooped earring in her left ear.

'You look my shop,' she said, rather than asked, and pointed to a tiny hut built by the side of the road. By the light of a kerosene lamp I could see pieces of jewellery on a small table.

'It's too dark. Not tonight,' I said.

'Then tomorrow you come. I give you good price for first business. My name is Rosa, remember me.'

'Rosa. Sure,' I replied, unconvincingly.

She turned away, probably knowing she would never see me again.

I got the guilts. 'Rosa. Do you have earrings?' I asked after her.

She turned around, smiled. 'Come. See.'

***

It was 10 pm when I got back to my hotel, feeling lonely and a little uneasy. I wasn't sure if I was ready for another dream about Anjali. For another disappointed awakening. Impulsively, I rang Bec, yearning to hear her voice. It was only after the third or fourth ring that I remembered about the time difference and was about to ring off when she answered.

'Sam, is everything okay?' she sounded alarmed.

'Bec, sorry, you must have been asleep. Go back to bed and I'll call later.'

The tension eased from her voice, 'Why did you call me so early? I thought something must be wrong.'

'I'm sorry, Bec. I just needed to hear your voice. I completely forgot about the time-zone.'

'Well, I'm awake now. How's it all going?'

'Well, I'm in Goa tonight. I had to interview an actress who was a friend of Subhani's.'

'An actress, huh. You move in all the right circles.' Bec's humour had returned. I updated her on what had been found in Subhani's backyard.

'Fucking hell, Sam. That sounds terrible. The Aboriginal elder you spoke to in Uluru also said something about spirits, didn't he? Are you sure you're alright?' I liked the concern she showed, felt comforted by it, felt loved.

'Yeah, I'm fine, Bec. The actress I spoke with also believes in spirits.' Bec listened quietly as I recounted the conversation with Anveeta Khan. She took it all in, processed the information, before responding to me.

'You know, Sam, that actress was really open with you. She said she told you things she never told anyone else. Things you wouldn't normally offer up freely to a stranger. Why do you think she did that?' Bec's voice had lost all remnant of drowsiness and her tone was now professional, honed by years of experience dealing with witnesses.

'My boyish charm?' I postured.

'If you ask me, I think she was a little too forthcoming.'

Bec's perspective took me by surprise. Could I have been blindsided by Khan, beguiled by her confidence? On reflection, she had been *very* open with me. Told me lots of stuff, even things that were deeply personal, and without much egging on from me. Sure, she was an actress, and I guessed actresses like to talk a lot, especially about themselves. But Bec was right, I was a stranger to her and the information she volunteered came too easy.

'Bec, now that you say it you may be right. I'll have to think more about it, but not now.'

I changed the subject and told Bec about Goa, about the Basilica of Bom Jesus, and said we should have a holiday here together one day.

'A holiday together? Are we coupling, Sam?' The way she said it made it feel like it was only half a tease. 'Actually, I do have some leave coming up. An exotic holiday may be fun.'

After Bec rung off I slumped on the bed, wearing only boxers, and looked up at the ceiling. The air conditioner had rattled louder than a beggar's tin, so I shut it down. With it, it was too noisy to sleep, even in India. Without it, it was too warm to sleep. The overhead fan spun at half speed, directing a relieving breeze onto the bed. A coil of sticky tape fluttered in the turbulence, spotted with the remnants of its flying victims. A small flag of victory in the midnight battle between mammals and mosquitos. I lay in bed and thought about Khan some more, found myself concluding that Bec's reasoning was solid. Khan did give me lots of information. Now I couldn't help feeling there was a lot more she didn't say.

CHAPTER 27

'So Subhani had a boyfriend,' Mabel called from her bedroom. 'He could be the father.'

'From the way Khan put it, he was more like a toy boy than anything serious for Subhani. I can't see her having his baby. Are abortions hard to get in India?'

'Not if you have the money and know the right people,' she said, walking back into the living room. 'Ta da, what do you think?' she said, turning her head to show her newly adorned earrings.

'Nice, they suit you' I said, pleased that she liked them. 'Somehow, I think Subhani would have those two boxes ticked.'

Mabel nodded, making the earrings swing like pendulums.

'What she said about Jogesh Nadar was interesting,' I said.

'What do you mean?'

'Well, if Khan is right then Nadar needs to have a hit. This movie might have been his last chance. When I interviewed him, he said he knew Subhani was trying to get rid of him. It was either him or her. That gives him a pretty strong motive to get rid of her.'

'And if he believes in curses, like Anveeta Khan said they all do, then he may also know how to cast a curse, or know someone who can,' Mabel added.

'So, what's the story? He tells her she's cursed. Gets her scared and anxious, stressing her out. Then makes her do really physically challenging things like climbing Uluru. Hopes it's the final straw?'

'I don't know, Sam. I still don't think the curse was just meant to scare her.'

I didn't like the scenario either. Too much left to chance. It wouldn't be the way I'd set out to kill someone.

'There's also another problem,' I said after thinking about it some more. 'If he was the one who told her she was cursed, why would she continue filming with him?'

'Maybe that's why she wanted to kick him out?'

'I suppose that's possible,' I said.

'Do you think Nadar could be the father?' asked Mabel.

I thought back to the unimpressive man in the editing booth. 'No, not really.'

'What about Davindar Singh. I'll bet he also believes in curses.'

'Yeah. But he has no motive. Nothing to gain from Subhani's death.'

'Where does that leave us?' asked Mabel. So it was '*us*' now.

'Not sure. There was also something else about Anveeta Khan. I feel she is hiding something from me.'

Mabel's crooked smile grew as I spoke.

'Maybe I know what. I have some gossip about her,' she said.

'What? You? Gossip? No!' I teased.

'Very smart. Listen, I told the girls at Mass that you were going to meet with Anveeta Khan and...'

'Mabel, you did what?'

She noted the exasperation in my voice, raised her hand. 'Wait until I've finished. Did you know that they had a big fight?'

'Who had a fight?'

Now Mabel was the exasperated one, she rolled her eyes. 'Anveeta Khan and Subhani Mehta, of course.'

'Really! What happened?'

'About a year ago they were in a movie together. I don't know which one. Anyway, Subhani was being interviewed on television about it and she said that Anveeta was very good at playing older women. A role model for the next generation of actresses.'

Mabel grinned. 'You can imagine what Anveeta Khan must have felt hearing that. It's the kiss of death for any actress. Apparently, they had a big argument about it. Ever since then Anveeta has had few roles.'

Khan told me that she had been close to Subhani, but that they hadn't spoken recently.

'How did you find this out?' This information would have been useful to me before meeting Khan.

'One of my friends read it in a magazine.'

That blew its credibility.

'Mabel, you can't believe what they write in those things.'

'I didn't say it was true, just that I had some gossip.'

Later that evening Silvia Dias called and gave me the address and phone number of Subhani Mehta's boyfriend, Pradeep Nair. She was nothing if not efficient. According to

Dias, Nair used to work as a dancer for Namaste Studios but hasn't been with them for a few months. She was about to end the call when I jumped in.

'Ms Dias. Can you tell me what the relationship was like between Ms Khan and Ms Mehta?'

For a while there was silence on the other end of the phone.

'Oh, they were very good friends,' she said, too casually.

'Are you sure, Ms Dias? You see, I've just finished interviewing another associate of Ms Mehta's who told me they had a falling out over something Subhani said on TV.'

I hoped she'd take the bait.

Her throat must have tightened, making her swallow before speaking. 'Who...who told you that?'

'I cannot say. Although the person who told me said it was reported in the media,' I replied.

Again silence.

'It's true they had a disagreement. But it was blown all out of proportion,' she said.

'I heard it was far worse than that. That they had become enemies.'

Dias sighed, flustered. 'What do you want me to say?'

'I'm just trying to confirm the truth of what I've been told.'

'Yes, they were no longer friends. How could they be after Subhani Mehta stabbed her in the back?'

'Thank you, Ms Dias. That's all I wanted to clarify.'

'Please. You didn't hear anything of this from me. I will lose my job.' She sounded close to tears now.

'Don't worry, Ms Dias. I won't say a thing.'

CHAPTER 28

It took almost two hours to get to the outskirts of New Mumbai, stop–start all the way. The sweat trickling down my back could've filled an Olympic-sized pool. The main hold-up was a traffic jam opposite a slum that took slumming down to new lows. The people who lived in decrepit concrete boxes were the lucky ones. The less fortunate made to do with canvas walls and sheets of blue plastic for roofs, held down by scraps of wood. The air was thick with flies, attracted by the ammonia stink of urine. A mangy pack of dogs tried to sleep in the shade of a pile of rubble while half-dressed children threw stones at them. An old, emaciated man squatted near the kerbside, looking at the traffic and defecating for all to see. He seemed to have no shame, maybe having no other options, but I felt ashamed for him.

In the midst of all this filth, a young woman washed her clothes in a trough by the side of the street, her baby tied to her back with rags. She scrubbed the fabric with a cake of soap, dunked it back in the trough to rinse, then slapped it mercilessly against a rock, beating the dirt out. She looked up and saw me staring at her through the window, smiled an angelic smile at no one in particular and turned away. The traffic lifted shortly after.

Pradeep Nair no longer worked as a dancer. Now he worked nightshifts in a call centre, 3 pm to 3 am, dealing with irate Western customers about their phone bills. I rang him in the mid-morning. He had just woken up. At first, he didn't want to speak with me, didn't want anything more to do with Subhani Mehta. I told him that was fine, suggested that he may want to get a lawyer since he was the prime suspect in Subhani's murder. I hoped referring to murder would confuse him, catch him off guard, cause him to panic. After calling me all sorts of things, some of which I recognised, he agreed to meet me at the call centre cafeteria at 2 pm that day.

The ten-storey building looked new, like most of the other buildings in New Mumbai, all glass and polished stone. The banner above the tenth floor read 'Vani Communications'. It could have been any building in any Western city, except for the leper who pulled himself along the broken footpath on a homemade skateboard, what was left of his hands wrapped in rags.

The cafeteria was to the left of the lobby. Inside, groups of young Indians sat around aluminium tables and spoke excitedly about whatever young people get excited about. They all spoke in English and dressed in western-brand-label clothes, taking care over their appearance. For a country that had restrained male–female social interaction for so long, this place was charged with sexual tension. A sign stretched along the far wall: 'Vani Employees of the Month'. Underneath the sign were portraits of bright young things with beaming smiles.

A guy who was sitting by himself walked over, a worried look on his face. 'Ryder?'

'Yes,' I replied. 'Thank you for meeting with me, Mr Nair.'

'Like I had a choice.'

We walked back to his table. I looked at the people sitting around us, they were all far too interested in each other to pay us any attention.

Nair was fine-looking, with piercing Tom Cruise eyes and cheekbones so high you'd need a crane to reach them. He was in his mid-twenties, tallish and clean-shaven. Through his T-shirt I could see that he was toned, a dancer's build. He was nervous and fired off a list of questions as soon as we sat down.

'Who are you? How did you know about Subhani and me? What do you mean I am the prime suspect? I wasn't even there when Subhani died!' The last sentence sounded more like a plea.

'I'm a private investigator. Subhani's father engaged me to investigate her death.' I fished out a card from my wallet and passed it to him. He looked at the card intently.

'Now, let's start at the beginning. Tell me what happened between you and Subhani?'

'How did you know about us?' he asked.

'That doesn't matter. Tell me what happened?'

Nair became indignant, he folded his arms. 'You're the detective. When you find out why don't you tell me?'

The taxi ride had exhausted whatever patience the heat had left me. I raised my voice slightly. 'Listen. Subhani was pregnant when she died. We have reason to believe that whoever was the father of that baby may have had something to do with her death. Right now, you're the one in the hot seat.'

Nair's face flared with panic, his eyes darted around the room to make sure nobody heard me. 'Okay. I'll tell you what I know.'

'From the beginning,' I said.

'Okay. We met at a film shoot about two and a half years ago. I had a solo dance sequence with Subhani. It was a difficult routine and we used to practice together after all the others had left. It took a long time to get it right. Often, we would fall over each other and laugh.' He paused, as a melancholy smile etched across his face.

'That's when I fell in love with her. I know it took her much longer to fall for me. She was a movie star and I was an up and coming dancer. Eventually she did. We kept it as quiet as we could. Didn't go out in public together. But Subhani organised it so that I was in every movie that she was in. We could sneak away then.'

Nair closed his eyes, smiled sadly again. 'We had great plans. She would make me into a star and then we would be equal. We could get married.'

I listened, nodded, knowing that this was not the story Anveeta Khan told me.

'Then one day, about a year ago, she told me it was over. Just like that.' He snapped his fingers. 'I asked her to tell me why? I wanted a reason. Perhaps I could make things okay between us, but she never told me. In fact, she just stopped talking to me completely, didn't return my messages. Then my dance roles started to dry up.' Nair closed his eyes and exhaled. 'That's how I ended up working here. Dealing with abusive people who want to complain about their phone service.'

A single tear left a snail trail down the contour of his cheek. Nair wiped it with the back of his hand. I pretended not to notice.

He sniffed hard and a wry smile grew across his face. 'I guess it's not all bad. You get a free mobile phone working here.' He pulled out a red phone from his pocket, slid it carelessly on the table.

'So Subhani broke up with you about a year ago and you still don't know why.'

'Oh no, I know why now.' His voice steeled. 'You see, it was killing me. I needed to know why. So I followed her.'

'You followed her? When?'

'About a month after we broke up. I knew where she lived. It was easy.'

'What did you find out?'

'I found out that she was a whore. That's what! All this time telling me she loved me.' Nair fisted one hand with the other. On the surface he looked docile enough, but underneath he harboured a rage.

'What do you mean?' I said.

'She was with that man. Davindar Singh. He would come to her house in the morning, spend a few hours, then leave. A little later she would leave also. *Whore!*'

Singh! I tried to keep a poker face.

'When did you stop following her?'

Nair's demeanour changed. He looked down, embarrassed. 'I did it on and off for a few months. Then, about six months ago I think Subhani saw me waiting outside her house. I'm not sure. Anyway, soon after that I lost my contract with Namaste.'

'Do you think Subhani pulled some strings?'

'Who knows? But now I have to share my flat just to pay the bills.' Nair screwed up his empty paper cup and tossed it away. 'So you see, I cannot be your prime suspect. I have had nothing to do with Subhani for months.'

'Thanks for talking to me. I know it must be difficult. Just one last thing. What was the relationship between Subhani and Anveeta Khan like?'

Nair snorted. 'Anveeta! They were friendly when I was around. Although it always seemed like they were being friendly for the cameras. Then they had a big fight after Subhani said Anveeta was too old,' he said, chuckling to himself.

Mabel's gossip had been right on the money.

'There was also something about a film script, but I was not with Subhani when that happened,' he added.

I thanked Nair again and got up to leave.

'The papers never said how Subhani died. Do you really think it was murder?' Nair asked.

I sat back down, was about to say something non-committal, then something struck me. Here was a man who was angry with Subhani for ending their affair and suspected her of ending his career. Rejection and vengeance have always been good motives for murder. Shakespeare once wrote, '... *the play's the thing wherein I'll catch the conscience of the king*'. I decided to test the Bard's logic.

'Look, it's nothing really. But if what I tell you makes it into the papers, I am sure Subhani's father will have you sued.' He'd also have my balls on toast.

Nair surrendered with both hands. 'Okay, okay. Like I have that much to lose.'

'Do you believe in curses?' I asked, gravely.

'Are you joking? I feel like my whole life has been cursed!'

I looked around us, checking the surrounds, then spoke so softly that Nair had to lean forward to hear. 'Subhani may have been cursed by a black magician.'

Nair's face grew taut, his eyes widened and his lower jaw opened. He looked genuinely shocked and I wondered what Shakespeare would make of that.

'Black magic? Are you sure?'

'I'm not sure about anything right now,' I said.

CHAPTER 29

By the time I got back to Mahim I was as stale and dry as a day-old samosa. I dragged myself out of the taxi and heard someone call out my name from behind. I turned around to see Father Joseph waving at me from the drab-looking foyer of Saint Mark's Church. I headed towards him, ignoring the vigil of beggars outside the church.

His dog collar was missing today. Instead, he teamed his black trousers with a white short-sleeved top, a tiny silver cross on each corner of his collar.

'Sam, what perfect timing! Do you have five minutes? I need to speak with you.'

He ushered me in to the church. The inside of which was functional, bordering on dreary: concrete tiled floor; orderly rows of wooden pews, spaced equidistantly; above them banks of dusty fans hanging like stalactites from the ceiling. Fading pictures of the *Stations of the Cross* alternated with barred windows along the grey walls. A heavy-duty church for a heavy-duty city. As if he had gleaned my thoughts, Father Joseph smiled. 'It's not pretty, but it works.'

Our footsteps echoed as we walked. We stopped in front of the uninspiring altar: empty stone altar table, a functional podium. A large brown wood-look crucifix dominated the front wall. Father Joseph bent down on one knee and made the sign of the cross. I had done this same gesture many times as a child, found myself doing it again now for some reason.

A doorway led through the cramped vestry and into his private quarters. It was simple and practical, like the man himself. A couch with teak arms and beige fabric faced a large television set still wrapped in the manufacturer's plastic. A brass, glass-topped coffee table was spaced far enough so that he could rest his feet. Further back was a table built for four, half of which was covered by different piles of papers. The seats of the chairs had a similar beige fabric as the couch, but not exactly. A good attempt at coordination all the same. On the wall, opposite the couch, hung the classic picture of the *Last Supper*. Thanks to Dan Brown, I knew it was DaVinci.

'Nice TV,' I said.

Father Joseph chuckled sheepishly. 'It's new. The cricket World Cup is starting soon.' Nothing more needed to be said. Cricket was the real religion in this country.

'Would you like a drink?' he asked.

'Sounds good.'

He motioned me to sit on couch, then dashed off into an adjoining room, returning soon after with a glass.

'Will whisky do?'

I took the glass, noticed he didn't pour himself one. I had no idea what he wanted to see me about. This was his dance and he'd have to lead.

'I spoke with Sri Chandrapathy,' he said, as he sat down beside me. 'He told me what you found in that poor girl's garden.'

I should have figured. It was a small world for a country of a billion people.

I gulped half of the drink down. 'He told you about the curse?'

'Yes. He also told me he is very worried about you.' He turned to face me. 'He thinks you're treating this flippantly.'

I put my drink down on the coffee table, carefully so as not to clink against the glass top.

'That's not exactly true, Father. I saw what was buried in Subhani Mehta's garden. I agree with him that someone put a curse on Subhani. There is no debate about that. What I can't accept is that it actually killed her. If you ask me, the fear and stress Subhani felt contributed to a heart attack. The person who cursed her may have some responsibility for her death and I intend to find out who that person was.'

I wanted to convince him, perhaps because by persuading him I would reassure myself in the process. Father Joseph wasn't taking the bait. He looked down again, gripping the edge of the couch with both hands, his shoulders tensed.

'I hope you are right,' his tone meant he thought I was wrong.

I turned to him. 'Father! I know what you said about that village leader, but you don't seriously believe in curses, do you?'

He looked up and blinked a couple of times before turning back towards me.

'I believe in good and evil, Sam. But this is not about me.' He angled his body to face me more squarely. 'You know,

I'm also worried about you. I think you're getting involved in things you do not understand. Dangerous things.' He placed his hand on my shoulder, tenderly, for a brief moment.

I dropped my head, closed my eyes and exhaled wearily, like a ship bellowing its last gasp before it sinks into the abyss.

'Father, why is it I get the feeling I'm the only person in India who doesn't believe in curses, or tantrics, or black magic, or even the Easter Bunny for that matter.'

The question hung in the room like the DaVinci.

'Do you know what evil is capable of?' The question came from his eyes as much as his mouth.

I'd seen some bad things in the past, particularly in the sexual crimes unit. Terrible things that people did to each other: paedophilia, gang rapes, incest. Things that helped me shake off any lingering doubts about the existence of either god or devil. These were very *human* crimes. In every case there was a rational explanation about *how* the crime was done. The *why* was usually lust, or rage, or anger or any other combination of emotions that made us human.

The Subhani Mehta case was different. If I looked at it objectively all I had was a lot of different pieces to a jigsaw puzzle, without knowing if they even came from the same set. I didn't have a *how*. Instead, I had a dead person with no obvious causes, a theory about Long QT Syndrome, a foetus nailed to a lemon, some hocus pocus about curses and spirits and a shot in the dark that all this somehow contributed to a heart attack. I hadn't even come to the *why*. There were too many variables, and being honest with myself, I was struggling to find any sense, any pattern that seemed logical.

Rather than being money for jam this case had made me flustered and flummoxed, grappling for a thread that could tether me back to reason. I looked at Father Joseph, this man of God. He was offering me a lifeline and I had nothing to lose.

'Tell me.'

He faced the front again, a hand placed on each thigh. 'Have you ever heard of the *Roman Ritual*?'

I shook my head.

'You may know it better as an exorcism.' He snuck a furtive glance to gauge my reaction. I said nothing for a little while. Memories of my younger self watching the movie *The Exorcist* flooded back to me. At the time it left me sleeping with the lights on.

'I don't understand.' I lowered my voice, out of instinct more than anything else. 'What has this got to do with exorcisms?'

'It has long been believed in the Church that being cursed is one of the major forms of possession. A curse is really a way of using demons to harm others.'

He fidgeted, brought both hands together in front of him. 'It's very difficult to explain. First, we have to make sure that the person is truly possessed, and not suffering from some other form of affliction like mental illness. When we are convinced, we perform an exorcism. It's a sad thing because in most cases the person who is cursed is usually an innocent victim. Somebody else has sent the demons.'

'How does someone cast a curse?' I asked, now intrigued.

'If you ask me, it is a through a pact with the devil, made with a spell.'

'You mean like the foetus and the lemon?'

'According to Sri Chandrapathy, those things were used as an offering.'

I sat back on the couch, wondering how I had stumbled into a world of aboriginal spirits, curses, black magic and now, exorcisms. Then something he said got me thinking.

'Father, have you ever performed an exorcism?' I asked.

It was a while before he answered. 'A priest can only perform the Roman ritual of exorcism in Christ's name. And not just any priest.' He raised a finger. 'He must be appointed by the Bishop and undergo special training. Some years ago the Bishop chose me.' He pressed his palm to his chest, humbly.

'Tell me, is it real?' I asked

'Believe me Sam, it is *very* real. For the person possessed it is the most dehumanising experience.'

'Could I watch an exorcism?' I asked, the voyeur in me coming out.

'Sam, only those who are pious and have complete trust in God can attend an exorcism. I don't think you are ready.' We both knew he was right.

'How many exorcisms have you done?'

'Many, too many,' now he sounded tired also. 'This is why I want you to understand what you may be dealing with. You may not believe in spirits and demons, but they *are* real.'

He reached into his shirt pocket. 'Here, this is for you. It is a medal of Saint Benedict, the guardian against possession. He will help protect you.'

Father Joseph passed me a silver chain with a small medallion attached. On one face was an image of Saint Benedict thrusting forth a crucifix, the way people do to vampires in the movies.

The opposite face was divided into four sections by a cross, each section filled with a sacred symbol.

'I have put a special blessing on the medal. Especially for you.' From the way he said it, it seemed the medallion meant a lot to the priest. I put it on out of respect. Another talisman.

'Thanks, Father. I hope it helps me sort out what happened to Subhani,' I said, being polite.

He clapped his hands together. 'I have no doubt you will get to the bottom of this, Sam. I think you are a good PI. I suspect you were also a good policeman.'

I smiled. 'It depends who you ask.'

He looked at me for a long time, saw beyond the cynicism in my eyes, saw the hurt. 'Whatever happened still upsets you, doesn't it? Do you want to talk about it?'

I looked back at him. It was hard not to like the guy. He had been good to Mabel. To me, also. There was something else about him, an inner strength, a calmness, a safety. I took a breath, forced myself to sit up straight.

'About ten years ago my partner Brian and I were working in the sexual crimes unit. One day a frantic lady came in, all jittery and shaking, and made a claim that her neighbour had just tried to sexually assault her six-year-old daughter.'

I turned to face the priest. 'You should have seen this little girl, Father. She was so scared. In hindsight, she must have been severely traumatised. She never looked up, just gripped tightly to her mother with one hand. Our child counsellors couldn't get a word out of her. She wouldn't speak to anyone but her mother. Even then, her mother literally had to coax the words out of her, which made it look like she was being coached. We knew that wasn't the case, but that's what it looked like.'

I faced forward again, stared blankly at the wall. 'It was clear to us that the girl wouldn't be able to give evidence in a trial. There were also no physical signs of assault to support the claims. But we'd heard enough to pursue the case, anyway. The guy sounded like scum. What we didn't realise was that the guy was well connected politically.'

'With suspected paedophiles, we don't let them know we're on to them until we have enough evidence. Otherwise they can go underground very quickly, destroy hard drives, that sort of stuff. So we couldn't just go and interview him. It all had to be done on the quiet. We spent weeks following him, trying to learn his patterns. The end result was zilch.'

'Force Command were mindful of the guy's connections, so eventually they shut down the case. We couldn't believe it. Even though we had no hard evidence, we knew this guy was bad. We just needed more time. It was obvious that someone in high office had got wind of the case and applied pressure to pull us off.'

'Anyway, Brian and I talked about it and agreed we couldn't let him slip through. We decided to keep an eye on him while we were off duty. On our own time. Nobody would have to know.'

My eyes closed momentarily as I recalled what happened. 'About four nights into our surveillance he pulled up late and we watched as he literally dragged a young girl out of his car and into the house.'

I looked to the priest. 'It was clear she didn't want to be there.'

'What did you do?' asked Father Joseph.

'We knew we had to wait until we had reasonable cause to intervene. If we acted too early, we could be done for harassment. If we left it too late, well, that poor girl…' I shook my head, left the rest unsaid.

Father Joseph stroked his chin, picturing the predicament.

I continued: 'Brian crept up to the house. We figured if he heard anything unusual it would give us the probable cause we were looking for and we could then enter. I kept my eye on him as he crept from window to window, stooping below them. After a minute or so he waved me over. From under a side window we could hear the girl whimpering.'

My fists clenched of their own accord. 'We had to do something,' I said, sounding like I wanted the priest's approval. Father Joseph acquiesced with a nod.

I took another breath and exhaled deeply. 'We ended up kicking down his door and rushing inside. You should have seen his face when he saw us.' I smiled at the memory. 'Anyway, the little girl comes running up the hallway and into my arms. She was terrified. Brian asked the guy what he was doing with the girl. The guy made a fuss about us not having a warrant. By that stage we knew we had reasonable cause and so we took them both back to the station.'

My eyes grew heavy, I rubbed them the same way a child cries. 'It turned out she was his niece. He claimed he was looking after her as a favour to her father. We knew that was crap, but the girl's father ended up backing his story and she was too young to provide any evidence that would stick. Brian and I ended up being counselled and suspended for one month, which was no big deal. The real problem was that this guy was going to get away with it.'

'A few days later the story got leaked to the press and they had a field day with it. The guy's career was effectively ruined, and his name tarnished more permanently. He ended up suing the Victoria Police for megabucks.'

'Brian and I were questioned over the leak. I knew it wasn't me, and though Brian never admitted it to me I just assumed it was him. In any case I wasn't going to squeal.' I shrugged my shoulders. 'In the end both of our careers were done for then and there. They couldn't prove anything but our one-month suspension turned into having the option of taking a demotion or being asked to resign from the force. Brian accepted the demotion to a country posting and I took the redundancy and bought my house. But you know Father, every time I think of that little girl, I know we did the right thing.'

Father Joseph had listened to every word I said. 'It sounds to me like you did the right thing also.'

'What I didn't realise was the effect it would have on my parents, my father in particular. Even after I told him the truth, I think he still felt a little ashamed. The people at his church didn't know the full story, so all they thought was that I had left the police under some cloud. I was the source of my family's shame. Until people found out how Anjali died.'

CHAPTER 30

Mabel was playing solitaire when I opened the door. The empty glass in front of her had a foamy tell-tale residue.

'Another beer?' I asked.

She looked up and smiled, nodded, then laid the seven of diamonds on the eight of spades.

I placed the beer on the table. 'Cheers,' I said, collapsing on the couch.

Mabel took a sip from her refreshed glass. 'Now, what did you learn from the boyfriend?' Her mind was back on the case, the cards could wait.

For a moment I hesitated, wondering how much I could trust Mabel with the information Nair provided. If it got leaked it would be dynamite and Aamir Mehta would explode all over me; again. She must have sensed my tentativeness, her eyebrows knitted together in a silent plea for trust.

I took a sip from my beer. 'You'll keep this to yourself, yes?'

'Cross my heart,' she said, making the actions.

'Okay. According to Nair, Subhani ended the relationship about a year ago and took up with Davindar Singh, the producer.'

'No! Really?' Mabel's mouth dropped open in surprise, making her look like one of those sideshow clowns you feed five dollars' worth of balls to win two dollars' worth of crap.

'Yes. If that's true, then there's a chance that Singh is also the father of the unborn child.'

'That's what Aamir Mehta wants to know!' she said.

'Yes, but I have to be sure. I need proof.'

'You don't believe the boyfriend?'

'I don't know. There was something about him that worried me. Like he could go flying off the deep end at any minute.'

'You don't trust him? Do you think maybe he is telling lies about Singh? Covering up for his own crime?'

'I'm not sure. He was worried when I told him he was the prime suspect. When I mentioned the curse, he seemed genuinely shocked, rather than sheepish or guilty.'

'You know, if the boyfriend's right then Singh must have lied to your face when he told you he didn't know Subhani was pregnant.' Mabel tilted her glass at me, emphasising her point.

'Yes, I know. But his wife was in the house. Perhaps he didn't want to say anything that she could overhear. Just from the way she spoke I reckon she calls the shots in that house.'

'Well, if Singh is the father what would his wife think when the child was born?' pondered Mabel. 'Subhani would have to reveal who the father was. The media would not let her keep it a secret.'

'That's a good question. I think it's time to have a frank discussion with Davindar Singh.'

I called Singh. He seemed glad to hear from me. I reasoned that was how he sounded when anybody rang—

everyone's friend, Mr All Smiles. He told me to meet him at a bar called Rapid at 10 that evening, said to dress well.

I wanted to know as much as possible about the man before we met again. Google gave me plenty of information on Davindar Singh. A website listed all his credits. He made his first movie in 2004 and averaged about four per year ever since. About average for a Bollywood producer. Most of the information on the website was 'pat on the back' crap, but there was one thing of interest. The majority of his movies in the mid-2000s starred Anveeta Khan as the lead female. Then there was a string of movies in the later 2000s where Anveeta was supported by Subhani Mehta. By 2012, Subhani had replaced Khan altogether.

It was more difficult to get information on Davindar before 2004. The only thing I could find was a newspaper article announcing the marriage of Ms Leela Darparti to Mr Davindar Singh in 2002. According to the article, Leela Darparti came from old money. Tea plantations in Darjeeling. Singh was the son of a senior government bureaucrat. They had met at university and remained good friends ever since. The article called the marriage the 'fruition of a wonderful friendship'. There was nothing on Leela Darparti before the marriage.

The match seemed strange to me. Leela would have been a few rungs higher on the social ladder than Davindar. Why would she marry someone below her? On the face of it, they seemed such opposites. He was good looking, outgoing. She was much less so. But she was rich.

Before leaving, I thought I'd chase one more thing up. I cast an eye around the room to make sure Mabel could not see what I was doing, then ran a search on the *Roman Ritual.* It felt like I was doing something wrong, like downloading porn.

There was enough literature to spend a few days in front of the machine. I read a few pieces, which largely said the same thing and that sent a little shiver down my spine. It seemed there was a manner of different ways the devil could have his evil way with you. In addition to your stock standard possession, a person could also fall prey to oppression, obsession, infestation and subjugation. The symptoms of each were described in detail.

After a little while I found what I was looking for. It wasn't that I doubted Father Joseph, but I wanted to check it for myself. The article on the screen confirmed that being subject to a curse was one of the major ways a person became diabolically possessed. All the articles described possession and exorcism in an objective, almost academic, fashion, giving it a sense of credibility that made it harder for me to question. When coupled with the sincerity with which Sri Chandrapathy and Father Joseph spoke about curses, it was hard not to feel that there was something to this. I found myself becoming unsettled, starting to doubt what I thought was certain. I instinctively felt for the medal around my neck, then logged off, hoping that my misgivings would shut down also.

'Mabel, if they got married in 2002 then I guess they would've been in their early thirties. Is that a bit late for a society girl?'

Mabel thought about it for a while. 'Wealthy women can afford to get married later than poor girls, but yes, it does seem a little late in life. Do you know if either of them was married before?'

'No, I don't think so. If one of them were married before it would've been in the article. You know, "widower finds love again". That sort of thing.'

I put the information from the article together with what I felt when I saw them together.

'You know what? I think this is a marriage of convenience. She gets off the shelf, he gets money and status.'

'You're so cynical. They may be in love.'

'Mabel, there was little love in that house when I visited. And she was in control.'

'If what you think is right, then imagine what would have happened if the baby was born. The news would be in every paper and I bet Subhani would have named the father.'

'That's assuming the baby was his. Would Leela leave Davindar for something like that?'

Mabel considered this for a long time also. 'It's hard to say. It would be an embarrassment for her. People would consider her a laughing-stock, letting her husband have a baby with another woman. Under her nose.'

'A choice between marriage and dignity. Right now, I wouldn't be surprised if she chose dignity. Where would that leave Davindar?'

'Without her money,' answered Mabel.

CHAPTER 31

I dressed as well as my baggage would allow: black shoes, black trousers, striped blue and white shirt with the sleeves rolled half way up my arms. Not that it mattered, after five minutes sitting in the back of the auto-rickshaw from hell my clothes stank of diesel and my face felt matted with grime. Of all the rickshaw drivers in Mumbai, I had to get the guy with a death wish and dodgy brakes. Traffic wasn't an obstacle for this guy, it was a challenge. He weaved through it like he was playing a video game. Left of the bus, right of the lorry, around the car, even up on the kerb. We never slowed down, were never bottlenecked.

I tapped him on the shoulder as we approached Rapid. He turned sharply towards the kerb, making the rickshaw over-balance, one of its three wheels lifting off the ground. He got me there in record time. My stomach arrived shortly after.

Unlike Australian nightclubs, there was no queue of wannabe's lining up to get in. I got the feeling, people either walked straight into this place or didn't even bother trying, self-filtering by the size of their wallets. The burly guy underneath the flashing blue neon sign had a lot of time to do not much. Every now and then he'd run his thick pony-tail through his right hand.

He flexed up when he saw me approach. His muscles had muscles, but he was soft around the middle. Too much time focusing on biceps and triceps, not enough on the abs. He held his right hand out to stop me. It made him look like a cop conducting traffic. When he heard I was a guest of Davindar Singh he stepped back, let me through with a flourish of his hand.

Inside wasn't as dark as I thought it would be. It was a long room with a large central bar, serving punters from both sides. A glass wall in the middle of the bar reflected the multi-coloured bottles that lined up against it, making them look twice as nice. There were a few bar stools, but it was basically standing room only near the bar. Further back was a raised area with tables and booths. A DJ held court in a stall above the dance floor. The music wasn't too loud so you had to shout at each other, but loud enough to avoid overheard conversations. The tunes designed for dancing, not listening.

The place was packed with Mumbai's rich-list, each willing to pay a small fortune for a drink. I opted for the cheapest overpriced beer. Davindar Singh was sitting in one of the booths, a packet of cigarettes and a tall glass of something blue in front of him. He was staring at a girl on another table. I caught his attention and he waved me over.

'Sam, good to see you,' he stood to shake my hand, gestured me to take the seat across from him.

'Thank you for meeting me, Mr Singh,' I looked around. 'It's a nice place, this. Are you a regular?'

'I come here every now and then. It's a good place to meet new talent.' I figured he was always on the lookout for new talent.

'So, what did you want to talk about? You said you wanted to check something with me?'

'Yes. It's rather delicate. That's why I wanted to speak to you in person.'

A calculating glint appeared in his eyes, like a chess player trying to anticipate an opponent's moves. I had no hard evidence that Singh was Subhani's lover, the father of her child. Just the word of somebody harbouring a grudge. The only way to confirm it would be to make Singh admit it. I set the bait.

'I've discovered that Subhani did have a lover,' I said.

'Really? I never knew,' he said.

'Yes. She tried to keep it a secret. Anveeta Khan told me all about it.'

'Anveeta, huh.'

'Yes. The guy's name is Pradeep Nair. He was a dancer at Namaste Studios. That's how they met.'

Singh seemed to relax at the mention of Nair's name.

'A dancer! I would never have guessed. She kept it well hidden. But what did you want to speak to me about?'

'Well, I've contacted Nair. At first, he didn't want to speak with me, but I managed to convince him. Anyway, he didn't want to tell me too much on the phone. All he said was that he wasn't the father of Subhani's child, but that he knows who was.'

'He does?' That calculating look came back, he rubbed his chin.

'Yes. I'm going out to speak with him tomorrow, but I wanted to talk with you first. See if you knew this guy, Nair. I'd just like some background info on him.'

'I'm sorry. I've never heard of him. I don't really mix with support staff.'

'Oh, well then, in that case I'm sorry, I wasted your time.'

Singh smiled graciously. 'No problems, anytime.'

'I suppose it doesn't matter really. Nair said he followed Subhani and her lover for months. Took photos of them. He's showing them to me tomorrow.' I wasn't sure how far I could run with the photo angle, just hoped it would make Singh think I could get some physical proof of his relationship with Subhani, rather than just relying on Nair's hearsay.

'Photos?' The way the lines that ran across his forehead deepened I knew he took the bait.

'Yes. He said I wouldn't believe who it was.' I paused for half a breath. 'Although he did describe the person. Tall, thick dark hair, strong face, lots of jewellery. Actually, come to think of it, whoever it is must look a lot like you.'

Singh's demeanour changed. The tension in his face drained away, a flash of anger raged across his face before his mask of charm returned. He pushed his glass towards the cigarettes, clearing the table between him and me, lent his elbows on the table.

'I'm not stupid, Mr Ryder. No more games. You and I both know whose face will be in the photos.'

'I guess we do. So, tell me, are you the father of the baby Subhani carried?'

His gaze raised as he looked over my shoulder.

'Go on, tell him. I told you, it would come out.' Leela Singh stood behind me, a fresh drink in her hand. She had a knack of catching me unawares.

'How long were you standing behind me?' I asked her.

'Long enough to hear about the photos,' she replied.

Davindar Singh stared up at her as she squeezed her way past him into the booth.

Leela Singh looked at me. 'Don't be so surprised, Mr Ryder. Of course, I knew about Subhani Mehta. And Anveeta Khan. And the others. I'm not an idiot like Davindar here.' She flicked her husband as if he were a bug on her shoulder, then reached for the packet of cigarettes on the table. Davindar Singh's face blushed red.

Leela Singh continued, taunting her husband. 'Go on, *darling*, answer the man's question.'

Davindar Singh looked around the club again, then spoke quietly. 'Yes, okay. I had an affair with Subhani. But I tried to end it when she told me she was pregnant. It was nothing serious for me.'

'Subhani was about three months pregnant. She planned to have the baby. That sounds pretty serious to me,' I said.

'My husband is a weak man. When he found out she was pregnant, he didn't know what to do. He panicked. It was up to me to invite Subhani to our home to discuss the options,' Leela Singh said contemptuously.

'You spoke with Subhani about the baby?'

'Of course. I told her that we could help her find somewhere discreet to have an abortion, or if she didn't want to do that, we could get it adopted anonymously. These things would have been very simple to arrange and I only had her best interests in mind. But that selfish girl wanted to have the baby. You know what she told me?' Leela dropped her hand on the table, her bangles jingled.

I shrugged my shoulders.

'She said that once she had the baby, Davindar would leave me for her. Become her manager and her husband. Ha! Can you imagine him leaving all this?' Leela Singh gestured around the bar.

Davindar Singh broke in. 'I told her that I would never leave Leela, but she wouldn't listen. She just thought I would look at the baby and my heart would change. She just wouldn't accept that I was not going to be with her.'

'What about the scandal, Mrs Singh? How could you stay with Davindar after that?' I asked.

She reached over and held her husband's hand. 'Despite everything, Mr Ryder, I am still fond of my husband. I would not leave him over this. As for scandal, what would it do? Davindar's reputation would only be enhanced if his affairs were made public.'

'Only Subhani would suffer from having the baby,' said Davindar Singh. 'Nobody would pay good money to see a fallen woman on the big screen. I would never engage her again.'

I sat back, bemused. 'What about *your* reputation, Mrs Singh?'

'Me?' She touched her neck just below the string of pearls. 'I'm not in the spotlight. I avoid it at all costs. The media would splash it about but after a while nobody would care. Besides, that isn't an issue now. Is it?'

With Subhani gone she was right.

Leela sucked her cigarette quickly, the way I'd seen her do it before, then spoke through the smoke. 'So now you know our little secret. What do you plan to do with the photos?'

'Why do you care? From what you're saying, you guys have nothing to lose if the photos are made public?' I asked.

'That would be true if Subhani were still alive,' said Leela Singh. 'The media would ask why she was having an affair with a married man? They would want to know why she was having a bastard baby, things like that. She would be the main target and they wouldn't worry so much about Davindar.'

Leela Singh shared a glance with her husband, then continued, 'Now with Subhani out of the picture the media would have to focus on Davindar. They may ask why he didn't come forward about his affair with Subhani before? Some journalists may put two and two together and ask if he was the father of the child? And if so, why didn't he admit this before? These things could publicly embarrass Davindar, paint him as an irresponsible man or, even worse, as a coward. It could leave a bad after taste in some people's mouths, important people.'

The couple in front of me were as distasteful as the double standard in society that they were relying upon to protect them. It was all about perception. How things would run in the media. In another life Leela Singh would make a great politician.

'Mrs Singh, I'm here to try and find out if Subhani was killed, not to sell newspapers,' I said, hoping the bombshell would provoke a response.

Davindar Singh lent forward so far that he was almost lying on the table. 'Subhani was killed? You mean murdered?'

'There is a possibility, yes.'

'How? I was there and I didn't see anything,' he said.

'I'd rather not say at this stage.'

'And you thought we had something to hide. I understand.' Leela Singh said this in a matter of fact way, holding the cigarette away from her, behind her back. 'Other people have things to hide also. You visited Anveeta Khan, didn't you?'

I nodded in the affirmative.

'You may not have noticed this Mr Ryder, but Anveeta's career is suddenly blooming again since Subhani's death. Even the movie she is starring in now was meant for Subhani. Not bad for an old *has-been*. Wouldn't you think?'

'What are you suggesting?' I asked.

Leela Singh looked at her husband. 'Go on, tell him.' She gave him a nudge.

Davindar Singh cleared his throat. 'About six months ago, after Anveeta's career had been in limbo, she came here and gave me a script. She said she had written it herself, but it looked like so many other stories to me. Two women in a road movie. From Calcutta to Varanasi.' Singh grinned disparagingly.

'She wanted me to produce it for her and Subhani to play the other role. It was obvious to me that she was trying to revive her career by acting alongside Subhani. I said I would show it to Subhani. Which I did.'

'Anyway, sometime later Subhani rang me and told me she liked the script but would not act in it with Anveeta. She suggested another actress. Someone who would not be so desperate to steal every scene. It put me in a difficult position. As a producer, I knew that whatever film Subhani is in, makes money. Regardless of how bad it is. On the other hand, I knew this would crush Anveeta, and I had a...' Davindar paused to find the right word, looked uncomfortably at his wife. '...history... with her.'

He flicked his hand in the air, dismissively. 'To cut a long story short, when Anveeta found out the film would be made without her, she swore she would get back at Subhani. Both Leela and I were there when she did.'

'So you're suggesting that Anveeta Khan had a reason to kill Subhani?' I asked.

They looked at each other.

'Not at all,' said Leela Singh. 'Until you just told us we didn't even know Subhani could have been murdered. All we're saying is that we're not the only ones to benefit from her death,' she answered, smugly.

CHAPTER 32

The night markets were lit up with the same garish ferocity you find at carnivals. Above, naked light globes splashed electric reds, greens and blues against the moonless night sky. The smoke from a row of charcoal grills mingled with the lights, forming fuzzy, multi-coloured ribbons that stretched up and disappeared into the blackness.

Crowds of people wandered along, window-shopping without windows. Families came out for the evening, children holding their parents' hands. The men dressed casually: slacks, chappals, loose shirts. The women dressed up, wearing beautiful saris in spectacular combinations: salmon and mint, red and purple, dark green and yellow. They gave the overhead lights a run for their money.

Loud, shrill music competed with the sound of generators. Traffic slowed to a snail pace as the sheer volume of people took over the streets. Everywhere was a mass of humanity. It smelled of charcoal-barbequed chicken, of spices and diesel. The whole scene was chaotic and charismatic at once, a community outside my taxi window. I thought about the Anglo-Indian community in Melbourne, of New Years' dances when my family would share a table with the Simons' from Preston, of Mrs Simons who would always bring a tray of sweet, buttery kulkuls to ring in the New Year, and of Emily

Simons with whom I had my first fumbling kiss. Both Anjali and I stopped going to the dances when we hit our late teens, having found cooler ways to celebrate the New Year. Now, I found myself missing those community events, missing that immediate connection to my culture. The taxi crawled along with the flow of the traffic and part of me wanted to get out and merge with the scene surrounding me. Instead, I closed my eyes and reflected on the conversation with the Singhs.

Leela Singh turned out to be a barrel of contradictions. She mocked her husband in front of me and treated him like a fool. Yet underneath it all she loved Davindar, supported him when she found out about the pregnancy, was complicit with him against Subhani. It was like they had some crazy co-dependency thing going on. I had her pegged all wrong, she chose the marriage over her dignity. She knew the shame wouldn't last long.

Mabel was wearing her light cotton nightgown with the fading paisley print. She sat on the sofa, her feet up on a chair she had dragged across from the dining table. An empty whisky glass on the table beside her. The only light in the room came from the TV, an old Sherlock Holmes movie starring Basil Rathbone. She put the volume on mute when I sat down beside her, giving me the impression that she was just waiting for me to return. I filled her in, my very own Watson.

'Well, we definitely know who the father is now. If Aamir Mehta is right about the curse then the Singhs killed Subhani so that her baby wouldn't live,' she said.

'I'm not so sure about that. For one, we still don't know if

Subhani was killed at all.'

Mabel looked at me with weary eyes, 'What about the terrible thing you found at Subhani's house, and what Father Joseph and the pujari have said to you? Don't you believe even now?' Her question was peppered with incredulity and disappointment, making me feel foolish, slow.

I didn't like the feeling so ran with Mabel's thoughts. 'Even if she was though, the Singhs have no motive to kill Subhani, nothing for them to gain. In fact, from the way they put it, they would've preferred it if Subhani was alive. She had more to lose than them.'

'Do you believe them?'

'I don't know,' I said, shaking my head.

'What about what they said about Anveeta Khan? I was right about her, wasn't I?'

'Yes, you were. Assuming what the Singhs told was true. It gives her a pretty good motive for wanting Subhani dead.'

'You'll have to talk with her again. Make her tell the truth this time.'

'Yeah, although she's not the only one with a strong motive. We can't forget Nadar. His career was at the crossroads and Subhani was planning to get rid of him. Davindar Singh said any movie with Subhani in it made money, so I can't see him choosing a has-been director over a mega-star.'

'That makes three suspects,' said Mabel.

'Four, if you count both the Singhs. Five, if you count Pradeep Nair.'

'The boyfriend?'

'The ex-boyfriend. Subhani dumped him for Singh and then most likely got his contract at the studios cancelled. Jealousy and vengeance sound like good motives to me.'

Mabel shook her head, made the same disapproving 'tut, tut' noises that Father Joseph made a few days before.

'So we have plenty of people who benefit from Subhani's death, but still no hard proof she was killed,' I said.

'Imagine having so many people wanting you dead,' Mabel thought out aloud.

I glanced at the TV, mute images on the screen. Holmes and Watson were striding about the moors purposefully, Holmes wearing his Deerstalker, Watson a Derby Hat. *The Hound of the Baskervilles* perhaps.

'They all knew where she lived, so each would have had plenty of opportunity to bury the foetus in Subhani's backyard,' I said.

Mabel agreed. 'They all worked with her at one time or another, so yes, they could know where she lived.'

'Well, we know Singh certainly did. Nair admitted spying on her, so he did. Khan was a friend at one time, so she would. Even if Nadar didn't know before, he could have got that information from anyone in the industry. The trouble is Subhani must have had a guard. I saw the empty guardhouse at her home. I'm guessing that whoever buried the foetus didn't do it while Subhani was at home. So how did they get past the guard?'

Mabel sniggered. 'With money,' she said, rubbing her thumb and fingers together.

'As for means, well, like you said before, the foetus was buried away from where Subhani could find it easily. So whoever did it must really believe in black magic. They would have also needed to know that Subhani was superstitious and would be afraid when told she was cursed.' I said.

'Well, Khan said everyone in Bollywood is superstitious.'

'Yeah, so it doesn't rule anyone out. Even Nair believes in curses.'

'Still five suspects,' said Mabel, shrugging.

'Five that we know about, anyway. How many of them would know if Subhani had a heart condition?'

'From what you said, even her parents didn't know if she had a bad heart,' said Mabel. 'You still think she was scared to death?'

I left her question unanswered, though she was right about Subhani's parents. They said they didn't know about any heart issues. If Subhani had a problem, she'd tell them before telling any of her colleagues, that is if she told her colleagues anything at all.

Mabel stifled a yawn. 'So, the Singhs think there are photos of Davindar and Subhani, huh? I wonder what they will do about that?'

'I'm not sure. If they treat it seriously, they may try to get in touch with Nair, buy the photos.'

'Then they'll know you were lying.'

I smiled, 'Yes, but at least I won't be the only one on a wild goose chase.'

CHAPTER 33

I rang Silvia Dias first thing in the morning. The phone rang six or seven times before being answered. I wondered if Dias recognised the number and debated whether to pick up or not.

'Hello Ms Dias, it's Sam Ryder here.'

She sounded flustered straight away. 'Oh…Mr Ryder. What do you want?'

'It's okay, Ms Dias. I don't want anything from you. I gather Ms Khan is still in Goa?'

'Yes, why?' She sounded a little more relaxed.

'I would like you to ask Ms Khan to contact me as soon as possible, please. Let her know it's urgent.'

'Urgent? Is there something the matter?'

'Let Ms Khan know it's about a film script that she developed. That's what I'd like to talk to her about.'

'Ooh,' she said, knowingly. I recalled Dias was a person who knew things she shouldn't.

'You know which script I'm talking about, don't you?'

I could hear Dias' grip on the phone change. 'Mr Ryder, please. That's none of my business. I will pass your message on to Ms Khan, but I can't guarantee that she will contact you. It is something that she is still very upset about.'

I needed to raise the stakes, shake things up. 'Tell her it has to do with Subhani Mehta's murder.'

She gasped. 'Murder?'

'Thank you, Ms Dias.' I rung off, confident that the idea that Subhani was murdered would force Khan to ring me back. Another trip to Goa was not on the cards.

It was just past 11 am when my mobile phone sang and danced in my pocket.

'Hello, Sam Ryder speaking.'

For a long time there was nothing, just a hissing. Then there was a voice I recognised, it sounded pathetic, broken.

'He...Help....m....Help mmeee.' He sounded anguished, in pain.

'Pradeep, is that you? Pradeep?' I said.

Nair cried on the phone. A deep, mournful cry. The way a son cries at his mother's funeral. At times it came out with such force that there was no sound, just rushing air. At other times it was a deep, choking wail.

'Pradeep, what's the matter? Where are you?'

'I...It's...in...side...m...me,' he struggled to get the words out, like he was fighting against himself. 'I...I ca... can't...get...i...it...out.'

'Pradeep, what can't you get out? Where are you?'

The sobbing resumed, although this time there was another noise in the background. A male voice shouted 'Pradeep', followed it up with Hindi. That meant he wasn't at work, they'd speak English there. It also meant he was somewhere where people knew his name. He told me he had a flatmate, someone to share the bills with. I flicked through my notebook until I found the contact details for Nair that Dias had given me.

'Mabel, can you drive me to Andheri. Something's wrong,' I said.

Mabel nodded.

'I'm on my way, Pradeep,' I said on the phone. The call was already disconnected.

We headed east. Away from the glitz and glamour of the beachside suburbs and into working-class Mumbai. The dusty, grey highway seemed to stretch on forever, fenced in either side by concrete-box shops, parked cars and potholes.

A metre-high concrete barrier separated the opposing streams of traffic and served as a bed for a couple of filthy, exhausted men. I guessed they were untouchables, *dalits*, who worked at night piling up rubbish or digging trenches, away from the sensitive eyes of the higher castes. They slept like the dead, oblivious to the noise, heat and pollution, perhaps just thankful for a flat surface to lay their heads.

Mabel took the off-ramp left to Andheri. Here, single-storey buildings of ageing concrete were slowly being swallowed up by huge, uninspiring apartment blocks with grilled windows and fenced-in compounds. Though not very old, the apartments already looked like they'd seen better days. The ones that had been recently painted in bright colours looked gaudy, rather than fresh, like drunken aunties at a hen's night.

Nair lived in the building up ahead. I hoped he was home. He hadn't answered his phone when I rang back.

Mabel parked about 50 metres away from his apartment block, said she'd stay with the car.

The block was built in a square, with apartments on all sides and a paved courtyard in the middle. Tall pillars of reinforced concrete supported the building and served as undercover car parking spaces for the tenants. According to the information Dias gave me, Nair lived in apartment 56 of Building 'C'. I walked up the poured concrete pathway and around to the courtyard, didn't get much further.

A group of people gathered in a circle close to the middle of the courtyard. A lady screamed 'Eeee yahhh'. Others pulled their children away from the huddle, shielding their eyes. Three men with folded arms gawked at whatever was the centre of attention, shaking their heads and looking up, pointing. I walked up to the group of people and prised myself to the front.

Pradeep Nair's body was bent and broken. His left arm was twisted where it shouldn't be and lay below his back. His spine looked as if it had snapped in two over it. Both his feet turned to the right and his right elbow and hand rested at right angles, making that part of his body look like an Egyptian hieroglyph. His left shin bone jutted out through his torn jeans. Nair's bloodshot eyes looked up at the sky, a terrified look fused onto his face. His mouth half open, a trickle of blood and saliva in one corner. A growing pool of blood crowned his head.

'When did this happen?' I asked one of the three wise men.

He eyed me up and down for a couple of seconds before replying. 'Ten, fifteen minutes,' he said.

'Did anyone see what happened?'

He shrugged. 'I don't know, we just came to see.'

I'd only ever seen one jumper before, years ago, when I was a fresh-faced constable. The guy had leapt from the fourth floor of an office block in Treasury Place, the government district of Melbourne. We knew it was suicide because of where he landed. Jumpers tend to leap horizontally out of a building, meaning they land away from where they jumped. Their trajectory taking the shape of a parabola. People who accidentally fall or are pushed from windows usually land directly below. Sometimes hitting the building or cliff face on the way down.

To me, Nair was the former. I looked up at the fifth floor of the building marked with a black 'C', to where Nair's apartment would be. His final resting place was a good distance out from there, meaning he didn't fall accidentally. To end up close to the middle of the courtyard meant that he would have needed to take a running leap.

I moved in closer, squatted over his body. Nobody stopped me. In fact, the closer I got, the further away they moved. There were deep scratch marks on his cheeks, as if someone were trying hard to gouge something out. I leaned in closer, took a look at the fingers on his right hand. There was tissue under his fingernails. Self-inflicted. It would've hurt.

Half of a card was poking out of Nair's breast pocket. It looked familiar: off-white, recycled paper. The word 'Sam' was clearly distinguishable, underneath that and centred was the word 'Private', both written in bold, black, size 14 font. The first four digits of my mobile phone number could also be seen.

If the police found the card they'd want to talk to me and I did not want to have another conversation with Superintendent Rao. I pinched the card between my pointer finger and my thumb and slid it from Nair's pocket. It was blood free, like most of Nair's torso. I pocketed the card as I backed away from the body. Nobody attempted to stop me, or ask what I was doing, they were mesmerised by Nair's body. Voyeurs of the macabre.

The balustrade on Level Five was low, giving me a slight sense of vertigo looking down. It wouldn't take much to stumble and accidentally fall over the edge. Particularly if you were out of your senses, which was how Nair appeared to me on the phone. This didn't look like an accident, however, with Nair's mangled body a good 4 metres away from the edge.

From above, the circle of people looked like synchronised swimmers, moving in and out from the middle to the beat of some unheard rhythm. Standing outside Nair's apartment, the distance between the door and the balustrade was only about 2 metres. Not enough room to create the momentum needed to land that far away.

I knocked. A barrel-chested man with a glass in his hand and a face that needed to be shaved three times a day answered. I held up a five hundred rupee note, told him who I was and asked if we could talk. He snatched the money, walked away without saying a word, leaving the door open behind him.

The entry was at the corner of a tiny, square room, about a third the size of Mabel's living area. Along the far end, opposite the door, was a blue fabric two-seater sofa. An armchair made of the same material was placed along the wall to the right of the sofa. A television and stereo took up most of the wall opposite the sofa, just beside the doorway. On either side of the armchair were internal doorways leading to different rooms.

The flatmate slumped on the armchair, spilling some scotch on his shirt, and scratched his dark, densely stubbled cheek.

'Shit,' he said, swigging down another large mouthful. 'This is bloody shit. Now I'll have to find somewhere else to live.'

He showed no signs of shock, made no effort to feign sadness at Nair's death. This was just an inconvenience to him. His honesty was refreshing and reprehensible at the same time.

I sat down on the two-seater, smelt the chemical aroma of the cheap scotch.

'What happened?'

He shrugged. 'I don't know. When he came back home, he was acting weird. Didn't say anything, just crying. He spoke to someone on the phone. Then he went into his room, still crying, crying. I asked him what the matter was but he ignored me. The next thing I know he opened the door, walked to where you are and then ran out and jumped.

Just like that.' He raised a shaky hand to his mouth, scotch dripped from his chin over his shirt again.

It was about 3 metres from where I was to the door. Add that to the 2 metres outside and you'd get a reasonable run-up to launch yourself.

'You said he didn't say anything. Just crying?' I asked, not bothering to find out *Hairy Flatmate*'s name.

He took another gulp, finished his glass and rested it on his growing belly. 'You are the man he met yesterday. The investigator, yaah? It was only after meeting you that he started to act strange.'

Only after meeting with me. I thought back on my conversation with Nair at the cafeteria.

'What do you mean by acting strange?' I asked.

'I don't know, we shared the same flat but we were not friends. He came home early from work yesterday and started talking about Subhani Mehta again. Sometimes crying, sometimes shouting. That's all.'

Hairy Flatmate looked across at me. 'Then, this morning, he was in a good mood. He said something about working it out and that he was going to be rich. He went out early this morning. I wasn't really paying attention.'

He got up, walked to another room. A bottle was being unscrewed. Top-up time. I scanned the room, seeing nothing of interest until I noticed Nair's red mobile phone lying under the armchair. It must have fallen out of his pocket when he commenced his run up. If I was right, my number would be the last number dialled, just before he jumped. Any decent cop would check it and contact me. They'd want to know what he spoke to me about before he died. That could lead to the same awkward questions that my business card in his pocket would have resulted in. I moved across and swept up the phone from under the chair, stood up and put it in my pocket just before *Hairy Flatmate* returned.

He noticed I was now standing, looked at me suspiciously. 'What are you doing?'

'You said Pradeep spent some time in his bedroom. Which room is it?'

'Straight through there,' he said, pointing at a door with the hand that held his drink.

The bedroom was only about 3 metres square. Hairy Flatmate stood at the doorway behind me. A double bed took up most of the space, unmade. A wooden wardrobe the only other piece of furniture, the top half hanging space, the lower half divided into three drawers. I took a quick look through, nothing much. Nair left no note.

'Small room,' I said.

'He used to have the bigger room, but now I rent it.' He leaned heavily against the door mantel. 'Shit! I'll have to pack all my things up again.'

The police would arrive soon. Not a good time to be around. I took out another five hundred from my wallet.

'I wasn't here and Pradeep never mentioned me,' I said, holding it in front of his face, the same way I did the previous note.

He wiggled his head and took the cash.

CHAPTER 34

We drove home in silence, as silent as Indian roads can get anyway. The myriad of bike, car and truck horns created a discordant background score while my thoughts took centre stage. Why would Nair commit suicide? Was he depressed over Subhani's death, over his failed career? Maybe, but those things had happened before I met him. His flatmate said he changed *after* meeting with me. Did I say something that led to his death? I told him he was my prime suspect. Surely that didn't push him over the edge? Figuratively and literally.

It didn't make sense. His flatmate said he was in a good mood this morning. The calm before the storm? Many suicidal people attain a sense of peace before they kill themselves, comfortable with the decision they have made. Usually, they take the time to write a note, letting family members know why and that they shouldn't blame themselves. Nair didn't sound like he was at peace when he called me, though, and he left no note. I thought of his family, another set of parents with no answers.

Mabel broke the silence. 'What are you thinking?'

'Just trying to make some sense out of it. Why he would jump?'

'It must have been an awful sight, his body. Do you want to talk about it?'

I reached across to Mabel, held her arm. 'Thanks Mabel. I'm fine. I've seen my fair share of bodies.'

'Yes, but you knew this man.'

'No, not really. I only met him yesterday, so I'm not grieving or in shock, if that's what you're concerned about. I'm just trying to understand why he'd kill himself. Why he'd call me first?'

Mabel glanced down at the red mobile on my lap, must've figured out whom it belonged to. 'Are you sure you were the last person he rang?'

Nair's mobile was locked but it didn't take a genius to work out his passcode spelled 'Subhani'. I checked his call log and was sure enough, my number was the last one dialled.

'Yup. That's my number,' I said, switching the phone off.

'But why did he call you?'

'I don't know, but it must be something to do with Subhani.'

I thought back about the broken body on the pavement, lots of damage visible on the outside and no doubt much more on the inside. The uncontested results of gravity and concrete conspiring against the human form. To me though, the self-inflicted scratches on his face were of more interest. He'd had a red hot go at tearing his face out. Why? What was it he said to me? *Help me. It's inside me. I can't get it out.*

Whatever *it* was, he tried hard to get it out. What did he mean, *it*? Depression? It's been known to consume people, but so quickly, so dramatically? I wasn't sure.

Then I remembered what else I told Nair. I told him about the black magic. At the time I thought he accepted it too readily. He even joked that his own life was cursed.

I ran through the sequence again. Nair was getting on with his life until I met up with him, brought all those feelings he had for Subhani back to the surface. I told him about the black magic, that Subhani may have been cursed. That stirred him up. His flatmate said he came home early, upset. By the morning, Nair was in a good mood, told the flatmate that he'd worked it all out, would be rich.

Worked what out? Could he have figured out who tried to curse Subhani? Perhaps, he thought he'd get rich by blackmailing them? If so, why would he kill himself? It didn't add up, unless his plan didn't work out.

'Mabel, listen to this. Yesterday, I told Nair that Subhani was cursed. He seemed surprised at first but I'm pretty sure he believed it. What if he worked out who did it and tried to blackmail them? When he left the flat this morning he was in a good mood. His flatmate said he thought he was going to be rich. Perhaps he had arranged to meet the person who cursed Subhani and was expecting a big payout, but instead that person turned him down? If he was already suffering from depression, would that be enough to make him want to commit suicide? His last hope being crushed like that? Maybe that's what he meant by 'it' being inside him? Depression.'

Mabel thought for a while before responding. 'I suppose so, Sam, but I don't know much about depression. Are you sure he was depressed?'

'Not really,' I had to admit, 'his flatmate said he was crying and shouting last night, but then he was happy and confident this morning. Things must have changed dramatically by this afternoon. Manic, really.'

'So maybe manic depression?' offered Mabel. 'Like bi-polar disorder. Did he have any medications?'

'I didn't think to check and we can't go back now.'

We didn't speak again until Mabel parked her car and cranked the handbrake. She turned in her seat to face me.

'Sam, just thinking about your scenario, if Nair really knew who cursed Subhani why wouldn't that person pay the blackmail? Surely Nair would have threatened to go to the police or to the media?'

'Good question, Mabel. I don't know the answer. Maybe Nair got the wrong person after all, or if he got the right person, perhaps his threats weren't strong enough?

'Hmm,' Mabel sounded unconvinced. 'What did he say to you again?'

'He said that it was inside him and that he couldn't get it out. I think maybe he was referring to his depression.'

'It was inside him,' Mabel repeated to herself, emphasising the word 'it'. Her eyes closed as she processed this information. When she opened them again there was a determined certainty in her stare. She reached out and placed her hand on my shoulder.

'Sam, there is another scenario. What if Nair met the person who cursed Subhani this morning and tried to blackmail them as you suggest, but that instead of being refused Nair got cursed as well? That's what he meant by *it* being inside him. And that is why he called you, because you knew about the curse and he thought you could help him.'

'So now you think he died of a curse also?'

Mabel nodded, tentatively at first, but growing with confidence. 'Yes. That is exactly what I am saying. Something got inside Nair, something he tried to get out. Something that made him jump.'

I spent the rest of the day looking for a more logical connection between Subhani's death and Nair's suicide. While Mabel was yet to convince me that Nair was cursed, we were in agreement that he had probably met with the person who had cursed Subhani earlier this morning. That gave me two points for triangulation.

It was clear to me that Subhani didn't find the foetus and lemon buried in her garden. It was too well hidden, and in any case, if she had found it, I doubt she would have re-buried it. Still, she knew she was cursed and that's why she got the talisman. The only way she could have known that she had been cursed was by someone telling her, and the only person who could have told her was the person who had cursed her in the first place. But why tell her? Why go to all the trouble of cursing someone and then warning them about it?

As for Nair, well I had only told him about the curse yesterday, yet he was able to arrange a meeting with the tantric by this morning. That suggested he knew the tantric reasonably well, knew how to get in touch quickly. To me that meant there was a strong chance Nair, Subhani and the tantric were all known to each other. That kept Anveeta Khan in the picture. Nair danced in Singh's films, so he wasn't ruled out. I wasn't sure about Nadir and made a note to check whether Nadir directed any films Nair worked on.

By now it was evening and my head hurt. I wanted to switch my mind off the case but the question of why the tantric must have told Subhani that she had been cursed was never far from my mind. Did they think that the fear and terror associated with the knowledge that you're cursed would be more potent than the curse itself? If so, why not just tell Subhani she was cursed? Why go to all the trouble of actually burying a curse in her garden? That act in itself suggested that the tantric did believe in the power of curses.

'Ouch! Bloody hell,' yelled Mabel from the kitchen. I raced over to find her dowsing her forearm under the running tap. 'What happened?' I asked, voice raised over the spluttering chorus coming from the stove.

'Some mustard seeds jumped out of the oil and landed on my arm. Such a stupid bugger,' she replied.

I walked over to the pot on the stove, black mustard seeds were popping and dancing in the hot oil. I stirred them so they wouldn't catch on the bottom.

'Can you add those spices and keep stirring?' said Mabel as she turned the tap off and reached for the tea towel. Beside the pot was a well-used silver plate with different coloured spices placed in small mounds. I brought it closer to my nose and could smell the earthiness of the coriander, the punch of the cumin, the steeliness of the turmeric and the bite of the chilli.

I added the rainbow of spices to the pot and stirred, keeping my head back to avoid the steam. 'What are you making?'

Mabel patted her arm dry, gingerly. 'Pepper water,' she said, quickly followed by 'Oh shit, better add the pepper.' She opened a container and put two heaped tablespoons of ground black pepper into the dish, then took the wooden spoon from me and kept stirring. 'Can't have pepper water without pepper,' she said, her crooked smile returning.

We cooked the rest of the meal together, cold beers offsetting the heat in the kitchen. I was glad for the distraction and Mabel put me in charge of completing the pepper water, adding tomatoes, water, tamarind pulp and curry leaves to the spices, while she made the dry fry, a beef dish cooked with onions, ginger and more pepper.

'This used to be your mum's favourite dish,' she said, while rinsing the starch out of the uncooked rice.

'Still is,' I said, 'our whole family loves it.' I paused. 'It was Anjali's favourite also. Mum used to make it regularly for Sunday lunch when she knew Anjali was coming. I don't think she's made it since…since,' I could feel my voice tremble.

Mabel came over to me, placed her hands on my shoulders. 'Oh Sam, I am so, so sorry. She was such a beautiful, happy child. You must miss her very much.'

I couldn't talk, just nodded, nods turning to trembles. My eyes shut tight, so tight I hoped they'd never open, never see the world without my sister again. Then the grief became too much and I was overwhelmed, I buckled, crumbled, my weight transferred onto Mabel. She grabbed me, hugged me to her, held me as I wept ferocious tears that had I fought back all these years.

I don't know how long we were like that. Mabel cradled me as my sobs became whimpers, my anguish temporarily exhausted, all the time whispering 'it's okay' into my ear. Finally, I pulled myself together, ashamed, embarrassed and headachy. 'I'm sorry, Mabel. I didn't mean for that to happen,' I said as I wiped my face dry with my sleeve.

'It's okay Sam, in fact, it's healthy. Your parents have been worried about you for some time now. They don't think you've allowed yourself to grieve,'.

'My parents have been talking to you about me?'

'Don't look so surprised, Sam. After all, we're Anglo-Indians, we always talk about our children! It's either that or complain about something,' she managed a smile. That summed up my relationship with my parents, they felt more comfortable talking to others about their concerns for me than talking directly with me. I guess it was the same way with them, honest conversations being too difficult, one of the reasons why Anjali's death was unresolved for our family, haunting every interaction.

'Your parents think you blame yourself for Anjali's death. I know what it's like. When Franky died, I spent so much time and energy blaming myself, wondering if there was anything I could have done to change it. But really, there was nothing. It was Franky's time and our Lord called him. You can't go on blaming yourself for what happened to Anjali. Nobody knew she was taking drugs.'

'I knew,' I said, as fresh tears followed the snail trail paths on my face. It was the first time I had admitted it to anyone.

Sleep that night was fitful, over-tired. I tossed and turned like a fish out of water. My mind kept switching between Anjali and Nair. Two deaths, one of which I wished I could change and the other just understand. No wishes were coming true, though.

It was early morning when my mobile rang, the name on the screen said 'Bec'.

'Hi Bec, how are you?' my voice croaked as it came back to life.

'Hi Sam, I'm sorry to call you so early.' The tone in Bec's voice was professional, I pictured her in the uniform, realised this was not a personal call and sat up in bed.

'Is there a problem, Bec?' My immediate thoughts went to my parents.

'Sam, early this morning one of your neighbours reported hearing noises in your home, loud voices, things being smashed. He knew you were away, so called us. By the time we got there whoever it was had gone, but Sam, they've done a real number on your house. I'm sorry.'

'How bad is it, Bec?' the concern in my voice was slowly being replaced by anger.

'It's bad, Sam. Everything's been trashed. You'll need to come back and sort this out. Stuff from your filing cabinets have also been thrown around, some of it probably private stuff your clients don't want lying around.'

'Fuck!' I raged.

'We've secured it as best we could, Sam, but you need to come home. Do you have any idea who it could be?'

'I've got a pretty good idea, Bec. You remember that death threat I played you? They came from a gang of four international students I busted selling drugs on campus.'

'They? I thought it was just the once. How many threats did you receive?'

'A couple. I didn't think they were serious, just pissed off, but I obviously got that wrong.' My anger was being mellowed by feelings of vulnerability, thoughts of what might have happened if I was in the house crept into my mind.

'What type of drugs?'

'Ice, mainly. Pills, some other stuff.'

'So, are these guys dangerous? Will they come after you again?'

'Not sure, Bec.'

'Give me their names and details and I will make some enquiries,' said Bec. I could tell from her voice that the enquiries would be forceful. I relaxed a little and promised to send her an email with the details.

'You need to come home ASAP, Sam', repeated Bec, this time with a tenderness filling her voice.

'I will, Bec. I'll make arrangements today.'

'And you can stay with me until your home is fixed.'

'Thanks, Bec, that would be great. I don't want to be a burden, though.'

'I wouldn't ask you if I thought you would. Besides, I've got my leave coming up. If you get up my nose, I'll piss off to Bali.' I could hear the humour in her voice, pictured her smiling green eyes, ached to be with her there and then.

'I miss you, Bec.'

'You better,' she said, before ending the call.

I sat on the side of the bed, phone still in hand, trying to keep my anger in check and think logically about what to do. Bec said to return ASAP and leaving today was an attractive option. Leave the heat. Leave the filth. Leave the questions that Nair's death raised. Leave the unsettling doubt that this case had cast over me. It wouldn't be hard to get on a plane. There were always seats. Then I thought about my obligation to the Mehtas. Aamir Mehta wanted the name of the father of Subhani's child. I could give him that now, although it didn't prove that Davindar Singh killed Subhani, or that Subhani was even killed in the first place. It was the best that I could do.

The phone call must have woken Mabel. She walked into the room, fastening her dressing gown. 'Is anything the matter?' She asked.

She plonked herself beside me on the bed, listened silently as I told her what had happened.

'You need to go home, Sam. Tend to your house. That is the most important thing.'

'Yes, you're right. I'll organise it in the morning and get a flight later in the day. That will give me time to talk to the Mehtas. Tell them everything I know. I can't give them all that they want, but I can answer some of their questions. They deserve that much. I just hope that's enough.'

CHAPTER 35

At first Aamir Mehta sounded confused when I called him. It took a while for it to sink in that I was leaving the case. When it did, he became excited, anxious. He asked if I'd worked out who killed Subhani. When I said no, he sounded disappointed, deflated. He told me to come at 10.

The maid had been expecting me this time. I followed her barefoot shuffle into the same room in which the Mehtas had met me last time. The shutters were still closed and there was a rank mustiness in the air, making the room feel stagnant and gloomy. Sitting on the very edge in a corner of one of the sofas was Rekha Mehta.

I greeted her, trying to conceal my shock at how far she had deteriorated. Her face was swollen from crying. Her eyes were little more than dark, hollow sockets, surrounded by flaking, rashy skin. The same red rash was below her nose, like a sick child. She hadn't bothered about the state of her hair. Instead, covering her head with a white shawl. Her white sari was dirty along the hem. I wondered if she'd bothered to change her clothes since the last time we had met. I sat opposite her. We didn't speak.

Aamir Mehta breezed in a little while later, dressed Western: crisp light grey trousers, matching belt, a white short-sleeved shirt. A faint smell of camphor followed him, not too strong to be unpleasant.

'Mr Ryder. I didn't understand your phone call this morning. You want to leave the case? Why?' he asked.

I resumed my seat after he sat down. A sign of respect I knew he'd appreciate.

'Mr Mehta, Mrs Mehta. Thanks for meeting me at short notice.' I paused to look them both in the eye but couldn't make eye contact with Rekha Mehta.

'I'm here to tell you that I know who the father of Subhani's child is.'

At hearing this the corners of Aamir Mehta's mouth began to rise, he had to fight the smile back. She was emotionless.

'I also have to tell you that I can't prove that Subhani was killed. I have some suspicions, but they're not enough to continue the case.'

Aamir Mehta nodded sombrely, placed his hands between his knees. 'I see. Tell us what you know.'

'I'd like to start with the baby's father. First, I must warn you that you may find out things about your daughter that you would rather not hear. Are you both prepared for that?'

'Of course, we are,' he said. It was her I was more concerned about than him. She remained dumb.

'Okay.' I took a breath, watched to see their reaction. 'The father of Subhani's child is Davindar Singh.'

Two tears, one from each eye, slowly negotiated their way down the lunar landscape of Rekha Mehta's face. Aamir

Mehta's body stiffened, like the tin man from *The Wizard of Oz*. His face grew stern, jaw clenched. Neither of them said a word.

I continued: 'Subhani and Davindar Singh had been in a relationship for about a year. When Subhani fell pregnant, she asked Davindar to leave his wife and be with her. He refused. He told Subhani to get rid of the baby. According to him, Subhani couldn't accept that. She fooled herself that he would come around. That's why she kept the baby.'

Aamir Mehta sat rigid on the lounge. 'Davindar Singh has been our friend for years. He has always been welcome in this house. How could he betray me like this?' he spoke crossly, the question directed to nobody in particular.

Aamir Mehta fixed his reddening eyes at me. 'How do you know this?'

'Before Singh, Subhani had a relationship with a man called Pradeep Nair. When it ended, he followed Subhani out of jealousy. He told me he watched Subhani with Singh. When I confronted Singh about the relationship, he admitted it. Mrs Singh also knew about it.'

'I trusted Singh. Both of them I trusted,' Aamir Mehta shouted, flailing his right arm wildly.

I gave him time to calm down.

'About Subhani's death,' I continued. They both looked up at me. 'There is no doubt that somebody wanted to harm your daughter. What we found in her garden supports that. There is just no evidence to take it any further. All I can say with any certainty is that Subhani died from an unknown cause.'

I wanted to give them more than this. It just wasn't possible. I felt like I had let them down.

Aamir Mehta swallowed hard, closed his eyes. When he opened them again, they were glassy, the fight in them gone. It felt like a long time before he spoke again. 'I understand, Mr Ryder. Thank you very much for all you have done.'

'I'm sorry, I can't do any more.'

'I cannot convince you continue the investigation?' he asked.

'Mr Mehta, even if I spent the next year in India, I couldn't give you any more than what I have today. Also, like I told you on the phone, there's some urgent business I have to clear up back home.'

Aamir Mehta sighed deeply, dropped his eyes to my shoes. 'Okay,' he said. He stayed that way for about ten seconds, eyes down, dejected. Then he rose and swiftly left the room.

I didn't expect to be let off the hook so lightly. Right from the beginning it was he who questioned the autopsy report, believing that there was something sinister about his daughter's death. It was only after we found the buried bag that I started to believe he was right.

A chafed hiss came from Rekha Mehta's mouth before any words formed, even then it was a harsh whisper. 'What does the pujari think?'

I looked into her eyes, wondering whether this would do more harm than good. In the end it didn't matter, she was my client also and had a right to know.

I gathered my thoughts. 'You must understand I have no proof for what I am about to tell you.'

She gave the briefest of nods to continue.

'Sri Chandrapathy believes that Subhani was cursed. After he cleansed Subhani's house, he told me about mantras called "bow and arrows". He said black magicians can use these mantras to cast curses on people.'

'So my Subhani *was* cursed,' she said.

'Sri Chandrapathy thinks so. He told me whoever did this to Subhani was a powerful tantric.'

If Rekha Mehta's face could drop any further it did then.

'A tantric,' she repeated, more to herself than me.

Slowly, she lent forward and stretched out her hand. The skin looked two sizes too big for her bones, like she'd had a long soak in a bath. I took her hand in mine.

'Thank you,' she rasped. It lasted less than five seconds, but it was the best thanks I'd ever had.

Aamir Mehta walked back into the room, remained standing. He held out a piece of blue paper. 'Here you are Mr Ryder. I believe, this more than compensates for your time and any other incidentals. Thank you for all you have done.'

I took the cheque. It compensated nicely.

CHAPTER 36

It was just past noon by the time the taxi dropped me off in front of Saint Mark's Church; my flight booked for 5 pm. A group of pedestrians were waiting for the lights to change before crossing, not game to try the traffic two-step. I joined them, seeking protection in the herd.

The movement caught the corner of my eye. One moment the car was parked, the next it dived violently into the traffic, causing other vehicles to merge right. The rest happened in broken pieces, like watching through a strobe light. With a screech of its tyres the car swerved back to the left and headed exactly to where we were standing.

The group of pedestrians started to move. First slowly, then with a panicked urgency. People screamed and pushed each other out of the way. The very young and the very old left to their own devices. At first, I froze, trapped in a zen-like trance, watching the scene as if it was on TV, seconds feeling like minutes. Then I registered a newspaper boy standing between the oncoming car and me, screaming. I grabbed him under his arms and jumped out of the way just as the car clipped my left leg. I landed on my back, the boy on top of me, then the world went blank.

It was always the same dream. I was in my room, sprawled on my single bed with the stainless-steel frame, crying. Anjali was sitting next to me.

'I hate all this. My stupid name, my stupid skin. Why couldn't they call me something normal? Everybody laughs at me. Samson curry, Samson curry. I hate it! Hate them!'

I took my frustration out on the pillow, pummelling it with both fists, pretending it was the bullies at school.

Anjali tenderly placed her hand on the small of my back, applied gentle pressure. A calming gesture. 'I think your name is good. It's like Samson from the Bible. You must be strong and brave like he was. Then everything will be all right.'

Mum and Dad never knew what was going on at school. If they did, they would have tried to do something, make a complaint. That would've made things worse. Anjali only knew because we went to the same primary school. She saw what happened. I was pretty certain she got similar abuse from her classmates, though she never let on. The crap we copped at school was our secret.

Anjali lent over next to me, put her arms around my shoulder. 'You just be strong and everything will be okay,' she said.

'Nothing is okay,' I sobbed into my pillow.

That's how the dream usually ended. The same little snippet from the past played over and over again. This time it was different, the dream didn't end.

Anjali squeezed my shoulder. I turned around to look at her. Suddenly she was no longer twelve. Now she looked like the last time I saw her. A grown woman with long, straight, black hair and her mother's eyes. I had aged also. Everything else had changed also. We were no longer in my bedroom. Now we were in a large building, long and high. It looked familiar but I couldn't recognise it.

I stared at Anjali. Part of me knew it was a dream, part of me didn't care.

'Be strong, Samson and everything will be okay.' Her eyes told me she wasn't talking about being bullied anymore. I reached out, touched her face.

Anjali rose and walked down an aisle. I followed, not wanting to lose her. She stopped in front of a golden altar. It had a big golden sun in the middle. The Basilica!

'Anjali,' I called. 'Please stay.'

She turned to me and smiled.

'Are you okay?' I asked.

'Everything is okay,' she said and walked away.

I came around, though this time I wasn't sad to wake up. It felt like more than just a dream. It felt like a communion. A real exchange between Anjali and me, leaving me calm, at peace. Then the pain set in and I noticed the circle of faces looking down at me, reminding me of Nair.

'Are you okay?' some guy asked. I wasn't sure. In time the pain in my back subsided, leaving the throbbing in my leg. After a while I managed to wriggle my toes, suggesting nothing was broken.

'You're very lucky,' said the man with a broad smile as he helped me up. I was shaky, favoured my right leg and would probably hobble like Quasimodo for a little while, but at least I was on my feet. My trousers were torn where the car hit me. One hell of a bruise was already mottling my thigh. It would match the bruise on my back.

I looked around the street, a little embarrassed at being the centre of attention.

'The boy?' I asked the man.

'He's fine, he ran away. All his newspapers are scattered on the road,' he said with a chuckle.

'What about the car? Did the driver stop?'

'No, no. If he stopped, he'd get such a thrashing.' His head wiggled approvingly as he walked away, stopping only to pick up a free newspaper on the way.

CHAPTER 37

It was the sixth cup of tea that must have done it, my hand twitching of its own accord. Either tea or delayed shock. I was in no state to fly back to Melbourne, so I cancelled the ticket, got a partial refund. Mabel convinced me to call my parents to tell them what happened and let them know I was okay. I say convinced but it was more of a threat than a suggestion. I knew that if I didn't inform them, she would call them anyway. She felt responsible that this happened while I was staying with her.

As it turned out, it was one of the best, most animated conversations I had had with my father in years. He was genuinely interested in how I found India, the Subhani Metha case, and when he found out about my house being trashed, agreed to take care of things until I got back on my feet.

'Are you sure, Dad? It's in a pretty bad state.'

'It can't be any worse than your bedroom used to be,' he said, a gentle tease.

'Thanks, Dad. Just make sure it's secure and I will deal with it when I get back.'

'Just come home in one piece, son,' he said, the tease now replaced with concern.

I realised then that he must have felt like he'd come close to losing me. Maybe that's why he wanted to hold on to the conversation, grasp at any opportunity to engage, to cling on, because the possibility of losing another child was a reality too grim to bear.

'I'll be home soon, Dad, but I'd better ring off now.' I hesitated, then added, 'I love you, Dad.'

A slight pause, as if words were being caught in his throat, then 'I love you too, son.'

I then rang Bec. 'Fuck Sam, are you sure you shouldn't be in hospital?'

'I'm bruised and shaken, but nothing is broken.' I looked at the bruise mottling my thigh. 'My leg is killing me, though.'

'Well, if you start to feel worse you better get to a hospital quick smart, okay? You don't know if you have any internal injuries.'

'Thanks, Bec. Also, about the house. My parents will sort something out while I am recovering. In the meantime, if you could follow up with those enquiries that would be great. I don't want those guys to turn up to my house again, especially if my parents are there.'

'Sure Sam, I'll get onto it first thing. Will let you know how I go.'

That's all the shop we talked. I gave her a description of my bruised and beaten body—slowly turning a vibrant shade of eggplant. She responded with a teasing promise of what we would do when we next met. Some of the things she said would hurt like hell in my present condition, but what a way to go! I wanted her then and there. Wanted to wake up next to her again. We made some plans.

The rest of the day was spent applying balm to my ever-expanding bruises and feeling sorry for myself. The ointment did nothing except make my bruises burn and me smell like a eucalyptus forest. Even a couple of Mabel's sleeping tablets couldn't help me sleep well that night, every twist and turn accompanied by piercing darts of pain, sharp notes that punctuated the throbbing base. I woke up early the following day, swollen and seized, like a rusted engine in need of some heavy-duty chemical lubricant.

I grimaced my way to the bathroom, noticed for the first time the scratches on my face, the bruising and grazing on my back, did the minimum possible to make myself feel better, no visitors expected.

'Would you like a cup of tea?' Mabel asked as I shuffled into the lounge.

'Tea and painkillers would be great, thanks.'

'What about something to eat? Do you want me to make you some scrambled eggs?'

I couldn't stomach any food at the moment, worried the act of chewing would release new belts of pain in places that had so far remained neutral.

'No thanks, not unless there's a chance your eggs are scrambled with some morphine?' I said as I gingerly lowered myself onto a chair. 'Just some painkillers, please. What are your plans for today?'

Mabel filled the kettle with water she had sterilised earlier. 'Well, I am scheduled to help clean the church today and then I was planning to catch up with my friends later today, but I will cancel all that and stay with you.'

'Thanks Mabel, but you don't need to do that. You just continue on with your plans and I can take care of myself. After all, I need you to stay on top of all the gossip!'

'Very funny, you'd think that car could have knocked some sense into you,' Mabel retorted with a smirk.

I spent the next few hours on the couch, feet up, remote in hand, eyes heavy. The cricket was on, a 20–20 match, franchise teams, fireworks, cheerleaders. Sound and fury, signifying nothing.

I cursed when my mobile rang, managed a slow, stiff, Frankenstein-like walk to the table to pick it up, didn't recognise the number.

'Ryder?' Anveeta Khan sounded *five parts terrified to one part* frantic. A paranoid martini. The message I asked Dias to pass on must have really spooked her.

'Hello, Ms Khan. Thank you for returning my call.'

'Put the TV on. Watch the news.' Her heavy breath hitting the receiver sounded like a storm growing in the background.

I flicked the channel, a live cross to a reporter, some sort of commotion going on in the background. I raised the volume. The reporter spoke into the microphone in his right hand, his left hand cupped over his earpiece, as if he were reporting from Baghdad.

'...giant fireball in the middle of the city. It looks as if the Mercedes' brakes failed at an intersection and it ploughed into the petrol tanker.'

The camera focused over the reporter's shoulder and onto the blazing scene behind. The initial explosion had engulfed at least two other cars. A ring of police kept the crowd of people away from the fireball while four firemen, two holding each hose, sprayed water onto the wreckage. In hindsight, it *was* reminiscent of a war-zone.

The camera pulled back to the reporter. 'While the total number of casualties is still unclear, it is believed that film producer Davindar Singh and his wife Leela Singh, along with their driver, were in the Mercedes when it exploded.'

Khan's voice chirped frantically on the mobile. I raised it to my ear.

'So! What do you have to say?' she asked.

The question made no sense, what was I supposed to say?

'I'm sorry, I don't know what you mean. It looks like a terrible accident,' I replied.

'Accident! This was no accident. Davindar's driver was too skilful to have an accident.'

'I'm sorry, Ms Khan. What are you saying exactly? This looks like an accident to me,' I said.

'Of course, you would say that,' she replied.

'I don't understand what you're getting at.'

'Listen to me. First, Subhani dies in Australia. Then all of a sudden you arrive from there. Then I tell you about

Nair. The next thing I hear is that he is dead. You speak to Davindar and now he turns up dead. What do you say about that?'

She was really ranting now.

'Calm down, Ms Khan. All I…'

She chopped me off. 'You are the common denominator,' she shouted. 'You asked me about curses and black magic. You are the one. Whoever you meet, dies.'

This was crazy talk, one too many gin and tonics talk.

'This is ridiculous, I'm not…'

'Just stay away from me. Pleeeaaassse. Staaaayyy awaaaayyy,' she cried into the phone before hanging up.

I turned my attention back to the screen, watched the burning, molten inferno. Despite the attempts of the firemen, the flames stretched at least 10 metres into the air. From this angle you could just make out the smouldering rear of the Mercedes. Not much else. Nobody could have survived that.

My thoughts swirled like the smoke above the fire. The reporter said brake failure. It wasn't that long ago that I saw Singh's car brakes being serviced. Perhaps they missed something? That fire was intense. What did Khan mean I was the only thing they had in common? I'd never met Subhani. Khan blamed me, which meant either she was innocent, or a damn good actress. I told myself I didn't care anymore, yet focused back at the screen anyway. *A raging blaze*. Something Aamir Mehta said leapt about in my mind like the flames on the screen.

Fire. *Hell's Fire!* I remembered the hatred in Mehta's cold eyes when he spoke, his hot breath, '*He deserves to burn in hell's fire*'.

Mehta? My skin began to tingle, my face flushed, as if I was too close to the fire. Khan may have been half right. They did have someone in common, just not me. Something else he said sprung to mind, '*Money is not my motivation*'. Then I remembered why the pujari's picture of Kali looked so familiar.

I shuffled to my suitcase, tossed around my clothing until I found Nair's red mobile phone, searched the 'Outgoing Calls' menu once again. My number was the last one dialled. I looked at the number before it, dialled at 7:03 am the day Nair died, checked it against the number I had on my phone, knowing I'd find the same number.

CHAPTER 38

Mabel still hadn't returned from Saint Marks, which was convenient. She would have told me there was nothing I could do, to let it go, recover, then return home. Instead, I got changed, gingerly, trying hard not to twist my back, unsuccessfully, painfully; then shuffled my way slowly to the main street. Another maimed person in Mumbai.

I levered myself into the taxi, butt first then swung my legs inside, told the driver that I'd give him an extra hundred rupees if he took me straight to Malabar Hill, no tourist route. He wore a stark white cotton outfit with a white cloth cap, said in perfect English that there was only one way to get to Malabar Hill, so there was no need for the extra hundred.

It took an hour to get to there, time I took to think. The link between Mehta and Singh was clear. The families were close. Although Singh and Subhani had taken it much further. I was certain now that Nair had worked it out. He called Aamir Mehta in the morning. Whatever Nair said must have struck a chord with Mehta. He must have agreed to meet. That's why Nair was pleased, he probably thought he was going to be rich.

As for Subhani, well, Aamir Mehta was her father. That's about all I knew. What would compel a father to curse his only child? In between the logic, other thoughts came. The concern of the pujari and Father Joseph and the warnings of an old man in Uluru.

Shadows were beginning to creep up the walls of the mansion, following the tributaries left by the long-gone creeper. The house was quiet, shutters closed. When you were a kid, every neighbourhood had a scary old house where a wicked witch lived. You'd dare each other to creep up and knock on the door. Then run. Just then, I felt like a kid again, taking each painful step with trepidation. The house looked sinister, malicious.

I took a deep breath, rang the bell. The young housekeeper answered, this time her eyes narrowed with hostility. She was about to close the door when I barged my way in. She yelped, but the action hurt me more than her. She turned and ran down the hallway, shouting out in Hindi.

The room where the Mehtas had greeted me was to my left. I walked up near the picture of the deity on the wall. It was stylised, but the tongue gave her away. In the picture Kali was coloured deep blue, with ten arms. Each hand held an article of war, with one holding a severed head. She wore the same garland of skulls and belt of heads as in the picture that the pujari had shown me. The splashes of red and gold that I recalled came from the beams of light that radiated from her crown.

I hobbled to the corner of the room, where the dark shrine hid. Now it was covered under a black shawl. I lifted the fabric and there she stood, about two feet tall, little more than a fearsome face. The statue was made of the blackest stone. Her face had two large, terrible eyes, outlined in blood red. A large red tongue stuck out through her red lips, her upper lip curled in a snarl. The statue was adorned with gilded earrings and a golden crown, serving to make her blackness even deeper. The pujari said Kali was neutral, malevolent and benevolent. This version looked terrifying.

I turned to leave the room, only to be stopped by Rekha Mehta at the door.

'You must go, you must go.' Her voice was coarse and quivered nervously. Her hands clasped together, fear on her face.

I grabbed her hands in mine, the adrenaline dulling my pains. 'Where is Aamir?'

She shook her head, began to cry. 'Please, you must go. Enough has been done already.'

I held her hands tighter. 'Aamir. Where is he?'

She shook her head, fell to her knees and sobbed. She was afraid of him, afraid for me.

I pushed my way around her, shuffled down the hallway, checking every doorway as I passed. Everything seemed normal, formal dining room, living room, kitchen, spare bedroom. There was one more room downstairs, right at the end of the hallway. I tried the handle but the door was locked. That seemed strange—locked doors within a family household.

I made my way back to the front room, past the still sobbing Rekha Mehta, towards the statue of Kali. Pain pierced through my torso, like daggers with red-hot blades, as I bent down and lifted the statue. I stumbled back down the hallway, raised the statue as high as my remaining strength would allow and brought it down upon the locked handle. The idol chipped as the handle broke.

Rekha Mehta crawled out from the greeting room and looked at me from the other end of the hallway. She put her hand up, begging me not to enter.

It was dark inside, black like an abyss. The smell of moth balls burnt my nose. That was the camphor I'd smelt on Aamir Mehta the other day. I fumbled along the side of the door for the light switch. Flicked it on. The lights were so dim they only managed to put a sheen on the shadows. I stepped in, couldn't see it, but could feel a haze in the room, as if it brushed against my skin.

It took a couple of seconds for my eyes to adjust. The room was long, perhaps 3 metres wide by 5 metres deep. I was right about no windows. At the end, directly opposite the doorway and dominating the room, stood another black statue of Kali, this one much larger. Three candles with tiny flames burnt at her feet, giving off the camphor smell. A red cape was draped over the shoulders, hiding the rest of her body. I drew closer. Her crazed eyes stared me down. On her forehead, between her eyes, a large smudge of red looked like it was still wet. A thick, slow drop was forming.

Beside Kali, to her right, was a large black lingam. Its circular base was covered in old flowers and a dusting of brown powder. Its tip was smeared with the same red. I touched it, brought the sticky substance to my nose. It smelt like rust. Blood.

A solid-looking bookcase filled the entire left-hand side wall. Heavy lattice doors inlaid with glass squares protected the contents. There were rows upon rows of books, most looked very old, and all had Hindi script on their spines. Another section of the bookcase held cherry-coloured glass jars of different sizes. I opened a couple to see what was inside: dried chillies, some type of round, brown seeds, green powder that smelt of vomit, rusty nails, oils and grains.

Another row of jars caught my attention, larger than the others and separated by an empty shelf. I chose one at random and opened it and almost instantly a musty smell made me cough. Inside the jar was a collection of dried bones of different sizes, bleached white. I couldn't tell if they were human or animal.

I opened a second jar. The piercing smell of formaldehyde made me turn away. I caught myself and looked again, tilting the jar to get a better look at its contents. A head was visible, two little arms. I moaned as my stomach turned.

A fireplace occupied the right-hand side wall, too big for a room this size. In front of it sat a large stone mortar and pestle. Recently cleaned. Up close, I could still feel the heat from the coals, meaning the fire had been alit recently. I used the poker to stir about in the ashes, wondering what had been burnt. At first, nothing caught my attention, then, after a little more probing, something white stood out.

I gingerly eased myself to my knees and plucked out a triangular remnant of paper. The corner of a photo. It was badly singed, but I could still make out a man's arm around a woman's shoulder. His hand draped loosely, covering her breast. The rings were familiar. Davindar Singh loved his bling.

'Ma Kali is beautiful, isn't she?'

Aamir Mehta stood at the door, a silhouette in a room full of shadows.

CHAPTER 39

Mehta wore a single-breasted white Nehru Suit, a band substituting for a collar. His pants were designed a little short, revealing white socks. White shoes completed the look. He looked like a modern-day Bond villain. Mehta stood tall, hands by his sides, his voice firm. The feeble man I'd met at Vivienne Fredricks' house was long gone, if he ever existed in the first place.

He wasn't armed, but he still seemed cocky. As if he had all the cards. I thought about rushing him, but in my present condition I wouldn't have gotten very far. We both knew that. Mehta allowed himself a couple of seconds to examine the broken lock, then took a few steps inside the room. Closing the gap between us.

'It was you all along. You're the tantric,' I shouted, startled.

'I was under the impression our business had concluded. What are you doing here, Mr Ryder?' he asked, coolly.

I pointed to the glass jars. 'The black magic, the foetus. You did all that. Why?'

He looked over to the bookcase, then back at me. 'I do not expect a person like you to understand,' he said condescendingly. 'Subhani was my creation,' he thumped his chest. 'I made her what she was. I gave her everything. All I asked for in return was respect. But do you know how she was going to repay me? By casting me aside. Me!' He sneered. 'As if she had a choice.'

'So you cursed Subhani, why?' I asked.

Mehta continued: 'I warned her that I would kill her if she tried to leave me. Disrespected me.' He spoke of her as if she were yesterday's leftovers, rather than his daughter. 'She knew how powerful I am. That's why she got the talisman.' A vicious grin broke across his face. 'As if that little thing was going to stop me.'

He walked over to the Kali statue, straightened the cape. 'All I had to do was provide an offering to the Goddess and chant the sacred mantras for her intervention.'

That explained why the foetus was buried. It was never meant to be found. This was never *just* about scaring Subhani to death. He *meant* to kill her with black magic. But Subhani knew her father. Knew he didn't just threaten. That's why she was scared. Why she got the talisman.

There was nothing between me and the door now. I thought about making a run for it, a very quick shuffle more likely, but didn't. For some reason I was drawn to him, to his charisma, he was the Venus Fly Trap and I was a fly that should've known better. I asked him the questions that had bothered me since day one.

'Why did you hire me?'

His smile contorted into a grimace. 'Because that bloody child was pregnant. That's why. Do you know how much shame it brought on me when that autopsy report was publicised?' His fists formed clenched pendulums by his side. 'My daughter was nothing more than a common slut. Whoever was the father of that bastard child needed to be punished.'

So this was all about Mehta's pride. The real reason he hired me was to find out who fathered her child, not to find who killed her. That's what he wanted from the beginning. I gave him that name and now that man was dead. *Hell's fire.*

I looked at the photo remnant in my hand. 'So you cursed the Singhs?'

Mehta looked pleased with himself. 'All I needed was that photo. Kali is very powerful. She has seldom refused any of my requests.'

'And Nair?' I asked.

He snorted disdainfully, walked around the room, deliberately stopped between me and the exit. 'I thought I'd seen the last of that low-class hoodlum a year ago. Then he called me and asked to meet. He told me that he knew about my powers. That stupid girl of mine told him. He wanted money to keep quiet.'

Mehta smirked. 'He acted like he was too smart. He thought he was safe from me.'

Mehta turned his attention towards me. 'When he came here, I asked him to write down how much he wanted, and his bank account details. Ha!' Mehta laughed. 'That piece of paper was all I needed. That idiot gave me his own death warrant.'

'So Kali made the Singhs' car crash into that tanker and Nair jump from his balcony?' It sounded fantastical, but Mehta truly believed it. And now, in this grotesque room filled with evil, I was beginning to believe it too. All the puzzle pieces were beginning to fit.

'Why me?' I asked, 'Really.'

Mehta paused before he answered, looked at me derisively. 'It didn't have to be you. Just someone from Australia. For two reasons. First, Subhani died in Australia, so any investigation into her death would need to start there. Second, I wanted a Westerner. Just in case the talisman drew attention. If an Indian investigator found out about it, they may have either been frightened off the case, or, worse, they could have gone to the media. More scandal.'

He snorted. 'As it turned out, I got someone who struggled to believe in anything. Even when you found my offering to Kali in the garden, which I deliberately overlooked, you were not convinced. Although I think you may have changed your mind since then.' A tight smile slithered across his face and his stare intensified, like a snake eyeing its prey.

'Why did you allow the pujari into Subhani's house? You knew what he would find.'

Mehta held both hands behind his back, nodded sombrely. 'Yes. That was a risk. But even if the offering was found, there was no way to link it back to me. Not after that girl was dead.'

His daughter was now 'that girl'. 'It was the only way you would stay on the case. Besides, I was able to turn it to my advantage.'

'What about your wife? Does she know you killed Subhani?' I asked, wondering if Rekha Mehta could be putting on a show also?

He pressed his lips together, forming dimples on his cheeks, 'My wife is a respectful woman. She knows her place'

'Davindar Singh wasn't going to leave his wife. You cursed Subhani and the others for nothing,' I said, not able understand how someone could place their ego over their daughter's life. Surely, he must have loved Subhani at some stage.

He raised a finger, sharply. 'Not for nothing,' he snapped. 'For disloyalty to me. All of them.'

We stood there like bookends for a little while, him blocking the only way out. I had no idea where this would end. His confession was useless without proof, and there would never be any proof. The perfect crime, too perfect for me. He had played me like a puppet and I was beat. In every sense of the word.

'Okay. What happens now?' I said, feeling that there was more to come but hoping there wasn't.

'What do you mean?' His eyes narrowed.

'You've told me you killed them, but I have no evidence. I'm also not going to the cops with some story about black magic. They'll think I'm crazy. So, the way I see it, you've got what you wanted. I'm going to walk out that door and hope to God that I never see you again.'

'You know that can't happen.' The snake in him reared, prepared to strike. 'I underestimated you. I had no idea you would get this far. Now I can't just let you fly away, can I?'

Even though we were both unarmed, he was in the better condition. A fair fight wouldn't end the way I wanted so I scanned the room for something to use as a weapon. The poker was my best bet and I lunged for it, felt sharp stabs of pain down my back as I did. I held the iron bar like a sword.

Mehta watched me with bitter amusement. 'Come, come, Mr Ryder. Do you really think I would resort to physical violence? Besides, I am just an old man. If you harm me with that rod the police will be less than gentle with you. What would you claim, self-defence?' He allowed himself to laugh.

He was right, but I wasn't about to let go of the poker. I jabbed it at him, hoping he would move out of the way, but he stayed put. The force of my thrusts about as intimidating as a Girl Guide with a sharp cookie. I lowered the poker.

'That's better,' he said, condescendingly. 'I'm not stopping you from leaving here, Mr Ryder. But you will not live much longer.'

'What do you propose to do, set Kali on to me?' I was only half mocking.

Mehta smiled conceitedly then pulled out something from the breast pocket of his jacket and held it up. 'All I need is this.'

It was a business card that read, *Samson Ryder, Australian-Indian Investigations*. I had given it to him at Vivienne Fredricks' house. He kept it all this time. Had he always planned to use it this way?

I tried not to care, laugh it off. 'Your black magic won't work on me. I don't believe in it.'

He sensed the hesitancy in my voice, saw the flash of panic that I tried to hide.

'I wouldn't be so sure. After what you have seen and heard. It's starting to make sense to you now, isn't it? You're beginning to believe.' He smiled again and put the card back in his pocket, patted it safe.

Adrenaline made the veins in my neck and forehead pulse. My grip on the cold iron poker became tighter, something to grasp on to. I tried not to be scared, but I was. My breaths became short, sharp, like an animal caught in a trap. I scanned the room frantically, searching for a way out, an escape from this room, from him and from this case. Then something broke the ray of light coming from the hall, behind Mehta's back. Something silver caught the light.

'So, you killed Subhani, Nair, the Singhs and now you plan to kill me. When will it stop?'

Mehta smirked, was about to reply, when a sharp, cracking sound pierced the room and seemed to echo forever. The look on his face changed from smug, to confused, to anger. He fell to his knees. Another shot rang out, forcing him to fall forward on the floor.

'Enough. It stops now.' Rekha Mehta stood inside the doorway, a pistol from the lounge in her hand, hatred smeared across her face. She didn't look at me, just down at the prostrate figure of Aamir Mehta and emptied the gun into her husband.

Surrounded by empty cartridges, Rekha Mehta closed her eyes and took a deep breath, as if it were her first. The hatred ebbed from her face and a forlorn sadness took control. It was the most pathetic look in the world, a person who has lost hope, love, everything. Her head tilted to the right and tears flowed at an angle, she fell in slow motion to the floor, letting the gun fall.

'My Subhani,' she whispered between sobs, over and over again.

CHAPTER 40

We sat on the lounge, both my arms wrapped around her, gently rocking. Her head buried in my shoulder. I had called Vincent Patel and we waited for the sirens. She had told me her story by then.

She was there when Subhani told her father that she would be getting a new manager, someone who could take her career to the next level, someone who could look after her forever. Subhani didn't need Aamir Mehta anymore.

They'd had a huge argument. Aamir Mehta didn't take this news kindly. He saw it as a betrayal. A very public humiliation. He wanted to know who this new manager was. Subhani wouldn't tell him. He warned her not to speak like this in front of him. Not to ever think about doing something like this. If she did, it would be the last thing she would ever do.

Rekha Mehta knew her husband never made empty threats, so she took Subhani aside, begged her to stop talking about leaving her father. When they were alone, Subhani told her that she had some good news that would change everything. This just wasn't the right time to tell them.

Then Subhani died. Just like that. At first Rekha wondered whether Aamir had anything to do with it but pushed those thoughts aside. After all, he was her father, surely he must have loved her. However, when the autopsy was leaked, he became very angry. He was more worried about the family name than about his dead daughter, his dead grandchild. It made her wonder just how much he really loved Subhani.

That's when I came into the picture. Rekha Mehta never expected me to find anything. I was just another reminder that her daughter was gone. But when she heard about the pujari, she became wary. Despite her husband's protests she insisted on attending when the pujari visited Subhani's house. It was the first time she could recall going against Aamir's wishes, risking his wrath.

Ever since Rekha knew him, Aamir Mehta worshipped Kali. At first it was only the occasional puja. Then he became a devotee, constantly offering her sacrifices and prayers. Over the years he became more serious, more selfish, about his intentions. He began to pray to the darker side of Kali, destruction rather than creation.

He also became more secretive. A little while after becoming a Kali devotee, Aamir cleared a room in the house which he kept locked. Rekha and Subhani could guess what went on in that room and often the smell the camphor leaked into the main house. Sometimes they would even hear his chanting, but they were never allowed in. Unlike the housekeeper; occasionally Rekha would hear them together, chanting and moaning.

She and Subhani became suspicious of Aamir when terrible things started to happen to people that he didn't like, business associates or competitors. Untimely heart attacks, bouts of paralysing fever, madness, one person was even mauled by a pack of dogs. As his power grew, so did his ego. He began to scare them.

The buried foetus confirmed Aamir's involvement in this matter for Rekha. He and his curses and spells. She had spent her whole married life being subservient to him, afraid of him. Now she felt helpless. There was nothing she could do. Nobody would believe her. Her only option was to wait until death.

Until today. She listened at the door as he described what he'd done. Listened to how he described his daughter. Her daughter. It was enough. Too much. She finally had a choice and she made it.

Rekha Mehta lifted her face from my shoulder as the sirens grew louder. She sat at the edge of the lounge, facing forward, hands on laps, composed. She took a few deep breaths and asked me to open the shutters.

I made my way to the front of the house, began to unhinge the shutters. The young housekeeper with the taut midriff was slinking away down the driveway, a packed bag in her right hand. She looked at me with a poisonous face and spat in my direction. A *shakti* in search of a new master.

Rekha was sitting in the same position when I went back in, only now her face was turned to the window. The once gloomy room was now bathed in light, and for the first time, she looked at peace. I sat back down next to her.

'That day you came here and asked about my Subhani, about whether she ever fainted. Why did you want to know about that?'

'I was working on a lead. That maybe Subhani had a heart condition that led to her death. It doesn't matter now.' I held her hands, her skin like a tissue.

'Aamir always expected perfection. He thought he was perfect and everything around him needed to be perfect also. He never really loved me, I know, but I thought if Subhani was perfect, he would love her.'

Rekha Mehta slowly rose and walked to the window. When she looked out her face was deep in reflection, looking into the past.

'My Subhani was such a beautiful girl,' she said, then turned to face me. 'But she was also a sickly child. She did faint, Mr Ryder. Not often, just three or four times, but enough to worry me. We hid that from Aamir, so that he would continue to love her.'

EPILOGUE

Mabel and I stood away from the crowd. The late afternoon sun had lost its intensity but the humidity kept building like a pressure cooker. The terminal was still off limits to visitors, so we stood outside in the soupy carpark. Another sacrifice for security.

A long line of taxis waited not so patiently for a fare. The drivers milled about in huddles, sharing stories. Everybody smoked, everybody spat. The solitary coffee dispenser was out of order and the little stall only had warm bottles of water left. Family groups joined the reception party, waiting for loved ones to walk through the doors. The taxi drivers eyed them with thinly veiled resentment. Every family meaning one less fare.

It had been a week since I walked Rekha Mehta to the police car. Vincent Patel had made sure she wasn't treated like a common criminal. I had also given Naina Krishnan the scoop, the facts slightly distorted. She wrote that Rekha Mehta had a breakdown caused by Subhani's death and killed her husband while depressed. It was the approach her defence was likely to take. There was no link to either the Singhs' or Nair's death. In return, Krishnan had given me the name of the leak in the Coroner's Office. A name I'd passed on to Julie Mahoney.

I'd had a lot of time to think about what happened. Away from the heat of battle. About Old George, the pujari and the black magic. Aamir Mehta seemed sure he was responsible for the deaths. He took pride in this belief. Even Rekha and Subhani believed in his powers. So did I, for a terrifying moment. Now I thought again.

Subhani was scared, that much as certain, and she had a history of fainting. Whether she died from a curse or from a heart condition would never be determined. As for Nair, well, he *was* depressed. Maybe deep down he knew Mehta would never pay up? Anything could've happened in his state of mind. In the end, he jumped. The Singhs had a car accident, like many others do. I *did* see the car being serviced. But how good a job did the mechanics do? Maybe they missed something with the brakes in their rush to get the job done?

Still, it was one hell of a series of coincidences. That's what kept me awake at night, playing in the back of my mind. How close was I to becoming another coincidence?

I caught myself reaching for the medal around my neck more often. Good old Saint Benedict.

I'd been back to Saint Mark's to thank Father Joseph for the medal. We spoke during the drinks break. India was looking good against Sri Lanka. I watched the rest of the cricket with him, watched India win, then stayed on for Mass. I sat in the back of the church, where nobody could see me, said a prayer for Anjali.

Whether Aamir Mehta really had the powers he claimed or not didn't matter. He intended to cause harm to those people and had acted to make it happen, which was just as bad in my book. But why? Because of some overblown sense of pride? I found myself understanding him because I had been guilty of that too, at times. Not to the same extent, but enough. Being open and exposed was a sign of weakness. So my pride kept me alone, even when someone was sharing my bed. I wasn't going to let that happen again. Not this time.

Mabel nudged me, pointed to the monitor. A week ago, that would have caused me to scream blue murder. My bruises were healing now. My gait returning to normal.

On the monitor we could see passengers lining up at customs. It would take another five minutes before they'd start to stream out from the terminal, wide-eyed with culture shock. The taxi drivers started to jockey for position, like bears waiting for the salmon run.

'Tell me again what she looks like,' she said, her crooked grin playing with the mischief in her eyes.

I described her for the tenth time, leaving out the mole on her back.

'Where are you going to take her?'

'To Goa, there's a Basilica I want her to see. Miracles happen there. She'd like it.'

'I think it's a miracle that this girl likes you.' She laughed heartily at her own joke. It was infectious.

It wouldn't be the best time to go to Goa. The monsoon would be felt there before Mumbai. On the flip-side, it would be nearly empty. We'd have the place almost to ourselves, which would be a feat in India.

A few minutes later, the first of the passengers walked through the exit. The noise reached a new crescendo, with taxi drivers jumping over each other to get a fair. I looked eagerly in turns between the overhead screen and the exit.

Then I saw a face. A tired face. Long-haul, cattle-class tired. It was a face I liked a lot. Her brown hair was loose, hanging below her shoulders. Her green eyes were a little glassy, a little frightened. They smiled when they settled on me.

Patrick Lyons grew up in a house full of crime; literally. Almost every room had a crime novel lying around, spread-eagled, face down, his mother's ways of bookmarking. Christie in the bedroom, Rendell in the kitchen and Chandler in the lounge. It was only a matter of time before he picked these books up himself.

Patrick wrote his first crime story at the age of twelve. A school competition. He got an 'A'. He also got a talking to about the amount of violence in the story. It did not matter that Patrick didn't win; he was just thrilled with how the writing process seemed to flow. He's been arrested by crime writing ever since.

Writing about his experience as an Anglo-Indian growing up in Australia during the 1970s and 1980s is a good way for Patrick to explore broader concepts of exclusiveness, racism, identity and duality. These notions subtly pepper his work, bringing grit to his characters. The often-hilarious cultural clashes he witnessed provide plenty of scope for humour, and an opportunity to reflect on the universal desire to belong.

Patrick lives in Melbourne with his family and a pet bearded dragon called Rex. He is never far from a good coffee.

www.patricklyonsauthor.com

www.ingramcontent.com/pod-product-compliance
Lightning Source LLC
LaVergne TN
LVHW100519110826
845146LV00002B/701
* 9 7 8 9 3 9 1 1 2 5 1 5 8 *